The Persian Always Meows Twice

EILEEN WATKINS

KENSINGTON BOOKS
www.kensingtonbooks.com

KENSINGTON BOOKS are published by

Kensington Publishing Corp.
119 West 40th Street
New York, NY 10018

All Kensington Titles, Imprints, and Distributed Lines are available at special quantity discounts for bulk purchases for sales promotions, premiums, fund-raising, and educational or institutional use. Special book excerpts or customized printings can also be created to fit specific needs. For details, write or phone the office of the Kensington special sales manager: Kensington Publishing Corp., 119 West 40th Street, New York, NY 10018, attn: Special Sales Department, Phone: 1-800-221-2647.

Kensington Books and the K logo Reg. U.S. Pat. & TM Off.

ISBN-13: 978-1-4967-2289-8
ISBN-10: 1-4967-2289-2
First Kensington Trade Edition: October 2017
First Kensington Mass Market Edition: November 2019

ISBN-13: 978-1-4967-1057-4 (ebook)
ISBN-10: 1-4967-1057-6 (ebook)

10 9 8 7 6 5 4 3 2 1

Printed in the United States of America

For all the amazing cats that have
passed through my life so far:
Peppy, Topaz, Sable, Honey, Elvis,
Harley, Jasmine, Sheldon, and Bela.

Not all mine, but all irreplaceable
and unforgettable.

Acknowledgments

For his input on high technology, patents, and intellectual property, I'd like to thank my cousin Phil McCabe.

For answering my questions on cat grooming and boarding, and allowing me to visit their places of business and watch them work, I want to thank Lisa Condo Bartlow of Priceless Pets, Susan Spreder-Mohr of the Cat Chalet, and Doris Spreder of the Cozy Cat.

For information on police procedures in a small New Jersey town, I'm indebted to Anne-Marie Cottone and Susan Epstein of the *Star-Ledger* and my fellow member of Sisters in Crime/Central Jersey, Pat Marinelli.

For weekly feedback that kept me on the right path, I'm grateful to the members of my critique group: Elisa Chalem, Susan Moshiashwili, Harry Pollack, Ed Rand, Jeremy Salter, Janice Stucki, and Joanne Weck.

And for taking a chance on me and Cassie McGlone, many thanks to my agent, Evan Marshall, and my editor, John Scognamiglio.

Chapter 1

The orange tabby crouched on my stainless-steel table and hissed like a rattlesnake poised to strike.

"Yipes!" Sarah Wilcox, at my side, jumped back a step.

I worried. Would the sixtyish little woman lose her nerve?

I sure hoped not. I urgently needed her help, and so far I'd already eliminated three other candidates, all younger and faster on their feet. But with Sarah's background in the trenches, I thought she might have the necessary nerves of steel and cool head under pressure.

Professional cat grooming is not a job for . . . well, pussies.

"Mango, behave!" I scolded the tabby. Then I told Sarah, "With a resistant cat like this one, I generally use a grooming harness." I held up the thin webbing straps to show how they should fasten around the animal. "You just slip the kitty's head through this loop"—I worked quickly so "the kitty" didn't have a chance to sink his fangs into my hand—"pass this part under his elbow, and snap it together at the top."

Mango tried to bolt, but now I had a leash on him. He finally gave up and hunkered down on the table, still lashing his tail.

Sarah chuckled nervously. "You did that very well, Cassie!"

"I've had a lot of practice. But don't worry— we'll be working together, so most of the time I can do the tricky stuff. You'll just need to back me up."

I demonstrated how to start grooming with a natural-bristle brush to get any mats out of the cat's fur, and follow up with a slicker brush to smooth the coat and bring out the sheen. "Of course, Mango's got short hair and he's pretty clean. A lot of the cats I work on have long hair or have gotten into something messy. Sometimes the local shelter even sends over a feral that they want to put up for adoption."

Sarah dared to brush Mango's striped head, and I held my breath, hoping he wouldn't turn on her. Maybe because she was older than my own mom, I felt extra protective. But her stroking must have felt good, because the tabby finally relaxed and even half closed his eyes.

"He was just scared, weren't you, pretty boy?" she cooed.

This little woman with the coffee-brown skin

and salt-and-pepper curls had totally mellowed Mango out. I might finally have a winner!

I glanced at my wall clock, which was rimmed with black paw prints instead of numbers. I'd hoped to schedule Sarah's interview earlier in the day, but she'd been tied up until two. I'd have to move things along to make my biweekly visit to George DeLeuw's house.

I needed to keep him as a customer . . . but I also needed an assistant. And Sarah seemed the likeliest candidate so far.

"Is this cat a feral?" she asked me now.

"Not really, but he was a rescue. Mango's one of my own cats." I smiled at her surprise. "He just hates to be groomed, which makes him good for demos. I'll need your help most when I work with the bigger breeds. In school, I once had to shave a twenty-five-pound Maine Coon, and it took three of us just to keep her on the table."

"Wow, hope I'm up to that." Her dark eyes twinkled behind wire-rimmed glasses. "Though I did teach high school math for more than twenty years."

I laughed. "You told me on the phone. If you survived that, I'm sure you can handle a few cranky felines."

As I freed Mango and let him jump off the table, Sarah asked, "You said you went to school for this?"

"Yep, I'm a certified groomer and animal behaviorist." I nodded toward a framed document that hung above a row of white metal storage cabinets.

By now I'd gotten used to people scoffing at my degree and line of work, but again Sarah surprised me. "There's actually a school that teaches you how to understand animals? Isn't that wonderful! Most people never go to the trouble to learn."

"I also have a BA in regular psychology, which sometimes helps in dealing with the owners."

"I'll bet!" She laughed.

Sarah also didn't seem like the type to turn up her nose at my state college credentials. I considered not only hiring her, but doubling the hourly rate I'd planned to offer. "C'mon, I'll show you the boarding area."

I shooed Mango up the stairs that led to my living quarters and shut the door behind him. Then I escorted Sarah from the grooming studio to another first-floor space.

The building had started out, in the late 1800s, as a private two-story home just off the main drag of rural Chadwick, New Jersey. You could tell that once upon a time it had a front porch, but eventually that was enclosed to create a storefront with a big display window. My Realtor had lost track of how many other businesses had occupied the place before I bought it four months ago. I only know that the last tenant, a cut-rate beauty salon, had left behind peeling paint, a leaky roof, and a thriving colony of field mice. All of those factors helped lower the price of the building so I could afford a down payment.

I did the scraping and repainting myself. Nick Janos, a handyman about Sarah's age, fixed the roof for me at a bargain rate. And for some reason, shortly after I stenciled CASSIE'S COMFY CATS on the front window, the mice moved out of their own accord.

Now one section of the downstairs former retail space provided a dozen cat "condos" for boarders. Each was the size of a broom closet and outfitted with a litter box at the bottom, bowls for food and water on the next level, and a higher, carpeted perch with a half curtain.

As I showed Sarah this area, she gushed, "These are wonderful, Cassie. What a creative design!"

"Thanks. I admit, I found the idea online, but my handyman built them all. I've only been open for a couple of months, so I've got just half a dozen cats in residence right now. Four are in the condos, as you can see, and two are out in the playroom."

We moved on to a larger, more open space filled with multi-tiered cat trees and towers, some taller than either of us. All the vertical posts were wrapped in sisal rope, and the various carpeted levels ranged from low tunnels, for cats that liked to hide, to platforms of different heights for the climbers. To separate this middle area from the front sales counter, Nick had built a wall of fine wire mesh on a wood frame, with a similar door that could be closed when there was a cat turned loose.

Sarah grinned over the playroom, with its cat furniture in different muted colors and geometric shapes. "And look at those guys!" She pointed over our heads, where a pair of Siamese lounged at opposite ends of a long, wavy, floating shelf—also built by Mr. Janos.

I explained, "Usually I only turn out cats together that come from the same home, like these two. Even so, in a strange place they might tend to squabble over territory. The different levels let them keep their distance from each other."

"Very smart." With a glance toward the small display of cat furniture in my front window, Sarah asked, "Do you also sell the perches?"

I nodded. "One commercial line, yes. I'll want you to handle some of those sales for me too, though it's not like I get a steady stream of customers."

She nodded. "Glad to. Keep my math skills sharp, right?"

"I'm sure they're better than mine."

A stolen glance at my watch made my heart jump. I'd been enjoying Sarah's company so much that I'd let time slip away from me. I should leave for DeLeuw's soon—it was a fifteen-minute drive.

"Sorry to rush this, but I've got a three o'clock appointment across town," I told her. "Can you help me put the Siamese back in their cages?"

The chocolate-point cat on the lower end of the shelf gave us no trouble, but her lavender-point buddy, higher up, had to be coaxed down with treats. Sarah's eyes lit up as she admired their fine-boned faces, large batlike ears, and svelte bodies. Since she seemed to be taking to her responsibilities so well, I mentioned that she also would be helping me clean litter pans once a day and making sure the boarders had food and water. That didn't discourage her, and neither did the modest pay that I offered.

"I do think you have a real feel for the job," I said. "If you want, you can start tomorrow morning."

Sarah seemed delighted that she'd passed muster, and so was I. The rest of my week should go as well as this Monday!

I showed her out, with a warning to beware of the shaky railing on my back steps. She made it safely to her car and waved good-bye.

Watching her pull away, I let myself hope that finally I'd found someone reliable to help me juggle all the factors that went into running Cassie's Comfy Cats.

None too soon. For example, I had to close early now, just to make this house call.

Usually I insisted that customers bring their cats to my shop, where I had my grooming table set up close to my wall of brushes, combs, and clippers; a large bathing sink; and a special cage where a cat could be safely blow-dried. No way could I bring all of that to a customer's home, and I wouldn't expect any of them to have such a professional setup.

But George DeLeuw wasn't just any customer.

I locked my front door and turned the hanging sign to CLOSED. Then I grabbed a pink-and-black duffle already packed with my smock, head wrap, gloves, and extra grooming tools. I hurried out the back to my small parking lot and jumped into my four-year-old Honda CR-V.

* * *

Being new to Chadwick, and not a big reader of business magazines, I'd never heard of DeLeuw before he first contacted me. Actually, his executive assistant, Jerry Ross, made the call, asking if I could come out to groom DeLeuw's cat, Harpo, a cream-colored Persian. Trying to gauge how much might be involved, I asked if this was a show cat that would need a special cut.

No, Ross told me, Harpo was just a pet. "But his coat gets matted, and Mr. DeLeuw thinks that makes him . . . uncomfortable. The cat, I mean."

I heard skepticism in the man's voice, which told me he didn't know a lot about cats. I had seen a few longhairs with mats so bad that they could cause pain or even health problems.

When I started to explain why I preferred to work on the animals in my own shop, Ross cut me off a bit impatiently. "Mr. DeLeuw has a professional-quality grooming studio in his home. I'm sure it will provide everything you need."

By that time, I'd gotten the impression that George DeLeuw probably had major bucks and could be a good customer to cultivate, so I'd agreed to make the trip.

His palatial home confirmed that impression. Only about five years old, it resembled an updated Norman château, with a massive front door and a turret section to one side. In beige stucco with brown trim, its otherwise rather mismatched segments seemed to spread out forever. His sweet-faced, middle-aged housekeeper, Anita, had answered the door and shown me in.

Tall, lean, and gray-haired, DeLeuw usually dressed even around the house in a polo or button-down shirt and khakis. I thought sometimes that he had the fastidious air of a minister rather than an executive. On that first visit, he had confessed that he'd tried to groom Harpo himself, with some help from Anita, but the results never looked quite right. "I was delighted to hear that a certified cat groomer had opened up right here in Chadwick," he said. "I'm sure you'll do much better."

He'd shown me to the rear of the second floor, where I did indeed find a clean, well-equipped grooming studio outfitted with almost everything I could want. Harpo, despite his flat, grumpy-looking Persian face, turned out to be a good-natured boy who was used to being handled. I didn't even need a harness to keep him on the table while I worked, and by the time I gave him a final fluff, he actually was purring. DeLeuw also appeared happy with the results and booked me for biweekly two-hour appointments.

So far I'd been to his home three times, and those visits had gone a long way toward helping pay my mortgage.

On my visits, I always let Anita or George himself take me directly to the grooming studio, and resisted the urge to roam through any other areas. I was afraid not only of getting lost, but of being accused in case anything valuable got broken or went missing. DeLeuw had quite an art collection, ranging from modern abstract paintings and drawings to stone artifacts that could have come from an archeological dig. My college minor was art, so

I recognized the styles of some famous artists and got the idea that George collected only the best.

Harpo seemed the sole exception. Once, when I'd remarked on the way the cat's big, plumy tail curled up over his back, his owner chuckled and said that was one of a few flaws that would disqualify him as a show cat. "But to me, he's priceless," DeLeuw went on, scratching the Persian under the chin. "Harpo is my buddy, my confidante. I tell him all my secrets."

So, maybe a guy didn't have to be totally heartless to make a killing on Wall Street.

Stuck now at one of the two traffic lights on Center Street, I admired the cherry trees just starting to blossom in pink puffs along the curb. Chadwick's turn-of-the-century main drag had been idyllic enough in the past winter's snow—like something out of *It's a Wonderful Life*. I imagined spring and summer would bring out even more nostalgic charm.

I'd picked this town for a few reasons. Some practical, some emotional.

One of my high school friends, Dawn Tischler, operated a successful health food store just a few blocks from my new place. Visiting her over the years, I'd noticed that Chadwick was starting to "take off," becoming a desirable spot for urban and suburban folks who wanted to get away from it all for an afternoon or a weekend. It had sprouted a couple of bed-and-breakfasts, several antique and craft shops, a cute retro diner, and a few more upscale restaurants. Driving along Center Street, I passed an old theater that a local group recently had revived to show classic films. To the lakeside park, the town had added walking trails and a Victorian gazebo, where they'd planned a new series of concerts this spring.

Four months ago, when I'd decided to open my business, I'd also been one of those harried suburbanites who badly needed to get away from it all. My last romantic relationship had come to a disastrous and even violent end, and I wanted nothing more than to escape to a setting that promised peace and safety.

More trees and shrubs brightened my drive toward the outskirts of town with that unreal Day-Glo green of early spring. I rolled down my windows to better appreciate the clean, unpolluted air. I enjoyed the smell even when I passed the occasional small farm with grazing cows or horses. These alternated with new developments that boasted old-world names like Hunter's Chase and Regency Estates, trying to sound exclusive and expensive. I hoped the McMansion trend wouldn't creep any closer to Chadwick. I preferred the town's more genuine, historical appeal, even if it did come with a few mice or roof leaks.

Arriving at DeLeuw's place, I pulled into the long, curving driveway and parked in front of the detached garage, next to his silver Mercedes sedan. The front lawn was a perfect swath of emerald-green velour, kept that way by Louis, his landscaper, and smelled freshly mowed; as I left my car, I heard the whine of some type of machinery farther back on the property. Toting my duffle, I started around the front of the house, where purple and white crocuses peeked out from beneath the dark foundation shrubs.

Something else, cream-colored, flashed under the bushes and rustled away. Too fluffy and pretty to be any type of wild animal.

I set down my bag quietly and sank to my knees. "Harpo? That you, boy?"

It was him, all right, flattened beneath one of the bushes, his coppery eyes round and scared. Of course he would be—George had told me he never let the cat outside. Harpo must have darted out when somebody, maybe Anita, had opened the door.

I fished some cat treats from my duffle and made whispering noises until the Persian finally crept toward me. After a couple of minutes, I lured him close enough to scoop him up in my arms. Being about one-third fur, he was lighter than he looked.

"Let's get you back inside." I carried both my bag and the cat to the front stoop and started to ring the bell, then noticed the door stood a few inches ajar.

Weird . . . somebody was being very careless, for sure. I pushed the door open and called out, "Hello?"

No answer. Harpo began to fidget, so I stepped inside anyway and put him down. He trotted off, feet padding silently over the marble tiles of the entry hall, and I followed him. With his heightened senses of smell and hearing, he probably would know where to find whoever was at home. Ideally, his master.

I was right about that. The cat passed a couple

of open doorways before he veered into what I'd always taken to be the study.

There, we both found George DeLeuw sprawled facedown on the Oriental carpet, a bloody gash across the back of his head.

Chapter 2

I stood paralyzed for a full minute, and only snapped out of it when Harpo crept forward and nosed around his master's head. I stooped to push the cat away and, while I was down there, checked to see if the man might still have a pulse.

After college, while pondering career options, I'd put in a few months as a vet tech, so I'm less squeamish about medical things than some people might be. I did not want to turn DeLeuw over to search for the artery in his neck, though, so I tried his wrist.

No flutter of life. Anyway, his skin already had started to cool.

As if the cold had spread from him to me, I started to tremble. Before this, I'd seen dead people only in coffins, and had plenty of time to prepare myself. Much different to walk into a man's house, someone I expected to find perfectly well, and come across him like . . . this. It just seemed unreal.

A horrible scream shredded my eardrums and sent Harpo skittering away. Anita stood frozen in the doorway, her normally toasty complexion almost as pale as her apron. "*Dios mío!* What . . . what . . . happened?"

I sensed that she'd almost asked, *What did you do?* Realizing how guilty I must have looked, I sprang to my feet and backed away from the body. "I don't know. I had an appointment. I found Harpo out front and the door open. I brought him inside and he led me . . . here."

"Is Mister . . . is he . . ."

"G-gone, I'm afraid."

Anita dared to steal a little closer and I made way for her. "He . . . had accident?" I heard tears in her voice.

"I don't think so." The closest stairs were out in the hall, and there wasn't anything nearby that could have fallen on him. Did he pass out and hit his head on some furniture? Again, nothing close by could have made that kind of wound. Besides, would he have landed facedown?

The housekeeper reached out, possibly to turn him over, but I stopped her. "Don't touch anything. I'll call the police."

She stared at me. "You think that somebody did this?"

"If there's even a chance of that, we shouldn't disturb the scene." At least I'd learned something useful, I guess, from all those mystery novels and cop shows on TV.

I pulled out my phone and made the call. Meanwhile, Louis the landscaper, whom I'd seen from a distance but never met, came down the hall from the back entrance. The fit young black man, his green EDEN LANDSCAPING polo shirt lightly stained with perspiration, stopped in the study doorway when he saw Anita and me.

"Did one of you scream?" Then he looked past us and saw the reason. "What the—"

"Oh, Louis!" Anita burst into tears, crossed to him, and huddled against his shoulder. Louis took the fortyish woman in a kindly but awkward embrace, as if they weren't normally on such close terms. She explained what little I'd been able to tell her.

Meanwhile I told the two of them, "The police are on their way. Why don't we go wait in . . . some other part of the house?" Lord knows, there were plenty of other parts to choose from.

The three of us moved across the hall to what I assumed would have been called the great room. Like the study, this larger and brighter space had moldings, a fireplace, and a coffered ceiling all in a dark, polished wood. It was obviously designed for entertaining a large, and sophisticated, group. While the study revolved around George's desk, this room offered a central seating area of light, neutral, upholstered pieces that threw the emphasis on the artworks. And those were everywhere you looked. A big, abstract, multicolored drawing hung over the fireplace; a black geometric steel construction stood on a corner pedestal; and a glass sculpture like a wavy jellyfish rested on the low coffee table next to a small ancient-looking Oriental chest.

Anita, Louis, and I sat on the beige sectional, at discreet distances from one another.

Louis clasped his hands on his knees and shook his head. "Somebody killed DeLeuw? That's crazy. Why?"

"A thief!" Anita decided. "They must've tried to steal money, or maybe one of his art pieces. Mr. DeLeuw surprise them, an' they—" She mimed the killer bringing down a bludgeon on her employer's head.

I didn't find fault with her theory, since we were all upset and knew far too little to draw any conclusions. But DeLeuw couldn't have been facing his killer; he'd been hit from behind. It would take a very brave or stupid burglar to break into a house in midafternoon, with the owner and two of the staff on the premises. Also, judging from the keypad near the door, the place had a sophisticated alarm system. But the killer didn't need to jimmy a window if somebody had let him in.

Did Anita, and was she covering up now for her lapse in judgment? Or did DeLeuw himself open the front door? He only would have let in someone he trusted . . . most likely, someone he knew.

Detective Angela Bonelli of the Chadwick Police Department appeared to be thinking along the same lines. While her crime scene unit photographed the body and did whatever else they had to in the study, she took first Anita, then Louis, then me into the great room for questioning. She sat across from me on the chaise extension of the beige sectional, keeping her posture erect despite the soft cushions. Her powder-blue shirt barely softened the effect of her severe navy pantsuit and dark chin-length hair threaded with gray.

"You're a professional cat groomer." Her nearly black, heavy-lidded eyes locked on mine, and she paused her pen over her notebook as if waiting for the punch line. "I thought they groomed themselves."

"Yes and no. There are many situations . . ." But I could see Detective Bonelli wasn't interested in my usual sales pitch. "Longhaired cats, like Mr. DeLeuw's Persian, often need extra care so they don't get matted. I've been coming out here to work on Harpo every other week." In case that didn't sound legit enough, I also mentioned my boarding facility in downtown Chadwick.

Her skeptical air began to dissolve. "Oh yeah, I've driven past that place. You can see cats inside, at the back, sitting up high on shelves."

I smiled and nodded, hoping I'd established myself as a law-abiding resident and business-person.

"You said you found the body?" she asked.

I explained the order of events. Meanwhile, in the corner of my vision, I saw a uniformed officer in the hallway going through my duffle. Was he looking for the murder weapon? After a second of panic, I decided nothing that I'd brought along was heavy or sharp enough to have caused DeLeuw's head wound, even if swung with great force.

"Did you and the deceased have any differences?" The detective still held eye contact with me in a way that made me squirm.

"None at all. We didn't have a lot of personal conversation, but he did like to stay in the studio while I worked on Harpo. He was interested in learning my technique." *Did that sound arrogant, or even suggestive?* I twisted my hands together, then worried that Bonelli might read my tension as a sign of guilt. "I liked Mr. DeLeuw because he seemed genuinely concerned about his cat. And because he put me on a regular schedule, he was a valuable customer. I'm very sorry to lose him."

"Did he ever discuss his work with you?" she asked.

That surprised me a little. "No, never. After he hired me, I got curious and Googled him, so I know he 'semi-retired' last year from a big-deal Wall Street job. But most of the time we talked about his cat, and cats in general. And sometimes about art, because I minored in art in college, and he has such an amazing collection."

"Were you familiar with his collection? When you came in today, did you notice anything missing?"

I suppose she had to ask that question, but it was a stretch. I shook my head. "He's got so much, I never would have noticed. And after I found . . . the body, I pretty much blanked out on anything else."

For the moment, Detective Bonelli appeared satisfied that I had not bludgeoned George to make off with one of his Franz Kline lithographs or Peruvian fertility figures. *Is that what they expected to find in my duffle?*

Still, she asked, "Do we have your permission to search your car before you leave?"

Hoping no one had stashed stolen artwork in my hatch while my back was turned, I agreed. I handed over my keys, which Bonelli passed to one of her officers.

"You said you've only been in town a few months," she recalled, looking over her notes. "How did you decide to move to Chadwick?"

I explained that I'd been influenced by my friend Dawn's success with her store and the fact that the town seemed to be on the upswing. "Also, with wealthier people moving to the neighborhoods nearby—like this one—I thought I should be able to build a good customer base."

Bonelli doesn't need to know that I also wanted to put some distance between me and my abusive ex-boyfriend. After all, that's got nothing to do with DeLeuw's murder.

"And you live alone?"

"Yes, if you don't count my own three cats."

Though it was a sensible question, under the circumstances, I couldn't help thinking the detective sounded a bit like my mother. Or like Dawn, who kept trying to find a new guy for me. Even my handyman, Nick, had hinted more than once that I should meet his son, Dion. "He's an electronic genius and almost thirty. But he spends his weekends holed up in our basement, doing who knows what on his computers. Understands them better than women, I guess."

So far I'd tactfully dodged that matchup, because I prefer someone who's good with living things. Like maybe Dr. Mark Coccia, the very cute vet at the clinic a few blocks from my shop. I'd first met him when I dropped by to ask if the clinic would display some brochures for my business, and saw him a second time when I brought in a rescue cat that needed medical care more than grooming. I had no idea, though, whether Dr. Mark was spoken for.

Detective Bonelli snapped me out of this reverie with a few more personal questions about my age and background, including how I'd been able to afford my shop. I explained that I'd inherited a little money when my father passed away and also I'd qualified for a small business loan. She finally seemed satisfied that I wasn't the type of girl who went around endearing myself to wealthy men who could bankroll my business . . . then bumped them off when I got tired of them.

At last, the detective closed her notepad with a mild warning that I should stay in the area in case she had more questions, and I assured her I'd be tethered to my shop for the near future.

Following me into the front hall, she added, "Please stop by the station downtown on your way home, to give a statement," she said. "We'd also appreciate it if you'd let us fingerprint you. Just so we can determine if anyone was in the house this morning who didn't have a legitimate reason to be here."

I agreed, figuring that if I refused to give my prints, it would only make me look more like a suspect.

A subtle glance at my watch reminded me how late it was. The cats back home—the boarders and

my own—would be wailing for their dinners. Now
that I'd recovered a bit from the vision of George
bleeding onto his exotic carpet, my stomach was
starting to complain too.

The crime scene guys had finished going over
the front hall powder room, so I got permission
from Bonelli to use it. When I glanced in the mir-
ror, I understood better why she'd her doubts
about me. I wore jeans and a CAT HERDER sweatshirt, my usual grooming apparel, with my faded
denim jacket. Several long brown strands had
drifted loose from my ponytail, and my hazel eyes
peered like a wild animal's through my overgrown
bangs. What little makeup I'd put on that morning
no longer helped to relieve my pallor.

A sudden commotion outside in the hall startled me, because in spite of the tragedy, everyone
had been acting subdued and respectful. I eased
open the powder room door and saw a dark-
haired man, probably in his late thirties and only
about my height, demanding to know what had
happened and who was in charge. He wore a
blazer that gave a business twist to his khakis and
T-shirt. When Bonelli hurried over to intercept
him, the newcomer announced that he was "Jer-
rold Ross, executive assistant to Mr. DeLeuw."

I stepped into the hall but kept a low profile.
So this was the same guy I'd dealt with that first
time on the phone. I'd never seen Ross in person
before, but I might have known him anyway from
his overall air of impatience. On the other hand,
he did seem genuinely shocked to hear of his employer's death.

"I just spoke to George on the phone maybe two hours ago!"

"Yes," Bonelli responded calmly. "We think he expired not long after that."

The sight of the forensic team clustered just outside the study fanned Ross's agitation. "My God, what was it? A heart attack or—"

"We're not sure yet." A couple of inches taller than the assistant, Bonelli steered him away toward the family room. "Please come with me. You can help by telling us whatever you may know about Mr. DeLeuw's schedule for today . . . especially any appointments he may have had here at the house."

"Huh? Oh yeah. Of course." As if dazed with grief, Ross let her lead him across the hall. If he was so upset by the idea of George dying of a heart attack, I could only imagine how he'd react when Bonelli told him it almost certainly was murder.

I preferred not to be around when that happened, so I reclaimed my duffle and made for the front door. En route I passed poor Anita, who sat in one of those stately chairs that rich people put in their front halls, mostly for show. The almost medieval-looking throne made a strange contrast with the sleek white pedestal next to it, which displayed an abstract sculpture—a foot-tall piece of jagged stone like an oversized arrowhead. Anita had straightened her spine against the tall back of the chair and curled her hands tightly around the ends of the arms, her expression also tightly controlled.

"I'm so sorry. This must be such a shock for

you." Remembering she also had been questioned as a possible suspect, I added, "I hope everything works out okay."

Anita nodded her thanks.

"Where's Harpo?" I asked.

By shifting her focus, I guess, the question relaxed her a little. "I put him up in the studio. I should go feed him. Maybe the police will let me now."

"Poor cat, I'm sure he's wondering what the heck is going on."

Anita managed a crooked smile. "So am I!"

I stooped to give her a quick hug, handed her my business card, and told her to call if she needed anything. Then I let myself out, past another uniformed cop.

Outside, the CSI guys gave me the okay to move my car. They were busy now, spreading some kind of film over key areas of the driveway. It took me a minute to realize they must be checking for latent tire tracks. This was a thorough crew!

As I drove home, I reassured myself that Anita would take good care of George's cat as long as they both remained in the house. I wondered, though, how long that would be, and what would happen to Harpo in the future.

I remembered one of the few personal conversations I'd had with DeLeuw, on my last visit. While grooming the fluffy blond Persian, I'd asked lightly if he'd started off with four cats, one for each Marx brother.

Though I'd meant the question half as a joke, the man's long face clouded over. "Originally, I also had his brother, Groucho. He was black-and-white, with a spot right under his nose like a little mustache."

I smiled at the image, but since Groucho was no longer around, I sensed DeLeuw's story had a downbeat ending.

"In my divorce, two years ago, my ex-wife managed to convince the judge that both cats were extremely valuable, which of course was hogwash," he recalled. "I bought them as pets, they couldn't even be bred, so they were worth a few hundred dollars at most. But even though Marjorie paid no attention to them while she lived here—except to complain about the fur on the furniture—she insisted one cat should go to her."

"Oh, too bad," I sympathized. "So she's got Groucho?"

DeLeuw's normally pale complexion deepened a shade, and he grasped his remaining cat more tightly. "Not anymore. A few months after the divorce, she e-mailed me to say that Groucho 'got sick' and had to be put to sleep." A snide tone I'd never heard before crept into his voice. "The cat was only five years old. He got checked regularly by a vet while I had him and never had any health issues! Probably, he threw up a hairball in one of her designer shoes."

I paused in the middle of untangling one of Harpo's mats, because his master's mood—and the atmosphere in the grooming studio—suddenly had turned so dark.

"If she didn't want to take care of him, she could have just given him back to me," DeLeuw almost snarled. "I think she just did it out of spite, and for the satisfaction of letting me know."

As I turned back onto Center Street, the memory of this sad story troubled me even more than when I'd first heard it. With George gone, could his cruel ex-wife possibly inherit sweet, beautiful Harpo?

Maybe I could do one thing to honor DeLeuw's memory. In my mind, I promised him, *Don't worry. Your cat will go to a good, safe home. I'll do whatever I can to make sure of that!*

Chapter 3

The Chadwick Police Station inhabited a former bank building, which gave it a suitably dignified brick façade with steps up to a white-columned entrance. Inside, unfortunately, old-fashioned charm had given way to maximum efficiency, with a Scandinavian-modern front desk, gravel-colored tweed carpeting, and fake-maple paneling. At least it wasn't gloomy, though, and I didn't feel as if I were rubbing elbows with too many hardened criminals.

I checked in at the front desk, which was guarded by a bulletproof window, and was matched up with a serious blond male officer. In another room, he took down my statement and had me read and sign it. I felt a bit proud of myself for doing what I could to bring DeLeuw's killer to justice.

Being fingerprinted was another story. Having

a female officer roll each and every one of my fingers in ink and press them in their proper places on a card with my name and address made me feel like a criminal. By the time she finished, I'd begun to doubt the wisdom of agreeing to be printed, of giving my statement . . . and of driving to DeLeuw's house at all that day.

At least, after that unnerving experience, I finally got to go home.

Before I'd even unlocked my back door, I could hear the hungry cries of the six boarders. Inside, I quickly dished out their meals, according to what the owners had requested (some even supplied special food). Meanwhile, my own cats on the second floor also figured out that I was back. Mango, probably, started scratching the closed door at the bottom of the stairs. Good thing the distressed-wood look was in these days.

I opened the door carefully, nudging all three back as I went. They escorted me up the stairs, tails straight up and twitching with anticipation. In addition to Mango, I had Cole, solid black, and Matisse, a dilute calico. All were shorthairs—why bring more work home with me?—and rescues of one kind or another. Mango had been living out of a Dumpster behind a restaurant in my old Morristown neighborhood. I'd gotten Cole from a shelter during a Halloween Black Cat Special adoption event. A friend offered me Matisse, three years back, when his cat had an unexpected litter. (In exchange for the kitten, I'd given him a stern lecture on the importance of spaying and neutering.)

After feeding my three roommates, I found that my answering machine had a message from

Dawn. Possibly she'd left one on my cell phone also, and I'd just been too busy with the crisis at DeLeuw's place to notice.

"*We still on for tonight?*" her recording asked.

Oh crap. We were supposed to try that new Thai restaurant. I am so not up for that anymore!

Dawn would still be at her own shop, but probably ready to close. I called her back, apologized for forgetting, and told her very briefly what had happened.

"Ohmigod, are you serious? The guy was murdered? Are *you* okay?"

"Physically fine, just pretty shaken up. I don't really feel like going out, though. Plus, I'm a total mess. Stumbling upon a dead body has a way of making a girl's eyes bulge out and her hair stand on end."

Dawn scoffed. "Oh yes, I'm sure you're hideous. But if you want some company, I can bring dinner to you."

Though that sounded wonderful, I started to protest. "I don't want to put you to any trouble. . . ."

"I sell food, remember? I have some things we can heat up, fast but good."

And they'd also be good for *me,* I thought, which probably wasn't a bad idea. "Thanks, that might be best. I'll pull myself together—in every sense—before you get here."

Hanging up, I reflected that at least I probably didn't get close enough to DeLeuw to pick up any bloodstains. Even so, I might just burn my CAT HERDER sweatshirt.

* * *

Dinner at least was a bloodless affair, for which I was grateful. Dawn's vegetarian quinoa-and-black-bean burritos were delicious and filling, and went reasonably well with a bottle of Sauvignon Blanc left over from my New Year's shop-warming party. I drank an extra glass, hoping to wash from my memory that vision of DeLeuw splayed facedown on the study floor. It seemed like a humiliating end for someone I'd considered a dignified gentleman.

I remembered reading in a mystery novel that a blow to the nape of the neck, just below the back of the skull, is one of the few head injuries that can kill almost instantly, by severing the spinal cord from the brain. I wondered if the killer had known that.

"The creepiest part," I told Dawn, "is that it happened in the middle of the day, with other people around. And supposedly no one heard a thing!"

She faced me across my 1950s yellow kitchen table, which I'd covered with a vintage fruit-patterned tablecloth for the evening, and took another slow, thoughtful sip of her wine. "Not even that maid you mentioned, or the landscaper?"

"She was vacuuming upstairs, and he was wacking weeds out back with ear protection on. They might have heard a gunshot, but not someone being hit on the head."

"Convenient." Even while cutting another forkful from her burrito, Dawn reminded me of a heroine from a Rossetti painting. She had the same slightly long sharp nose, ivory complexion, and masses of wavy of auburn hair, which she controlled with assorted clips and braids. Her penchant for flowing tunics and ankle-length skirts enhanced that romantic impression, even if the overtones were more 1960s hippie than turn-of-the-century.

"So either one of them is lying, or it was a crime of opportunity." I slipped into cop jargon again. "Somebody George let into the house just saw a chance to whack him. I wonder if the police have any idea yet what the weapon was. I mean, if the killer planned it, he could have brought a gun, right?"

"Yeah, that does make it sound as if the murder wasn't really premeditated," Dawn said. "Could be, somebody just got into an argument with him and lost control. Or he surprised somebody who was trying to steal something."

I shuddered. If I'd gotten to my appointment earlier, and maybe gone up to the studio alone to groom Harpo, I might have been in the house when DeLeuw was attacked. If the killer had no idea I was there, I might have been the only one to hear the scuffle. I might even have come down the hall to check it out. . . .

And I might not be sitting in my apartment tonight, safely talking to my friend.

"You feeling all right?" she asked. "You just turned a little green."

I managed a smile. "Maybe overdid the wine. I'll make us some coffee."

"With what you've been through, I'd recommend herbal tea," she countered. "I brought just the thing. . . ."

In the past, Dawn had provided a few herbs that helped calm down fractious cats, so I was willing to let her prescribe for me.

We drank the sweet, musky brew while lounging at opposite ends of my sofa, a hand-me-down piece slipcovered in beige cotton. You could call my decorating style Tabby Chic. The furniture covers were washable and livened up with a few pastel fleece throws. The beige-tweed area rugs were a synthetic indoor/outdoor material for easy cleaning. The room's main window faced southeast toward the street, so I grew a few plants on the deep sill that were nontoxic to cats and didn't much appeal to them. I used pull-down shades instead of long draperies that would tempt climbers. Since I would never declaw, I kept a couple of tall, sturdy, sisal-covered scratching posts near the sofa and the upholstered chair.

In case you've wondered, cats aren't my only obsession. Before I turned my design talents toward animals, I'd dabbled in art, and my walls displayed a few of my best originals, which tended toward Pop and surrealism. I'd also hung up framed reproductions of some artworks by Klee and Magritte, and one vintage poster advertising the old PBS *Mystery!* series. A wide bookcase below held not only volumes on cat breeds, behavior, and care, but hardcover and paperback mystery novels and psychology texts from my college days.

After graduation, I'd soon realized that my mother and my career counselors were right, when they'd warned that a psych major with an art minor would not set me up for great career success. I was still searching in vain for a job when, a year later, I volunteered for a summer at an animal shelter. I'd always loved animals and had a knack for handling them, so I rethought my goals and looked for more training in that field.

On top of the bookcase, I kept a framed photo of my mom and dad, dressed up for some real estate dinner when his office had won a big award. Dad had been a "people person," more upbeat and easygoing than Mom, and had acted as a kind of buffer between us. Since the shock of his death three years ago, she and I had been awkwardly rebuilding our relationship.

The bookcase also served as a launching pad for my pets to access another series of stepped wall shelves built by Nick. Right now Matisse gazed down at us from the top level, her eyes contented slits. Cole had curled up on the sofa next to Dawn, while Mango, in a more sociable mood than earlier, perched on the arm next to me.

I scratched the side of his face until he closed his eyes, leaned into my hand, and purred. That made me think again of DeLeuw's poor frightened cat. I shared with Dawn my worries about what would become of Harpo.

"From what George told you, he probably wouldn't leave another cat to his ex-wife," Dawn pointed out. "Of course, he might not have made a will at all."

I hadn't considered that. I didn't have a will, but I was only twenty-seven and unmarried, with no kids and very little savings. "He must have—he was worth millions!"

"It's not unheard-of. Some rich celebrities have died without leaving wills, and then it all had to be hashed out in court. Cases like that can get very messy."

"But you're talking about actors and rock stars, right? DeLeuw was a money guy, and from what I saw, he was very methodical about his whole lifestyle. Anyhow, assuming he does have a will, how soon do you think the . . . heirs will know what it says?"

She raised an eyebrow at me. "You only groomed his cat three times, Cassie. I don't think you're in for a big windfall."

Again, I mustered a half smile. "I very much doubt that too. Though it would be nice, since without George, I'm losing a big part of my income! But I just hope he provided for Harpo. Suppose he never updated the will since his divorce? If the ex-wife has anything to say about it, that gorgeous cat could go to a shelter, or even . . ." I didn't want to consider the worst alternative.

Dawn waved one hand, a bracelet of small crystal nuggets dancing on her wrist. "If you want legal advice, you're asking the wrong person. Why don't you call your mother?"

That made good sense. Mom worked as a paralegal in a law office in Morristown. She must have handled some cases involving wills, maybe even those of murder victims. "Only one problem. I'd have to tell her about discovering the body today, and that will freak her out. You know how overprotective she is."

"You weren't going to tell her? It might even get into the papers or online."

"Crap, that's true. If she reads about it first,

she'll be even more upset." I glanced at the cell phone on my coffee table but couldn't make myself pick it up. At only ten o'clock, I was too emotionally drained for any more drama tonight.

Dawn read my mind and shrugged. "You can at least put it off till the morning."

I sighed. "And then I also have to figure out how I'm going to replace the steady income I was getting from those visits to DeLeuw's place."

"You should have signed up for the chamber of commerce small business expo next Sunday. Maybe there's still time."

In the recesses of my brain, I remembered seeing that advertised and Dawn mentioning it. I'd been busy, though, and didn't think I needed to bother. When I started Cassie's Comfy Cats, I had visited other businesses in town to introduce myself, and persuaded many of them to display my advertising brochures. I also took out ads regularly in the town weekly and the county daily newspaper. But with this loss of a major customer—even though it left me in anything but an upbeat frame of mind—I might have to get back to more aggressive marketing.

"I'll give it a thought," I said.

"You can at least take a table with your brochures. Keith will be there, and he doesn't bring much more than his portfolio. Of course, he also draws people on the spot."

Keith was Dawn's longtime boyfriend, who somehow made a good living doing caricatures at parties and more elaborate illustrations and videos for corporate clients.

"Easy enough for him," I said with a laugh, "but I am not going to try to groom strangers' cats in the middle of a busy trade show!"

"No," she agreed, "probably not the best idea."

The herbal tea had its intended effect on me, and a few minutes later even Dawn could see I was fading fast. As she left by the back door, she advised, "Get some rest, and things will look better tomorrow."

I was so tired, I forget to warn her about the loose right banister. Luckily, the motion-sensor light came on as she started down the short flight of steps, because when she leaned on the wooden rail, it wobbled dangerously.

"Sorry!" I told her. "I have *got* to get Nick out here to fix that."

Another call to make tomorrow, I thought as I left the cats food for the night and shambled off to bed.

That herbal tea was strong stuff, and despite everything I'd been through, I slept soundly. You might say, like the dead.

Chapter 4

People often act surprised when I tell them I don't let my cats sleep with me at night. Even when I lived at home with my parents, and different cats, I never did.

I acquired most of my pets when they were less than two years old, and to a young cat, nighttime is for hunting. They'll stalk feet and hands that move beneath the bedcovers, then pounce with great ferocity. They'll jump on top of your headboard, stare at the ceiling, and wail for the mother ship to come take them back to Alpha Centauri. Or they'll help declutter the top of the dresser by knocking off your watch, your keys, and your lipstick. If those don't get your attention, that nice bottle of perfume ought to roll real good. . . .

Crash!

Sure, it scares them a little when you finally lurch out of bed, half-blind with sleep, wave your arms, and scream very bad words. But at least it relieves the boredom.

Some people can't bear to listen to yowls outside the closed bedroom door, and claim their pets sleep quietly on their beds after, oh, a couple of years. Well, if I don't let mine in, they stop yowling a lot sooner than that, and in the meantime, I can wear earplugs. I make exceptions only during winter power outages, when we all need the extra body heat.

So it surprised me to hear them meowing loudly on Tuesday morning, until I checked my cell phone and realized I'd overslept. *Almost eight!* I'd have to scramble to feed them and myself, shower, and be ready at nine to open the door for my new assistant.

Two strong cups of coffee had perked me up by the time Sarah arrived. Her teal-green knit pants and a coordinating print tunic showed she was thinking ahead; they looked nice enough for the sales desk, but casual enough to let her handle the animals.

As Sarah mounted the back steps, I warned her about the shaky railing. I took a minute, while she was getting settled for the day, to leave Nick a phone message about fixing the rail when he could. Then Sarah and I fed the boarders, scooped out their litter, and gave them each a little TLC.

"The owner of the two Siamese is picking them up at ten," I told Sarah. "We'll wait until after he leaves to start letting the others out of their cages."

My new assistant had been throwing me occasional sideways looks, and when we took a break, she finally asked, "Cassie, did you know you were in this morning's paper?"

Uh-oh. There could be only one reason for that, but I played dumb. "I was?"

"Well, just your name. That appointment you went to yesterday . . . Was it some man named George DeLeuw?"

The taste of coffee rose again in my mouth. "Oh Lord, they mentioned me? What did it say?" Bad enough losing my best customer, but being named as a murder suspect could torpedo my business before it ever got off the ground.

"Just that you showed up to work on his cat and found him dead inside the house. Is that true? It must have been awful!"

"Yeah, it was." Relieved that the paper hadn't exaggerated my involvement, I briefly told Sarah the story. "I liked the guy okay, and he seemed to have a pretty quiet lifestyle, so I can't imagine who'd want to kill him. On the other hand, I really didn't know much about him."

"From the story, it sounds as if the police are looking into his business dealings, so maybe that's the explanation." My assistant shook her head, reflecting. "If he lived alone, who's looking after his cat?"

I smiled and rested a hand on her shoulder. "Sarah, you're my kind of people. That's exactly what I've been worried about ever since I came home from his place. I left my number with the housekeeper, and I just hope she'll call me if there's any problem."

Freddy, the elderly owner of Simone and

Samantha—the two Siamese—showed up just after ten to claim them. He and his longtime partner had enjoyed their week in Key West, he said, but would be happy to be reunited with their "girls." Sarah expertly settled up the bill so that Freddy left us two cats poorer and a few hundred dollars richer.

In the brief lull that followed, I used my phone to check whether DeLeuw's death had made the Internet. But when I saw I'd missed a call from my mother, that told me all I needed to know.

Mom never had understood why I couldn't use my degree in psychology to analyze human beings, a career that at least involved some prestige and real money. "Four years of college," she liked to remind me, "and you brush other people's animals for a living!"

Now I asked Sarah, "Can you handle things for a few minutes? I need to explain to my mom how I ended up in a house where a guy got murdered."

She winced in sympathy. "Good luck!"

I perched on a stool behind the sales counter to make the call. Mom sounded about as wound up as I'd expected, and thought I was keeping secrets from her because I hadn't told her immediately about the incident. My attempts to explain that I got home exhausted and depressed, and had been busy all morning with a new hire, only seemed to make things worse. I'd never figured out how to handle Mom when she got like this— even if I acted calm, she just thought I wasn't taking the situation seriously enough.

"I don't know why you had to move out to the sticks all by yourself," she fretted.

"Mom, this didn't happen at my store."

"No, but it happened when you went out to someone's house for your job. What if you'd walked in while the killer was still there?"

I had no real answer for that—I'd wondered the same thing, myself. "Well, I didn't. Two other people were on the property, and the killer avoided them, too. It had to be somebody with a personal grudge against DeLeuw."

"Maybe he was involved in something criminal. You don't know anything about these people you go out to work for!"

"He was the only customer who asked me to come to his home. So from now on, I'll insist they all bring their cats to me. Will that make you feel better? I'll tell them my mother worries too much when I make house calls."

"Don't be smart." Mom sniffed—just indignation or actual tears? She'd gotten even worse since starting her current job, as if reading about all of these lawsuits made her always imagine disasters. "Now that your name is in the paper, this person might think you know something and come after you. I wish you didn't live alone!"

I would not let our conversation veer onto the old subject of why I'd stopped seeing Andy. From my seat behind the sales counter, I could just glimpse the four-inch canister of pepper spray I kept hidden on the shelf underneath. I'd told my mother that Andy and I argued all the time over little things, but she'd rationalized that I was "too independent" and all couples had problems to work out. I'd never revealed that during our last argument, in his apartment, Andy shoved me backward against a metal bookcase. The gigantic multicolored bruise on my left shoulder blade took more than a week to heal.

No bones broken, but I wasn't giving him an opportunity to do worse. Safer to live in Chadwick by myself than back in Morristown, near him.

I steered the subject and tone of the conversation in a new direction. "Actually, Mom, on the subject of people living alone, I could use your professional expertise." *She'll stop worrying,* I thought, *if I give her a puzzle to figure out.* I explained DeLeuw's home situation and asked what she thought might happen with his cat.

My approach worked, and the more rational side of her brain kicked in. "If it looks like murder, they'll do an autopsy. That will hold everything up for a while, but at least it might narrow down their range of suspects. His killer won't be allowed to benefit from any inheritance . . . assuming the police can figure out who it is, which could also take a while. Even under less complicated circumstances, probating a will can drag on for a long time."

When my father had died, Mom handled all the interactions with their lawyer regarding his will, so I knew nothing about the process. "What exactly does 'probating' mean, anyway?"

She prefaced her answer with a little sigh of impatience; she'd never quite accepted the idea that I didn't inherit her analytical, methodical type of mind. I suppose I took after my father, a periodontist who painted watercolor landscapes in his spare time.

"Probate is the whole process of settling an estate," she explained. "The deceased person's property has to be inventoried, his debts have to be paid off, and whatever is left is divided among his heirs."

"This all happens even if he left a will?"

"Very often. In your Mr. DeLeuw's case, just the fact that he owns an expensive house and property and an art collection means his estate will be probated. But the fact that he was murdered complicates things too. . . ." I could almost hear Mom's shrug over the line. "It could take a year or more to settle everything."

I pictured all of this stretching out over time while poor, confused Harpo languished without his owner, and possibly without even the basics like food and water. "Would they let his housekeeper onto the property to keep it up? Somebody would have to pay her. . . ."

"His lawyer will take charge of all that, at least until they can find his nearest relative." With a warning in her voice, Mom added, "It's not your problem, Cassie. Don't get any more mixed up in this than you already are."

"I hear you, Mom." When call waiting beeped and my handyman's number showed up, I saw my chance to cut things short. "Oops, somebody's trying to reach me. Gotta go. Love ya!"

I caught my breath, then dialed Nick back, expecting a nice, boring conversation about the porch repair. But normally easygoing Mr. Janos sounded even more agitated than my mother.

"Cassie, I'm sorry I missed your call. I honestly don't know when I can get over there. There's another guy who covers for me sometimes. . . . I can give you his number. . . ."

Nick once mentioned that he'd been to the doctor for a heart problem, and from his tone now I expected the worst. "Don't worry about it. Are you okay?"

"It's my boy, Dion." I heard Nick swallow hard. "The cops are questioning him. . . ."

That quiet, nerdy guy who spent all his time tinkering with computers? *What did he do?* I wondered. *Knock over an electronics store?* "Oh no. What for?"

"It's just so crazy." Nick drew a long, shuddery breath. "They think he killed that rich fella, George DeLeuw!"

Chapter 5

I waved Sarah over, gave her my seat behind the sales counter, and took my phone to the rear condo area for privacy. "Nick, why would the police think your son was involved?"

"Because he was mad. He thought DeLeuw stole one of his ideas for some kind of invention." The handyman, normally upbeat and easygoing, sounded totally unraveled today.

"Did the cops hold Dion?" I asked.

"No, thank God. They got no proof, 'cause he didn't do it!" Nick sighed deeply. "Cassie, I can't go into it all now. I'm headed out to a job I put off from this morning. But I'll get over to your place later this afternoon, okay? Long as nothing else goes wrong . . ."

"I sure hope nothing else does." Thinking of his heart trouble, I added, "Take it easy, okay?"

As I hung up, I heard Sarah's voice at the front of the shop overlapping with Dawn's. The two huddled over something on the sales counter that turned out to be a bedraggled-looking brown tabby kitten, all legs, eyes, and ears.

"Cassie, isn't he the sweetest thing?" Sarah cooed.

"I found him hiding in my storeroom," Dawn said. "He's got no collar or license, but he doesn't seem awfully wild. When I called to him, he came right up to me."

"He does seem very tame," Sarah agreed as the kitten head-butted her arm, eyes blissfully squeezed shut.

"Could be he ran away from a home and got lost." I picked up the little guy, who introduced himself with a polite mew, and looked him over. Probably four or five months old, the age when mother cats usually wean their young. He might have been born feral, but if so, he had no fear of people.

"I'm usually more of a dog person," Dawn admitted, "but just look at dat pwecious widdle face! I'd keep him at my store, but I guess that wouldn't be fair if his owner is out looking for him. Or maybe you can hang on to him while I post signs around town and see if anybody claims him?"

"Before either of us takes him in, even temporarily, he should see a vet who can make sure he hasn't got any health problems," I warned her. "I can't endanger any of my boarders. Just at first glance, I can see he's got fleas and ear mites."

Both of the other women backed off from fondling the kitten after hearing this news, and my friend brushed off her silky sea-green tunic.

"Can we treat him for those things?" Sarah suggested. "I saw some flea medicine back in the grooming area."

"Yes, but if he's been neglected, he could have more serious issues that we can't see." I told Dawn, "I can lend you a carrier if you want to run him over to the clinic."

My friend responded with a sly grin. "Gee, I think you should do the honors. After all, you know much more about cats than I do!" She stage-whispered to Sarah, "Cassie's got a thing for the vet, Dr. Coccia."

Anticipating the bills for vaccinations and other treatment, I tried to pass the little tabby back to Dawn. "You know what they say—finders keepers."

She read my mind. "I'll gladly pay for whatever care he needs, but right now I've really got to get back to my store. And as you know, Cassie, I'm perfectly happy with Keith. However, I think you should seize this opportunity!"

I glanced to Sarah for support, but she abetted Dawn. "The clinic's just a few blocks away, right? I can handle things here, Cassie, until you get back."

"Mew!" added the kitten.

They were all ganging up on me. Who could resist that kind of pressure?

I called first to make sure Dr. Coccia could spare a few minutes to check out the little stray, which we temporarily named Tigger. Then I ran up to my apartment long enough to change into a clean T-shirt in a flattering coral shade, put on a touch of makeup, and quickly trim my bangs over the bathroom sink. (Grooming animals for a living does give a person some useful life skills.)

Back in the shop, I left Sarah instructions just in case anyone came by to pick up or drop off a cat. Then I packed Tigger into a spare carrier, shrugged into my short brown pleather jacket, and headed out on foot.

I always enjoyed strolling through downtown Chadwick. Alongside the trendier shops selling handmade jewelry, fine art, and high-end crafts, you still could find several mom-and-pop businesses that probably went back several generations. On the sidewalk outside a new clothing boutique, I dodged around a headless mannequin dressed in a flashy retro-inspired outfit; a few steps later I passed a homey hardware store with rakes and bags of fertilizer stacked out front. Delicious sugary smells wafted out of Cottone's Bakery, another long-time fixture on Center Street. A quick peek through the front window of Towne Antiques also made me drool, since I generally pick up my "antiques" at the Salvation Army and refresh them with a coat of paint.

A few people who passed me in the opposite direction glanced at the pet carrier and smiled at either me or Tigger. We animal lovers share an un-spoken bond.

Like my shop, the Chadwick Veterinary Clinic occupied what once had been a private home, but in this case a sizeable white ranch house with colonial overtones. A sign with the names of the two staff veterinarians, Mark Coccia and Elizabeth Reed, hung from a post near the front walk. The property included a good-sized rear parking lot, which so far I'd never needed to use.

The waiting room had a central modern reception desk in polished oak, and matching benches ran along two walls. I checked in and sat down, the carrier on my lap, as far away as I could manage from a lively Great Dane. The huge brindled dog kept straining at the end of his leash to get a better look at Tigger, which his owner found amusing. I turned the wire mesh front of the carrier toward my body.

A white-haired man stood at the desk, settling up a bill, his shoulders hunched and a small red collar poking out of his pocket. The receptionist spoke so softly to him that I couldn't overhear, but no doubt he'd just had to put some beloved pet to sleep. I ached for him, having been in that situation many times—not only with animals of my own, but during my brief stint as a vet tech. It never got easier.

I just hoped Tigger wouldn't turn out to have any dire, hidden ailment that was beyond treating. He seemed too bright-eyed and energetic, though, for that to be the case.

A tech called us into one of the examining rooms, where I set the carrier on a steel table similar to the type I used for grooming. A couple of minutes later Dr. Mark strode through the door, obviously in the middle of a busy schedule. It could have been just my imagination, but I thought his eyebrows did a little jump and his smile stretched extra wide when he recognized me.

"Ms. McGlone! Good to see you again. You were in here last month, right? With the stray kitten that had ringworm?" When I nodded confirmation, he asked, "How's she doing?"

I was flattered that he remembered my visit, even down to the gender of the kitten. "Great, as far as I know. The shelter put her up for adoption, and I think they already found her a home."

"That's terrific. Always glad to hear about a happy ending."

Mark himself was the type to inspire fantasies of happy endings. A little taller than me and a little older—perfect, right? Typical dark Italian good looks except for startling deep-blue eyes fringed by black lashes. He didn't wear a wedding ring, but I warned myself the guy *had* to be taken. His type never stayed on the loose for very long.

He glanced at the carrier and asked, "What've we got today? Another orphan of the storm?"

"You guessed it." I lifted Tigger out onto the table. "My friend Dawn—she owns the health-food store Nature's Way?—said this little guy sneaked into her storeroom somehow. She's thinking of keeping him, but I insisted you have a look at him first."

Mark noticed the same superficial health problems as I had, then checked Tigger's teeth, felt his belly, and drew some blood. "If he's been on his own for a while, he could have picked up some parasites. With any luck, he won't have caught any more serious diseases."

"Dawn was wondering if he might have belonged to someone, since he seems so friendly."

The vet took out a device resembling a supermarket scanner and passed it above the kitten's shoulder area. It didn't beep, which told both of us Tigger lacked a microchip that, in place of a license tag, would identify him as someone's pet. "If he did come from a home, it seems like the people didn't take very good care of him. Whether your friend keeps him or she finds the owner, this guy should be vaccinated against distemper, rhinotracheitis, calicivirus, and rabies."

I nodded. "Maybe I should leave him here today and let him get the works?"

Mark stroked the tiny striped head with just his fingertips, in a way that melted my heart. "Sounds good. We'll give him a bath this afternoon to get rid of the fleas, and test him for FIV, feline leukemia, and worms. You should be able to pick him up around this time tomorrow."

Much as I'd have liked the excuse to see Mark again, I knew I'd probably have things to tend to at my shop. "Dawn may be the one picking him up. In fact, maybe I should give her an idea of the cost."

Mark tallied it off the top of his head, and I texted my friend. "Okay, she's fine with that."

"The first visit is a little steep, I know," he sympathized. "Especially for a stray who might have been exposed to all kinds of problems."

"You'll be fine, Tigger," I told the little tabby as a tech took him away in his carrier.

It occurred to me then that Mark might be able to answer a nagging question for me, though I'd have to ask discreetly. "By the way, would you know what happens to a pet when the owner dies suddenly and didn't provide for it in his will?"

Understandably, he needed a minute to consider this. "I haven't run into too many situations like that, but . . . I guess any of the heirs would be free to claim the animal."

"What if none of them want it?"

He planted his hands on his hips, which were noticeably slim even in baggy blue scrubs. "Sounds like you've got a specific case in mind. You wouldn't be talking about George DeLeuw? Oh gosh, that's right—the newspaper said you were at his house!"

A polite knock at one of the room's two doors, and the vet tech put her head inside. "Mrs. Ostroff is here. The cocker spaniel with cherry eye?"

"Thanks, Debby. I'll be right with her."

I felt guilty to be keeping Mark from his other patients. "I don't want to take up your time. . . ."

"No, no, it's a worthwhile question. I just saw DeLeuw's cat once, when George brought him in for a booster shot. Harpo, wasn't it? Beautiful animal. Nice disposition, too."

"Yes, and I'm afraid he's going end up in a bad place, or maybe even euthanized. That's the last thing George would have wanted. But while everyone is concentrating on solving his murder, Harpo could slip through the cracks."

Mark glanced briefly toward the door, and I knew he was thinking about the other patients waiting for him. "Tell you what. I'll ask around, look into some of the options. Is there a number where I can reach you? I don't think we have one on file. . . ."

Always prepared, I grabbed a business card from my purse and also wrote my cell number on the back. "I really appreciate your help, and I'm sure George would too."

"Crazy thing, huh? A guy like that, killed in his own house, in a quiet town like this?" Mark shook his head. "Okay, Cassie. I'll call Dawn tomorrow when the kitten's ready to go home. And I'll also be in touch with you about . . . this other business."

I stepped back onto the sidewalk, feeling lighter, and not just because I'd left kitten and carrier behind. Tigger would get the treatment he needed, I should be getting information that would help me to look out for Harpo's best interests . . . and Mark Coccia now possessed my phone number and had promised to call.

All in all, a very productive morning.

Chapter 6

I headed back to the shop with a swing in my step, leaving my jacket open to the light breeze. The fresh air up here had taken some getting used to, compared to the other, more crowded New Jersey towns where I had grown up. I also enjoyed the absence of any really tall buildings in Chadwick. Even downtown, all I had to do was raise my sights a little to gaze out over rolling hills beyond. In any season, that view tended to improve my perspective in more ways than one.

Passing the drugstore, which still had Easter decorations in its window, I noticed a woman up the block who definitely did not look like a native. Tall and slim, she wore a sophisticated, minimalist outfit no Chadwick matron would consider—a loose linen-colored tunic with wide-leg brown pants, a stylish cross-body purse, and wedge shoes. Even the cut of her super-straight, shoulder-length blond hair looked expensive.

The other thing that set her apart was that she was having some kind of meltdown over her cell phone. People around here usually don't have such intense relationships with their electronic devices. She kept moaning to herself, "No-o-o, *no-o-o!*" and slapping the phone against her palm as if that would resuscitate it. Finally she slumped back against a nearby car, her face crumpled, as if on the verge of tears.

When I lived in a more urban setting, I might have passed by, not wanting to get involved in someone else's drama. But even though I'd only been a Chadwick resident for about four months, some of the town's friendliness had rubbed off on me. And though this woman looked stressed, she didn't appear dangerous . . . or crazy.

Nearing her, I asked quietly, "Is something wrong? Do you need help?"

She started, as if surprised that anyone had overheard her. "Oh . . . thanks. My stupid phone is dead, and I just realized I probably left my charger at home!" I must have looked puzzled—*So, go home and get it?*—because she added, "In California."

"Ah," I said.

She obviously needed to vent to someone. "It's got my whole calendar and all my contacts! And I was supposed to confirm an important delivery today to my San Jose store. . . ." She blew out her cheeks in frustration. "Guess I won't be doing *that.*"

"You just need another charger, right? Mind if I take a look?"

She paused, as if wary about trusting me, then handed over the phone. I'd held out a thin hope that it might be similar to my very basic model, but of course not. She had a top-of-the-line smartphone that could probably do everything but iron her hair.

"I thought maybe I could just lend you my charger," I said, "but guess not."

"Where can I even find another one around here?" she lamented. "Is there an electronics store out on the highway? But I don't have *time*. . . . I have so much else to do today!"

Tears finally welled up in her eyes, which were a distinctive silvery green that felt familiar to me. Fine lines fanned from the corners of her eyes and the edges of her lips, so I figured her to be around fifty. For someone so meticulously turned out otherwise, she wore no visible makeup.

I felt helpless at her distress. "I'm sure it'll be okay."

She blotted her tears on her sleeve and pulled herself together. "I'm sorry. I don't usually carry on like this, but . . . my brother just died. I flew east to make arrangements for his funeral."

The poor woman! "Well, of course you're upset. That's probably why you forgot to pack your charger, too." I had an idea. "Look, there's a little electronics store a few blocks down, on a side street. I bet they could fix you up."

The blond woman glanced up and down Center Street and took in the humble mom-and-pop businesses with a tight, skeptical smile. "Oh, I really don't think—"

"Seriously, you'd be amazed at the stuff Emmy keeps in stock. It's worth a try, right?"

She weighed the small effort against her desperation. "*Where* is this place?"

"Not far. I'll walk with you." I started down the block and coaxed her along like one of my finicky felines. "I'm Cassie, by the way."

"Danielle." The woman offered a slim hand with a perfect French manicure. "It's nice of you to do this."

On our way, I remembered her comment about an important shipment. "What kind of store do you have in California?"

"I'm a fashion designer, and I have retail shops in San Jose and San Francisco," she told me. "DeLeuw Designs."

I planted my heels, suddenly remembering where I'd seen those eyes before. "Oh my God. You're George DeLeuw's sister!"

"That's right." Danielle laughed uncomfortably. "This really *must* be a small town."

"No . . . I mean, he was pretty well-known, but . . . I groomed his cat, Harpo." To prove I wasn't a crackpot, I fished a business card out of my purse and handed it to her. "I'm so sorry for your loss. I didn't know your brother terribly well, but he seemed like a fine man."

"He did, didn't he? Anyhow, thank you, Cassie."

I wasn't about to mention that I'd found George's body, because I didn't think she needed that picture in her head. But Danielle brought it up herself, having heard about it from the police.

"It's been a double shock," she admitted as we started walking again. "To hear that he'd passed from natural causes would have been one thing. But murdered!"

"I think everyone here who knew him and worked for him felt the same way. At least the local police seem to be doing everything they can to figure out what happened."

Once we reached Emmy's Electronics, I sensed that the store's homey name and small square footage did nothing to boost Danielle's confidence. Neither did the sight of the desktop and laptop computers and smaller, older-model flat-screens TVs that cluttered the front of the shop.

"She does walk-in repairs," I explained to Danielle. "These are probably fixed and waiting for customers to pick up."

Danielle glanced restlessly toward the door. "Maybe I should drive out to the highway. This might just be a waste of—"

Emmy bustled out then, a round woman with a curly mop of graying black hair and a cheerful, rosy face. "Hi, folks. What can I do ya for today?"

Tentatively, as if she didn't quite expect the shopkeeper to speak her language, Danielle explained her problem and surrendered her phone. Emmy turned it over in her pillowy but skillful hands.

"Hey, that's a nice one," she said. "I think we got something that'll work with this. . . . Just got a new delivery last week . . ." She hunted through the overlapping stacks of high-tech accessories that packed her store to the rafters. In just a couple of minutes she produced a sleek black device the size of a pack of cards. "This is portable, and it'll have you recharged in two hours." Emmy ripped open its molded plastic casing to let Danielle test it on her phone.

DeLeuw's sister couldn't hide her surprise when the charger worked. She gladly paid what, for me, would have been a hefty price.

I smiled through the whole transaction without once whispering, "I told you so."

"Thanks for your help, Cassie," Danielle said as we left the store. "You saved me searching up and down the highway, which I don't know very well."

"Don't mention it," I said. "You've got enough problems right now without having to stress over your phone."

Back at her car, a rental, she hesitated. "I'd like to buy you a coffee or something, but—"

"That's okay. I need to get back to my own shop, and you have a lot to deal with today."

"I do." She looked down with a sigh at the sidewalk.

"Nice meeting you, though," I told her. "Good luck with . . . all the arrangements."

After we'd parted, I reflected on Danielle's odd response when I'd said her brother seemed like a fine man.

"He did, didn't he?"

Strange way to put it! I thought. *But heck, she's in mourning and under a lot of stress. It probably just came out wrong.*

Back at the shop, I apologized to Sarah for being gone so long and told her about encountering DeLeuw's sister. She agreed that it was one heck of a coincidence.

Then, with no more time to waste, my new assistant and I donned our official CCC smocks to groom Mystique, a boarder due to be picked up that evening. The stunning Birman cat provided us with a different experience from Mango, being a semi-longhair with a mellow temperament.

"I've never seen one like this before," my assistant commented, still with a girlish fascination. "Her coloring is so pretty, like a Siamese's. Look at those blue eyes!"

For a second I recalled Mark Coccia's sexy eyes, also unexpectedly blue, then snapped myself back into professional mode. "Some people think Birmans were developed from Siamese, maybe crossed with Persians, a long time ago," I told Sarah. "And see how her legs are dark, but with white feet?"

Mystique was so accustomed to being groomed that the two of us didn't need a harness to keep her on the table. The milky fur that covered most of her body had stayed pretty clean during her visit, so we mostly combed her to get rid of any dead hair and fluffed her up with baby powder. One of the things I enjoy most about my job is the beauty and variety of the animals' fur. Mystique's was silky, without the lush undercoat of a Persian like Harpo. Even among nonpedigreed shorthairs like my own three cats, Matisse's calico coat had a light, soft quality, while Mango's tabby hairs felt a bit crisper and Cole's black fur lay flat and smooth as satin. I'd be able to recognize any of my pets simply by touch.

We had just finished primping the boarder

when I heard a knock at my back door. "That's got to be Nick," I told Sarah. "Can you put Mystique back in her cage while I talk to him?"

"Sure." My assistant hugged the Birman with both arms, as if she might find it hard to say good-bye when the cat's owner arrived.

I found my thickset, balding handyman already checking out the wobbly post on my back steps. "Thanks for making time to come," I told him. "My friend Dawn leaned on that rail the other night and almost took a spill."

"Might be able to fix it with just a bolt or a bracket." Nick stroked the short fringe of his gray mustache. "I'll have to check underneath to see."

He had pulled his JANOS HOME REPAIR panel truck into my parking lot and opened the doors to get his toolbox. When he turned back around, I noticed his eyes looked red and tired behind his wire glasses. He spent a minute crouched next to the low flight of steps with a flashlight and a few mutters of concern.

Surfacing, he told me, "I probably can secure it okay for now, but that old wood's starting to split. You really need a new post. I can make you one, but I might not get back here to install it until the end of the week."

"That's fine," I assured him. "Do what you can now, and replace the post whenever you're able. I know you've got a lot on your mind these days. How is Dion doing?"

"He's home, anyway." Rummaging through different-sized brackets in his toolbox, Nick shook his head. "I still can't believe anyone could accuse him of murder! That Detective Bonelli, she's new around here. Just joined the force about six months ago."

Only a little longer than I'd been in town, but I got Nick's point. "She doesn't know the locals, I guess, so she suspects everyone."

"Course, I s'pose she's got good reason." He paused, a bracket in his hands, and sighed. "Damn, this is all *my* fault."

That made me stand up straighter. I couldn't help noticing all of the hammers, saws, crowbars, and other potentially lethal objects stockpiled in the back of Nick's van. And for a guy around sixty, he still looked strong enough to wield something like that with plenty of force. "Why do you say that?"

"'Cause I told him to go over there. Now I wish to God I never mentioned it!"

"You told him to go to DeLeuw's house yesterday?"

"No, no. Like, a month ago."

I leaned against the stairs' more solid railing, across from where Nick was working. "Why? And what would that have to do with George's . . . death?"

Nick sat on the gravel next to the steps and reached underneath with a bracket to see if it would do the job. "Dion has this idea for an invention, some kind of computer code that'd be real hard to crack and can handle big files or something. I don't understand much about it, but he thinks it could be a big deal. First, though, he needs money to develop it and patent it. Neither of us has got that kind of cash, so he needs a backer."

"Okay." I also didn't know much about patenting an invention, and even less about computer codes, but it all sounded logical.

"I say to him, 'Why don't you talk to that DeLeuw fella? I heard he used to work on Wall Street and he knows some people out there in California, in Silicone Valley.' "

I could hardly blame Nick for this malaprop, because he'd probably had a lot more experience with caulk than with high technology. And how could I feel superior when even I had no idea what "silicon" was?

He drilled under the steps for a minute, then took a break to continue his story. "So Dion goes over there, tells DeLeuw about his idea, and shows him the plans. I guess DeLeuw seemed interested and said he'd discuss it with his Silicone Valley buddies. After that, Dion checks with him every coupla days, e-mailing or calling. DeLeuw keeps telling him the computer guys are still testing the system and making up their minds. Finally he goes over there in person and DeLeuw blows up at him. Says these things take time, and if Dion doesn't stop bugging him, he's gonna just tell the California company to forget the whole thing."

Hardly a motive for murder, I thought, unless Dion was a major hothead. "He must have been pretty disappointed—"

Nick cut me off with a wave of his cordless drill. "*But* Dion reads all the computer-business news online. Last week he saw that some Chinese electronics firm came out with a new system that sounds just like his idea. So he thinks DeLeuw went behind his back and made a deal with somebody else, cutting him out."

That did sound like a good reason to lose your temper. "And somehow the police found out about all this?"

"Some people who worked for DeLeuw—his housekeeper and his assistant—they remembered Dion coming over that first time and then phoning and e-mailing a lot. The assistant guy said Dion kept 'hounding' DeLeuw about the invention. Made my boy sound like some kind of dangerous lunatic, which he's not! Besides, no matter how mad Dion got, he'd never hurt anybody."

I let Nick position the new bracket and screw it into place before I asked, "He could use a good alibi. Where was he yesterday afternoon?"

"Eh, where else? At our house, in his office in the basement, working on his computer. He said he was debugging a game for a client and was—whatcha-call-it—online. He told me his computer would have a record of the times he'd had the game open, modified the files, and stuff."

Of course, these days a person could be parked in his car and still be using a laptop or an iPad. It was hard to imagine a guy calmly playing a computer game right after having a violent argument and killing someone. But if Dion was clever enough to come up with a sophisticated encryption system, maybe he even could falsify the times he'd been working on his computer.

"At least you can vouch for him being at home, right?" I asked Nick.

"Sure, but how much do the cops trust me? I'm his dad. Besides, Dion's got a separate door to go in and out of the basement. It's convenient, because clients sometimes visit him. So if someone asked me to swear under oath, did I know he was in the house that whole afternoon . . . I guess I couldn't say for sure." His stubborn pride resurfaced. "Still, I know my boy, and that's enough for me."

I heard the frustration in his voice and felt sad that he had to go through this heartache. "Maybe when they find the murder weapon, it will have somebody else's fingerprints and that will clear Dion."

Nick had gone back to working under the stairs, so his face was half-hidden, but his tone remained grim. "Maybe they already found it. They asked Dion about the artworks DeLeuw had around the place. Like, did he ever look at them, touch anything?" Finished with his repair, the handyman sat up and faced me with a puzzled expression. "But that doesn't make sense either. How could you kill somebody with an artwork?"

Nick didn't charge me for the small repair and told me to save it for when he put in the new post. Once he left, I hurried back inside my shop to help Sarah return Mystique to her owner, Mrs. Nolan. The preppy-looking, fortyish woman commented on our grooming job, which brought a big smile to Sarah's face and also gave me a boost. Debby Nolan had told me in the past that her Birman often won prizes at cat shows, and I knew that folks on the show circuit took their grooming uber-seriously. Maybe she'd recommend me to her friends!

By now it was past five, so I thanked Sarah for

doing a great job on her first full day, and joked that I hoped I'd see her again tomorrow.

"You sure will," she promised on her way out. "I enjoyed every minute."

I marveled at her energy, because even though I was about thirty years younger, I felt wiped out. All I wanted was to feed my cats, pull together an easy dinner for myself, and hit the sack early.

Stress, I thought. Maybe a delayed reaction to the shock of yesterday.

And now the cops suspected Dion Janos? It didn't seem possible that a sweet guy like Nick could raise a son with that kind of temper.

While I spooned out canned food for my three roommates, then stir-fried some leftover chicken and vegetables for myself, I thought some more about how ridiculous that whole theory sounded. The police thought someone clocked George with one of his own artworks? That head wound wasn't made by a picture frame!

Only later, after I'd dropped into bed and turned out the light, did I remember one piece in DeLeuw's collection that could have done the deed. The foot-tall chunk of granite with one jagged edge, kind of like a giant arrowhead.

But if someone had used that to kill DeLeuw, the motive couldn't have been art theft. When I'd left George's house yesterday, the sculpture had still been on its pedestal in the front hall.

Chapter 7

I may be strict about no-cats-in-the-bedroom-while-I'm-sleeping, but I'll admit I've slacked off about cats on my dining table during meals. Cole and Matisse often try to join me, and no matter how often I remove them, one or both will sneak back up when I'm not looking. These days I let them as long as they keep their distance and don't try to actually take food off my plate . . . or out of my mouth. Since I always feed them before I eat, that seems only fair. They know they're banished when I have company, and I always wipe the table and put down a fresh cloth before another human joins me for dinner.

Wednesday morning, Matisse meditated on the table facing me, front paws neatly rolled under her (the feline version of the lotus position). I ate whole-grain cereal with skimmed milk and raspberries while I scanned the national news on my laptop. I always check the local stories too, which was how I came across George DeLeuw's obituary.

Even though the same news source had carried the initial story about DeLeuw's murder—or maybe for that reason—the obit made no mention of his violent death. It simply noted that the sixty-five-year-old had passed away on Monday at his home in Chadwick.

The full article stated that DeLeuw was a managing director with Redmond & Fowler Securities Management in New York City, where he formerly served as chairman of Hetherington Mutual Funds. He had graduated with an MBA from Columbia Business School and held analyst and associate positions with a couple of investment banks before his rise to power on Wall Street. A columnist from a major business publication was quoted as saying, "Over the years, George DeLeuw developed an outstanding reputation for generating revenue for his corporate clients. He also stood out for his low-key, cooperative approach in a profession that often breeds mercurial temperaments and big egos."

In the words of Charles Schroeder, another managing director at Redmond & Fowler, "George's business acumen was second to none, and was exceeded only by his high standards, which he never compromised." The article explained that DeLeuw had divested himself of some responsibilities in recent years "to spend more time traveling and adding to his prestigious art collection." He still kept his hand in, though, as an adviser on the boards of one major investment firm, of the Braff Museum of Art in New York, and of Encyte Cybersecurity, based in San Jose, California.

The article concluded, "DeLeuw is survived by his sister, Danielle, of San Jose. He was predeceased by a daughter, Renée."

Intrigued, I made an electronic copy of the obituary. George had never mentioned any children, and to have one die young must have been a wrenching experience. I wondered how long ago that had happened and how old Renée had been.

I searched under Redmond & Fowler, and among the dry reports from business magazines I found only one hint of scandal. A few years back, several Wall Street firms had been investigated for laundering money from drug cartels—cocaine from South America and heroin from Central Asia. One major international bank was found guilty, but because it was deemed "too big to fail," it paid a fine to settle out of court. Investment-banking firms such as Redmond & Fowler also came under scrutiny during that period, but in the end the Justice Department could not find enough proof of wrongdoing to bring a case against them.

One other detail that caught my eye in DeLeuw's obit was the mention of the Silicon Valley cybersecurity firm. No doubt this was the connection that had led Nick Janos to decide that DeLeuw might be able to help Dion patent his innovative coding system.

I guessed George's autopsy had been completed, because his funeral was set for Thursday at a local cemetery, with viewings tomorrow morning and evening at the Dewey Funeral Home in Chadwick. I considered going. Would that look weird, since I barely knew the man? And would I *feel* weird, rubbing elbows with people who knew him far better, and whom I did not know at all, such as his business associates?

Though, thanks to our chance meeting, I now sort of knew his sister, Danielle.

Of course, sometimes family connections could be more problematic than helpful. In my e-mail queue, I found one from my mother with the subject line, "Blast from the Past." That cheery title didn't prepare me for her alarming message: "Guess who I ran into at Headquarters Plaza yesterday? Your old boyfriend Andy! He's working there now as a 'loss-prevention officer.' I guess it's like what he did at the mall, while you two were dating, but at least it's a step up. He asked about you, of course, and I told him . . ."

No, no, Mom! You didn't—

". . . that you moved to Chadwick and started your own business. Andy sounded very impressed. Don't be surprised if he looks you up one of these days. Just to wish you well, of course!"

And she signed off with a damned wink emoticon.

Jeez, why did she have to do that? I'd told her, when I'd first moved away and she'd mentioned Andy, not to ever tell him where to find me. But of course, the few times she'd met him she had really liked him. Also, she thought I was still mad over some small issue and just didn't feel like talking to him. My fault, I guess, for letting her go on thinking that.

He got a job in the same complex where my mom works? Was that just a coincidence?

Maybe I'm panicking over nothing. With any luck,

he's totally given up on me by now. If he's got a new job, maybe he's also got a new girlfriend.

Though if I knew that for sure, I'd be tempted to call the poor woman and warn her about Andy's temper.

Shutting off the computer, I showered, dressed, and welcomed Sarah's arrival. We had a fairly busy day to distract me from my worries.

Linda, a plump, bushy-haired young woman, brought in a fourteen-year-old Abyssinian with kidney problems named Ali. She gave us prescription food to tide him over while he boarded for a week. She'd had him since her high school days and obviously loved the old guy a lot. Fortunately, the cat was not so far along that he needed any medical procedures, such as subcutaneous fluids. We don't handle anything that tricky, and I would have had to refer her to the clinic.

"I'm so glad you only take cats," Linda told me on her way out. "I boarded Ali once at a place full of barking dogs, and he was a nervous wreck by the time I got him home."

Smiling, I told her that was a common problem, and one of the reasons I'd decided to specialize.

Sarah and I groomed the lean, chestnut-colored cat before putting him in his cage. His health problems made his coat dry and dull, but a gentle brushing did improve it somewhat, and Ali seemed to appreciate the attention.

Again, I noticed how kindly Sarah dealt with all the animals, and asked her, "Do you have any cats of your own?"

"Not right now," she said. "I did when I was younger, and while my husband was alive, we sometimes fostered kittens for the local shelter. The little ones have so much energy, though!" She rolled her eyes and laughed. "I'm not sure I'm up to chasing after them anymore. But sometimes I do miss the company of a pet around the house."

"You just need an older, quieter cat," I advised. "There are a lot of nice ones stuck in shelters, because so many people prefer kittens."

"Maybe so," Sarah said noncommittally.

While we settled Ali into his temporary home, with a bowl of water and his special food, my cell phone vibrated. My mother again.

Better answer, so you can nip her new scheme in the bud! I took the phone to the back of the grooming area for privacy.

"Did you get my message?" she asked coyly.

Her tone irritated me, but I tried to be patient. "Yes. Mom, I understand you probably were caught off guard, running into Andy like that. But I specifically asked you *not* to tell him where I'd moved to or what I'm doing these days."

"Oh, honestly. I just told him you'd started a business. I didn't even say anything more about it."

"Yeah, like Cassie's Comfy Cats in Chadwick would be that hard for him to track down. I'm serious—you had no right to violate my privacy like that."

At least the legalese got her attention, and she huffed in surprise. "Really, Cassie, aren't you being melodramatic? Even if you don't want to date him anymore, what's the harm in—"

"There just might be a lot of harm in it, Mom."

When Sarah threw a concerned glance in my direction, I dialed down the volume. "I'm working now, so we'll have to talk about this another time. Meanwhile, you need to trust my judgment."

After I hung up and rejoined my assistant, I felt I owed her some explanation. "She thinks I should get back together with my last boyfriend. She doesn't get it, that he's one of the reasons I moved all the way out here."

Sarah nodded toward the sales counter. "I hope he's not the reason you keep that pepper spray around."

I felt my face warm. "You don't miss much, do you?"

"Not after all those years teaching high school!" She hesitated before adding, "I had a student once who was being stalked by a boy she'd broken up with. It got to be a very scary situation—her family ended up calling the police."

"Well . . . I never had to go that far." Noticing that it was past noon, I suggested we take a lunch break. "I'll fill you in on the whole drama, just in case you ever need to know."

Over our sandwiches, I told Sarah more about my history with Andy than I'd ever revealed to my mother. "Looking back, I can see he fit the classic profile. He could be charming and funny and very romantic, but he also had a mean streak. He used to torment Cole until he got scratched, then grouse about my 'crazy cat.' After we'd been dating a couple of months, he started blowing up at me over small, stupid things, even calling me nasty names. One time he grabbed me so hard by the wrist, I swear he sprained it. He was floor manager for a sports-equipment store that was having financial problems. I knew his boss put him under a lot of pressure, so I rationalized it that way. The second time he hurt me physically, though, I heard the warning sirens loud and clear. I told him we were done."

Gently, Sarah asked, "How did he take it?"

"Oh, he apologized and swore he'd never do it again. I was tempted to give in, but I was just too scared to trust him. You hear stories about guys who swear they're sorry and then beat you up even worse. Besides, he said, 'You just made me so mad. . . .' as an excuse."

Sarah nodded. "Right—putting the blame on you!"

Memories I'd suppressed came flooding back now, signs of trouble I'd missed at first but that became obvious in hindsight. And I'd never forget that shocking moment when suddenly Andy had turned his full strength against me and I'd been too stunned to even fight back. Come to think of it, no wonder I hadn't wanted to date anybody since then!

"For a while after that he did some minor stalking stuff," I told Sarah. "Leaving phone messages and driving slowly by my apartment building. I told him to knock it off and blocked all his e-mails and his calls. When I moved to Chadwick, I tried to cover my tracks so he wouldn't follow me here. Of course, then I was brilliant enough to use my nickname in the name of the shop!"

"You never told your mother any of this?"

"I should have, right after it happened. But I was afraid either she'd accuse me of exaggerating or she'd fly off the handle and call the police. I know that technically Andy assaulted me, but I couldn't actually prove that. And once it was over between us, I thought, why make a lot of trouble for him?"

Sarah's canny eyes glinted behind her lenses. "So he couldn't do it again to someone else?"

I dropped my gaze to my half-eaten sandwich. "Well, yeah. There is that."

My phone rang in time to save me from making any more excuses. The veterinary clinic!

I expected a receptionist on the line, so it was a pleasant surprise when a familiar baritone said, "Hi, this is Dr. Coccia." Then I worried that he'd called in person to give me bad news about Tigger.

Fortunately not. "The kitten has had his shots and flea treatment—didn't need worming—and he's doing great. I just left your friend Dawn a message, telling her she can pick him up around four."

"Okay," I said. "I'll check with her to make sure she got it."

"As for the other question you asked me about, I didn't find out anything too helpful." In his tone and wording, Mark sounded guarded; maybe he didn't want the staff to overhear him discussing the DeLeuw murder. "Under most circumstances, if an owner dies and hasn't provided for a pet in his will, it's up to the surviving family members to deal with it. If there is no family, or no one wants the animal, usually it will go to a shelter. A shame, of course, but it happens all too often."

"That's what I was afraid of," I told him. "But thanks for double-checking. You've given me a lot to think about."

A warm chuckle on the line. "Uh-oh, I can hear the gears turning! If you do find a way to help Harpo, keep me posted."

After I clicked off, I found Sarah smiling at me. "Now, *that* young man sounds like a much better prospect for you."

"Huh . . . if he's a prospect at all. But at least we both feel the same way about trying to protect DeLeuw's cat."

Mark was right about one thing. Now that he'd confirmed my worst fears about Harpo's probable fate, the gears in my mind had started spinning at an even faster pace.

After closing up my shop for the day, I decided to stop by Nature's Way to see how Dawn was making out. Her building was one of the nicest small renovations in town, I thought. It originally had served as a feed store, then a humble five-and-ten. But Dawn brought out the Victorian details of its façade with a multicolored paint job in soft, harmonious shades of green. She believed in offering her customers a bit of pizzazz they wouldn't get by ordering their supplements and gluten-free cookie batter online. In her front window, a jungle of thriving plants surrounded a display of books and other products relating to nutrition, exercise, relaxation, and specialized New Age topics.

Dawn also had turned the sign on her front door to CLOSED for the day, and when I stepped inside, she shrieked, "Cassie! Watch out!"

But although Tigger dashed in my direction, my reflexes were pretty sharp too, and I shut the door before he escaped. "Just where do you think you're going?"

The striped kitten stared up at me. "Eeeep!"

Dawn giggled and scooped him into her arms. "I'm so glad you stopped by, Cassie. I don't know what to do with him! This must be what it's like to come home from the hospital with a new baby."

"I hear he did well at the vet," I said.

"Yes. Thank goodness he has no icky worms or diseases. If nobody claims him by next month, he goes back to get"—she dropped her voice to a stage whisper—"neutered."

Tigger tried to squirm out of her grasp, as if he'd understood completely.

"Want to hold on to him for a second, Cassie, while I get us some tea?"

She passed the little tabby to me. I cuddled him against my shoulder, where he purred in my ear like a motorboat.

"He looks so relaxed!" Dawn sounded accusing. "How do you do that?"

"Just hold him nice and secure against your body. Not upside down in your arms, or in any way that he thinks you might drop him."

"Lord," she said, "it is almost like dealing with a human baby."

"Worse, in some ways. He'll be able to run faster, squeeze into smaller spaces, and climb onto higher shelves."

While she disappeared into her rear kitchenette, I assessed the potential kitten hazards of her rustic but welcoming store. She had sanded down the old oak floorboards but otherwise left them unfinished, and the original wood-burning stove still occupied a central spot in the sales area. She'd painted the barnlike wallboards and built-in shelving a pale sage green that nicely set off her merchandise. But I could imagine Tigger frolicking along those open shelves and knocking fifteen-dollar bottles of essential oils to the floor, where they'd mingle to create some truly overpowering scents. And of course, every time a customer arrived or departed, the kitten might make a dash for freedom. Dawn and I hadn't gone to all this trouble just to have Tigger end up back on the streets, with all the dangers that involved.

She carried in a tray with two steaming mugs and assorted herbal teas. She set it on an over-turned barrel near the stove, between two salvaged club chairs she had covered with Indian paisley throws. I pawed through the teas and picked a ginger blend that sounded as if it would perk me up rather than tranquilize me like the one the night before.

Meanwhile, we let Tigger roam. I crumpled an empty tea bag wrapper and tossed it to him. He leaped on it as if it was a killer scorpion that he needed to slay to keep us all from harm. His manic dance of destruction soon had Dawn laughing hysterically.

"He's a cutie," I agreed.

She met my gaze again with a rueful smile. "I really should make a good-faith effort to see if he already belongs to someone. Can you put a sign in your shop?" She brought her iPad over from the sales counter. "How does this sound? 'Did you lose a brown tabby kitten, white-tipped tail, about three months old? Check with Dawn at Nature's Way.'"

I considered this. "Not sure. If you found a valuable necklace, would you describe it in detail so just anybody come could and say, 'Oh yes, that's mine!'"

"Well, no. But he's not—"

"I know, but there might be people who'd be happy to take him off your hands for bad reasons. Medical experiments and . . . other things you probably don't want to know about." I thought of stories I'd heard about stolen kittens and puppies being used as bait animals for fighting dogs.

"No description?"

"Stick with 'Did you lose a kitten?' and the bit about checking with you."

She deleted everything else. "You're the expert."

By now Tigger had easily made the leap onto her sales counter and was eyeing a shelf filled with crystal knickknacks. I retrieved him and sat down again with him on my lap. "Are you going to leave him here overnight?"

"I intended to," Dawn said. "My apartment's kind of small, so I thought he could be, like, a store cat. But now I'm afraid he's going to be lonely."

"Well, you said he's been camping out in your storeroom. If there's no way he can hurt himself, maybe that would be a good spot for him. Give him something soft to lie on, some water and dry food, and a litter box."

She brightened, as if feeling more competent. "Got all of that covered. I found a shallow cardboard box that I lined with a plastic garbage bag, and I already stocked some all-natural cat food and litter."

"Great! That should get him through the night." I tasted my tea and savored the kick of the ginger. "Still, if he's going to live here at the store, you'll have to figure out some strategies to keep him—and your merchandise—safe."

Dawn buried a hand in her cascade of wavy reddish hair, braided across the top today. "This is what I get for falling in love at first sight. You'd think at my age I'd know better." Her head popped up at a new thought. "Speaking of which, Dr. Mark seemed a little disappointed that I came by for Tigger instead of you."

"Well, we did talk afterward on the phone," I reminded her. "Unfortunately, he just confirmed everything my mother said about what happens to pets when their owner dies and nobody else wants to take them in."

Possibly because she now was a pet owner herself, Dawn looked dismayed. "Do they get put to sleep?"

"Well, they usually go to a shelter. But depending on the shelter's policies, and how long they stay there without anyone adopting them . . . yeah, that could happen."

"How sad for DeLeuw, if with all his money, he couldn't prevent that from happening. And since you're not related to him—and it's not likely that he left you the cat in his will—there's probably nothing you can do to stop it either."

"We'll see about that." I took another slow, thoughtful sip of my tea. "I haven't quite exhausted all of my options."

"Such as?"

"Mingling with the rich and semi-famous. Asking some discreet questions. I've decided to go to his viewing tomorrow."

Dawn tilted her pale Renaissance-goddess profile at me. "You don't think people will wonder why his twice-a-month cat groomer felt she had to pay her respects?"

I told her about my encounter with Danielle, and how we'd discussed the murder while I helped her find a new charger for her cell phone.

"Well, that's better," my friend decided. "You'll have at least one person there you know."

I nodded. "And besides, I have the best reason in the world to feel awful about George's death. After all, I *am* the one who found his body."

Chapter 8

It's not easy to decide what to wear to a funeral-home viewing, scheduled midmorning, when the deceased is someone you hardly knew and probably everyone else in attendance will be a lot richer than you are.

Fortunately, my wardrobe was small enough to limit my choices. I own very few dresses, none of them black. Anyway, I figured it might almost be in bad taste for someone like me, no relation, to show up in full mourning. So I opted for what could have passed for a modest date outfit—slim black pants and a fitted, long-sleeved top in a teal-green-and-black abstract print. After I added drop earrings in the same shade of green, I at least looked presentable and pulled together, if still not wealthy.

The Dewey Funeral Home occupied a Queen Anne Victorian structure in the older residential neighborhood of Chadwick. Its corner site offered plenty of room for parking, but I'd bet the lot rarely overflowed the way it did that morning. It surprised me to think very private George DeLeuw had that many friends in town, until I noticed license plates from New York and Connecticut, plus a few rental cars. Perhaps many former colleagues from Redmond & Fowler, and other business associates, had traveled to pay their respects. If some distant relatives also had shown up, maybe one could be persuaded to give Harpo a loving home?

I parked on the street and fell in step behind a tall, broad-shouldered man in a well-cut dark gray business suit, accompanied by a sophisticated brunette in a black skirt suit that might have cost as much as one of my mortgage payments. The handful of mourners gathered just inside the front door also looked seriously decked out for ten thirty a.m. Suddenly I felt as if I'd shown up in overalls with hayseeds in my hair.

Surrounded by all of these impressive strangers, the natural introvert in me wanted to slink quietly back out again, or at least hide in a corner. Then I reminded myself that the amateur sleuths in my favorite mysteries did this sort of thing all the time— attended the funeral of the murder victim to get a sense of who might have had a motive to kill him.

And I'm not even doing that! I just want to get a feel for who might be willing to look after the guy's cat. Remembering the forlorn expression on the lovely Persian when Anita had whisked him away from his master's corpse, I had to make the effort.

A couple of the Victorian's original first-floor rooms probably had been combined to form Reception 1, where DeLeuw lay in repose. The rosy tweed carpeting here coordinated with two sofas and two armchairs, all upholstered in rose-and-green floral stripes. The rest of the seating consisted of rows of folding chairs with flat burgundy seat cushions. Murals on two of the walls depicted similar pastel country landscapes; a burgundy curtain hid the area behind the casket.

I did a quick scan of the mourners—who numbered about thirty—and recognized only three of them. Luckily, Anita sat toward the back where I could easily say hello to her.

She acted both surprised and happy to see me. Her deep-blue wrap dress might have come from a discount rack at the same big-box store where I'd gotten my outfit. She introduced me to her husband, Hector, who had a shiny dome, a kind smile, and a mustache as black as his loose-fitting suit.

"I'm so glad you guys are here," I whispered. "I feel a little out of place among all these high-powered folks."

The housekeeper smiled. "So do I. A few, I just know their names, or they came to Mr. DeLeuw's house once in a while. I'm sure they wouldn't remember me. But I wanted to come for his sake. He always treated me well. He was a good man, I think, deep down."

I wondered what Anita meant by that last comment. Maybe just that nobody got to be a big success in the business world with having a bit of the shark in him?

"How are you doing?" I asked her. "Still keeping up the house?"

She nodded. "The police made me stay away

for the first day, because they went over the whole
place—looking for clues, I guess. When they let
me come back, I had a mess to clean up, because
they went through drawers, closets, everything.
They took all of Mr. DeLeuw's electronic stuff and
work papers, even some of his artworks."

I saw a chance to confirm one of my suspicions. "Do they think something like that could
have been used as the murder weapon?"

"Could be." She glanced around to see if anyone else was listening. "I probably shouldn't talk
about it . . . but they took the big rock that was on
the stand in the hall. They packed that up real
careful, like they thought it was important." Anita
shuddered. "Gives me chills, to think of somebody
hitting Mr. DeLeuw with that!"

Silently, Hector reached for his wife's hand
and squeezed it.

"I know. The whole thing is very upsetting." I
decided to change the subject. "So there's no one
actually living in the house now? What's happening with Harpo?"

Anita's soft features frowned in sympathy.
"That poor kitty. I come at least once a day—the
lawyer pays me, for now—and I feed him. Mr.
DeLeuw had one of those timed feeders, so I leave
a few meals. I keep him shut up in the master
suite, where he's got some room and can sleep on
Mr. DeLeuw's bed. But he's still lonely. He cries
when he hears me come up the stairs, and he cries
again when I leave him. It's really no way for an animal to live."

I laid a hand the little woman's shoulder. "That's

one of the reasons I'm here today, Anita. If you want to help, you can tell me who some of these people are. . . ."

She identified half a dozen gathered at the front of the room who seemed to be accepting most of the condolences. Of course I'd already met George's sister, so I decided to approach her next.

First, I knelt down in front of the polished cherrywood casket and tried to accept that the waxy-faced corpse resting on tufted ivory velvet was all that remained of my best client. If he could speak from the Beyond, would he be able to tell us who killed him? Or had his assailant crept up from behind, so that DeLeuw literally never knew what—or who—hit him?

Silently, I again promised George that I'd find a way to at least protect his cat. Then I edged away from the casket and slipped into the cluster of people around Danielle.

Her mourning garb couldn't have been simpler—a straight black knit dress with three-quarter sleeves, hemmed just past her knees. Simple to pack, I figured, if you were flying in from California. But her big hammered-silver earrings added style and picked up the highlights in her straight ash-blond hair. Her pale green eyes again reminded me of her late brother's, as did her narrow, ascetic face and high cheekbones. Today she wore a little more makeup, which shaved a few years off her appearance.

At least she recognized me, remembering that I'd helped her with the cell phone charger and that I had found George's body. With a thin smile, she added, "D'you know, I didn't even realize my brother still had a cat until I read the news story. George and I got together from time to time, when he had business on the Coast, but the subject just never came up."

"I hear his lawyer is checking around to see if someone will take Harpo," I said, trying to be tactful. "Unless Mr. DeLeuw provided for him in his will . . ."

"Well, God knows how long it will be before we know that." Danielle edged away from the casket, as if her late brother shouldn't overhear this conversation. "Possibly the police have had a look at the will. If so, they're keeping it a big secret. As if anyone close to George could possibly have done this to him, and over something as ridiculous as an inheritance."

I was sure George would have had quite a lot to leave his heirs, so it spoke volumes about Danielle's own financial situation that she couldn't imagine anyone harming her brother to hurry the process along. Or so she said.

"If you ask me," Danielle said with a sniff, "it was that gardener."

"Louis?" I asked in surprise. "You think he stood to inherit something?"

"No, of course not. But he could've had his eye on some of the artworks. George told me every now and then he noticed some small piece missing from its spot and didn't remember moving it. His housekeeper or even his gardener might have pocketed those things, although I don't suppose the woman would haven been capable of . . . doing what was done to George."

I thought of Anita's grief when she saw her employer's body. "I don't think so either."

Danielle met my eyes with a cool, confidential gaze. "It would have to have been someone taller and stronger, right? That's why I suspect the gardener."

I didn't bother to explain that Louis was a landscaper, not just a gardener. Or that people had seen him working in the yard throughout the period when DeLeuw probably was killed.

It wasn't my place, anyway, to discuss possible suspects with Danielle. I steered the conversation back to a situation I could do something about. "You're right about one thing. While the police are still investigating, it could take a while before the will is probated. Meanwhile, Harpo really needs a new home."

"Harpo? Oh, the cat." Danielle shook her sleek head. "Won't be with me, I'm afraid. I'm too busy for a pet. I'm always off on buying trips or visiting my boutiques—I'm opening another one in LA next month—so I'm always traveling, hardly ever home."

"That's too bad. Do you know of any other family members who—"

"No, I don't. Sorry." She turned her attention then to someone else who embraced her and offered condolences.

Time for me to step away, but I pondered my next move. While waiting, I glanced at the small screen set up near the casket, playing a memorial video. The loop included a 1950s-era photo of George as a child, with his younger sister and his parents; a shot of him on the basketball court in high school; his college graduation. From there on, the images showed him shaking hands with another man at some business function, studying an abstract painting at an art gallery, and accepting a plaque at what looked like his retirement party. No personal pictures from his adult years, I noticed.

Backing up a step, I jostled a statuesque redhead in a form-fitting black sheath and high heels. "Excuse me!" I said. Then I recognized the woman Anita had identified as Marjorie, DeLeuw's ex-wife.

She ignored both my clumsiness and my apology, but nodded toward the slideshow. "Pretty spare, isn't it?"

"I guess his sister must have put it together in a hurry," I said. "But I did notice there aren't many family pictures—mostly business."

Marjorie's red lips twisted. "Well, that was George, mostly business. I see Danielle managed to get a shot of him at an art gallery, but nothing with our daughter."

She must have meant Renée, the one who had died. "Maybe she thought that would be too painful?"

The woman responded with a cynical shrug. "Probably right about that. I'm sure there are more than a few people here who'd rather not be reminded of Renée's death."

Marjorie started to turn away, but I saw my chance to find out more, and offered my hand. "By the way, I'm Cassie McGlone. I was coming by the house twice a month to groom George's cat. I actually . . . found him."

"You mean—" Her penciled eyebrows rose in

two perfect arcs. "Really! I heard that an employee had discovered his body, but I thought it was one of the staff."

This time I heard a slight slur in her speech. Had she been drinking this early? No hint of alcohol on her breath, but maybe too many Bloody Marys at brunch? That might explain why she was sharing her opinions so freely with a complete stranger.

I tried to forget that DeLeuw had blamed this woman for euthanizing his other cat out of pure spite; otherwise, I'd find it impossible to carry on a civil conversation with her.

"It was a terrible shock for everyone," I told her. "None of us who worked for George could imagine why anyone would want to hurt him."

I purposely threw out this idea to see how Marjorie would react, and could see her moderating her response. "I guess the police are looking into the possibility of art theft," she said vaguely. "And there was some business with a local man who thought George stole his idea for an invention. But it's anyone's guess, really, who might have killed him. You don't get to his level without getting your hands dirty . . . and making some enemies."

She glanced in the direction of the well-dressed businessman I had followed into the funeral home, now in deep conversation with Jerry Ross. According to Anita, that was Charles Schroeder, the R&F exec who had been quoted in DeLeuw's obituary.

Marjorie's offhanded demeanor bothered me, and I wondered if she counted herself among

George's enemies. Since I had no intention of asking *her* to provide a home for Harpo, I said I was sorry for her loss and moved on.

I pretended to admire one enormous spray of all-white roses, Asian lilies, carnations, and chrysanthemums displayed on its own easel. At my right, I could hear snatches of the conversation between Ross and Schroeder.

"They've moved his whole art collection to a warehouse." Jerry sounded bewildered.

"That's to be expected," said Schroeder. "George had a lot of valuable things, and they have to be assessed. Easier to move them to a secure location than to post a guard round the clock at his house."

"Do you know yet who's taking over the Foxfire account?"

"They're giving it to Rachel Dominitz. Just for the time being."

"I thought—"

"This is an unexpected emergency, Jerry. The transition needs to be handled as smoothly as possible. Once things shake down . . . we'll see." After a pause, he added airily, "But we'll survive!"

At that point, Jerry noticed my glancing in their direction and asked rather sharply, "Can I help you?"

"Sorry, I don't mean to interrupt," I lied. "I just wanted to introduce myself, since we've never actually met. You're Jerry Ross, right? I'm Cassandra McGlone, the groomer Mr. DeLeuw hired for Harpo."

"Oh . . . of course. We've spoken on the phone." His handshake was professional, just firm enough.

"Great of you to come. This is Charles Schroeder, one of George's colleagues at Redmond & Fowler."

The fellow with the ramrod posture and silver temples also shook my hand and murmured some acknowledgment, but I had the sense that both of them wondered why I'd shown up for the viewing. Suddenly a light came on in Schroeder's eyes. "You're the one who found George's body!"

That announcement startled Jerry, who apparently hadn't read the newspaper story, or at least hadn't remembered that detail. "You were at the house that day?" he asked me.

I explained briefly how I'd happened upon the murder scene. "You arrived just as I was leaving. I saw you, but I guess you didn't see me."

They both looked taken aback by that comment, and I wondered if it sounded too creepy. Had I accidentally made myself sound like a suspect?

In a hurry to change this impression, I complimented Schroeder on the kind things he'd said about DeLeuw in the newspaper story.

He nodded soberly, with a faraway expression. "George and I went back thirteen years. We both started as vice presidents around the same time, and worked side by side on a few accounts. When he took a step back from the firm, a year ago, we felt the loss. But George was an independent thinker, always followed his own instincts." With a thin smile, Schroeder added, "Those instincts brought him great success . . . most of the time."

I wondered if he was implying that George's

instincts had somehow put him on a dangerous path. Probably he was just referring to a few financial gambles that went south.

Meanwhile, Schroeder's eye was caught by something happening behind me. "Rachel and her husband just came in," he told Jerry. "Excuse me, won't you?" And he strode toward the doorway of Reception 1.

Left to make conversation with me, Jerry looked a bit uncomfortable. He ran one hand back over his head, the dark hair cut very short, no doubt to camouflage some thinning. In spite of his boyish demeanor, up close I figured him to be nearing forty.

"I still can't get my mind around it," he said. "I talked to George maybe two hours before the police called me. I guess he had my number posted somewhere to contact in case of an emergency. But you got there first."

"Yes. Too late to be of any help, unfortunately."

Jerry stuffed his hands into his pants pockets, pushing up his suit jacket on either side. "They asked me about his schedule—did he have any appointments at his home that afternoon. At first I thought it was a ridiculous question, as if a murderer would call up and make an appointment! But of course, it could have been someone he was doing business with."

"Possibly someone who'd arranged to buy a piece of art from him, but planned to steal it instead," I suggested.

"As far as I know, though, nothing was taken."

A crease deepened between his eyes. "No, I've got my theory, even though they might never be able to prove it. There was this local guy who came to George with an idea he wanted to develop, some new kind of computer encryption." His hands came out and gestured cluelessly. "I didn't understand how it worked, but George seemed to. Anyway, the kid got it into his head that George stole his idea and sold it to somebody else. Got to be a real pain about it. Once, he left this angry message on the house phone while we were working there, and I said, 'You really oughta tell the cops about this guy. He could be dangerous.' But George didn't take it seriously."

I imagined Jerry telling this story to the police—no wonder they had pulled Dion in for questioning. Too bad Nick's son didn't have a better alibi for that afternoon.

"Well, as you say, we may never know," I commented. "The only witness to the crime may be Harpo, and he's not talking."

Jerry looked startled for a split second, until he realized I meant the cat, then laughed. "No, I guess he isn't."

I used that segue to make my pitch about liberating the Persian from his solitude in the master suite and finding him a new home.

"I sure can't take him," Jerry declared. "I'm allergic. Had to take an antihistamine every time I went over to the house to coordinate things with George. Even though he had you grooming the cat, and the housekeeper was always dusting and vacuuming, I'd still sneeze my head off without the medication."

"That's too bad. Do you have any idea if George provided for the cat in his will?"

He blanked. "None at all. George didn't discuss private matters like that with me. Guess we'll find out when the will is probated . . . whenever that might be."

"That's just the trouble." I explained the consequences that might be in store for Harpo. "Jerry, you must have influence with George's lawyer. Could you ask if I might be able to board Harpo at my facility until we find out if George left him to anyone? It would be safer than a shelter in every sense. He wouldn't be around sick cats or barking dogs, and he wouldn't be in any danger of being put to sleep."

The man's brown eyes turned wary. "Gee, I dunno. What do you charge?"

"I wouldn't, for this. I just want to make sure he's safe."

"He's not very valuable, y'know."

Ross thinks I'm going to steal him or sell him? I had to smile at that notion. "I know; George explained that to me. Really, the minute anyone comes forward to give him a good home, they can have him."

Ross pursed his mouth while considering this offer. "Sure, I'll talk to the lawyer. He'll probably want you to sign a paper, but . . . why not?"

Minutes later I quit the overly floral-scented atmosphere of the funeral home for the brisk April day outside. It had taken some work, and getting to know more than I'd ever wanted to about DeLeuw's family and friends, but I just might have achieved my goal of providing a safe haven for Harpo.

In the process, though, I might have set a tougher goal for myself. Now I really did want to find out who murdered George DeLeuw.

Chapter 9

I'd left Sarah in charge of the shop a couple of times now since hiring her, and she'd managed well. As a thank-you, I stopped at a take-out place on my way back and picked up wraps for the two of us. She was pleasantly surprised by the free lunch, and also to learn that Harpo might soon join our roster of boarders.

"Guess your idea of going to the viewing and asking questions paid off," she said, pouring herself a mug of coffee from the pot I kept going in the back room.

"It did, though I probably found out more than I wanted to know about George's close relationships . . . or lack of them."

Ironically, what I'd learned had left me even more curious than before. While I ate, I opened my laptop on the front counter, typed "Renée DeLeuw," and hit search. The name turned out to be pretty rare, at least on the Internet, but I found one reference that seemed to fit. About four years ago, a woman in her late twenties—my age now— had died alone of an apparent heroin overdose in her apartment in Philadelphia. I searched further and turned up an obituary that, like George's, omitted the cause of death but did identify the overdose victim as the daughter he'd had with Marjorie. Renée had graduated from Penn State with an MBA, but at the time of her death was supposedly working at a fast-food restaurant.

The story struck me as both tragic and mysterious. Renée came from a wealthy, privileged background, had gotten a solid education, and should have had a bright future. But for some reason she'd turned to hard drugs, which undermined all of that potential. I didn't know at what point George and his wife divorced, or how long they might have had their differences, but I suspected Renée's death was the final blow. I thought of Marjorie's bitter tone when she'd commented that the funeral-home slideshow didn't include even one photo of their daughter.

Could something have reopened that painful wound recently, and made her so angry that she'd killed her ex-husband? In heels, Marjorie would be tall enough to have swung that chunk of stone. Or she could have hired someone to do it . . . ? But again, a hit man surely would have used a gun. If that stone sculpture really had been used to strike George, it looked like a crime of impulse.

Sarah and I had just finished eating when we got a drop-in customer who taxed all of our skills. A middle-aged bearded man named Luke brought us a cat his wife had adopted from a shelter a few months back, a pale gray longhair mix that they called Stormy. He wanted to board the cat for a couple of weeks while they took their two preteens on a spring break trip to Disney World. And as long as Stormy was in my care, they figured they'd have him professionally groomed. I could tell at first glance, even through the grill of the carrier, that he needed it.

This could be a lucrative arrangement, I knew. Unfortunately, certain clues told me that Stormy lived up to his name in temperament.

"The folks at the shelter told us we'd have to groom him a couple of times a week," Luke admitted. "We tried in the beginning, but he put up such a fight, we finally gave up. I don't know what he went through as a kitten, but sometimes he can be a little tough to handle."

I heard a hiss before Luke even opened the carrier, and suggested he bring it straight back to the grooming studio. At that moment I wished I had two assistants, because we had to leave the front counter unstaffed—I figured I'd need Sarah's hands along with my own for this job. Fortunately, a few months back Nick had installed a video intercom that was triggered when someone came in the front door. It let me see who it was and tell them I'd be out in just a minute.

Sarah and I had to tip Stormy out of the molded-plastic carrier, and he still tried to hang on to it with his front claws. Once on the table, he calmed a little as his owner petted and talked to him. But his long silvery coat was a mess, full of obvious mats.

"These are probably causing him pain," I explained to Luke, "which isn't making him any happier. I think it's going to take too long, and stress him too much, to comb and cut out every mat separately. If you want to leave him for a couple of hours, what I'll do is a lion cut."

I explained that this involved shaving almost the whole cat, except for the face, the neck ruff, the paws, and the end of the tail. "It will take a while for the coat to grow back, but meanwhile, he'll have no matting and you'll have less shedding."

When I showed Luke a picture of the typical result, he chuckled uneasily. "Oh man. If I bring him home looking like that, my wife might kill me!"

"Do you want to call her and put me on so I can explain? Maybe you can e-mail her a picture of it too, so it's not as much of a shock."

I did spend about ten minutes on the phone with his wife, and in the end they agreed to leave the cat with me to be shaved.

That was the easy part. After Luke had gone, Sarah and I got Stormy onto the grooming table and into a harness. She held the leash while I took on the challenge of maneuvering an electric shaver without cutting him. A cat has very thin skin, and the mats of hair pulling on it didn't help, even without his attempts to twist around and bite or scratch me. Halfway through, I wished I'd gotten permission to give the animal some kind of natural sedative to ease his stress . . . and mine.

As I was concentrating, my cell phone rang twice, but I couldn't stop to answer it.

Finally, with Sarah's invaluable help, I had turned Stormy into a miniature and very grumpy silver lion. We removed his harness to shave the last few spots, shooed him into an empty cage, and gave him some food to help him recover from the assault upon his dignity.

At that point I finally checked my phone messages. The first was from Jerry Ross. He said George's lawyer had agreed to let me keep Harpo at my facility until the will was probated or someone from DeLeuw's circle offered to take the cat.

"To make it clear that this is a business arrangement," Jerry added, "George's trust is willing to pay seventy-five percent of your boarding fee for as long as the cat is in your care. Is that acceptable?"

"Certainly." I wasn't going to risk queering the deal by bargaining for more. It would be guaranteed income for weeks, maybe even months, to come.

"Okay. They'll probably e-mail the contract over to you this afternoon."

I waited until I'd hung up to cheer, "Yesss!" and high-five Sarah. When I told her the good news, she grinned. "We'll have to make up a *real* nice condo for Harpo. He's used to the best."

The second call also was a welcome one— Mark, checking to see if I'd learned anything helpful at George's viewing. Since the vet had no real stake in solving DeLeuw's murder, I dared to think his interest was more personal than professional. His message did allow me to tell the clinic receptionist that I was "returning a call from Dr. Coccia," which got a quick response.

"The best result from the viewing," I told him, "is that they're going to let me board Harpo until all of this is decided. No more worries about him going to a shelter."

"That is terrific," Mark agreed. "No family members stepped up, I gather?"

"No. I asked around, but . . . they're a strange crowd."

Some clinic staffer interrupted Mark to ask about X-ray results. When he got back on the line, he said with a chuckle, "Never easy to carry on a long phone conversation here, but I'm curious to hear what else you found out. We don't have many murders in Chadwick, and people are kind of anxious to get this one solved."

I saw my opening. "When do you get off work? Want to grab a bite to eat?"

"Hey, that sounds good. Maybe the diner?"

We made plans to meet there at six thirty. My heart was still pounding from my bold move when I clicked off.

Sarah noticed, of course. "It must be more than just rescuing DeLeuw's cat to make you smile that big."

"Got a late appointment with the vet," I said. "Actually, more of a dinner date."

"Congratulations, girl! You're on a roll today."

I tucked my cell back into my purse. "Seems that way. I just might start looking forward to phone calls if they all turn out like this."

The diner, Chad's, occupied a prominent spot toward the north end of Center Street, along the now-defunct railroad line. Its façade was chrome, embossed with an Art Deco sunburst pattern, and its name blazed in neon turquoise above the door. Someone obviously chose "Chad's" because it sounded cool and retro. I doubt that the town's founder, Revolutionary War general Grayson Chadwick, ever went by that nickname, and the owners of the diner were Phil and Addy Panopoulos. They did have a framed head shot of actor Chad Everett—very young, in a cardigan, with slicked-down 1960s hair—just inside the glass-walled vestibule. Maybe that explained it.

A drizzle had started after sundown, and even from a distance I could spot Mark already waiting in the vestibule. I normally saw him in scrubs, but he'd changed into a more approachable combination of dark jeans, a plum button-down shirt, and a hooded rain jacket. With little time to plan, I'd fallen back on the same outfit I'd worn to DeLeuw's viewing.

I was only a few minutes late, and hoped he'd accept my excuse. "I spent a couple of hours this afternoon giving a lion cut to a very uncooperative longhair, so it took some time to make myself presentable."

"Well, you definitely succeeded." His admiring smile set my pulse racing again as he held open the diner's inner door for me.

The nostalgic décor of Chad's always boosted my spirits, even though it re-created an era long before I was born. The booths, chairs, and counter stools all were upholstered in turquoise vinyl, which popped nicely against the black-and-white checkered floor. Cream-colored walls displayed not the clichéd shots of old movie and TV stars, but photos from Chadwick's own past. These included a sock hop in the high school gym and an exterior view of the old movie theater with people lined up for a 1940s war bonds drive. As a new resident, I enjoyed perusing these glimpses into the town's history.

The place was bustling that evening, as usual. I'd been perfectly happy for us to meet at an informal restaurant with reasonable prices, but it suddenly occurred to me that *everybody* in Chadwick came here. Did I want the whole town buzzing about the cat groomer having dinner with the local vet? Not since high school had I worried about being the subject of gossip. I'd gone to a big college and had my first apartment in a sizable town, where I'd felt pretty anonymous.

But hey, Dr. Coccia and I were just getting together to discuss our mutual interest in Harpo's welfare. And, of course, in the DeLeuw murder. *That* was a much hotter topic of gossip around town these days.

At least with our animal-oriented jobs, we found plenty to talk about. While scanning the menus, we discussed Dawn's new kitten. I said she already was becoming so attached that it would be a shame if anyone did claim Tigger.

"She may not have much to worry about," Mark said. "I have a feeling someone's pet had a litter in the garage and that little guy just wandered off on his own. Any owner who didn't bother to spay the mother or take care of the babies is probably glad to be rid of him. Too many people out there like that. But you were smart to warn her not to give him away to just anyone."

I savored the compliment. "I told her, if somebody says they lost a kitten, ask how old it was, what color it was, and if it was a boy or a girl. If they answer wrong, or even seem like they're guessing, don't hand him over."

Our waitress showed up then, dressed in black pants, a turquoise blouse, and a white apron—the last two trimmed in black-and-white checkers. Her white name tag identified her as Ashley. She was as adorable as her retro outfit, with a high ponytail, rosy cheeks, and rosebud lips.

"Doctor Coccia!" she greeted him in a chirpy voice. "So nice to see you again. You're getting to be a regular here."

"Why not? Can't beat the food . . . or the service," he responded with a smile.

I suffered a pang of jealousy. Not "he belongs to me" jealousy, but "it's our first date, darn it, don't rock the boat" jealousy. All right, I might have been a little paranoid; I'd once gone out with a guy from an online dating site who spent most of the evening ogling our waitress, making it clear that he'd rather be with her than with me. Would Mark turn out to be that kind of jerk?

Ashley took our nonalcoholic drink orders and talked us into a hummus dip with pita wedges as a shared appetizer. After I ordered a dinner-sized Caesar salad and Mark requested the spinach pie, the waitress kept asking sweetly if there was anything else *at all* she could get for us (*or at least Mark*, I thought). But whether she was just hoping for a generous tip or really flirting, he remained oblivious, and once she had left, his vivid blue eyes zeroed back in on me.

He asked, "So what does Cassie stand for? Cassandra?"

I nodded. "A strange name for an Irish girl, maybe, but it was my grandmother's."

"It's originally Greek, I think," he said, still studying me. "Cassandra was a prophetess . . . a wise woman."

"Not so sure that applies!" I laughed. The offhanded compliment flustered me, and I deliberately shifted to a more neutral subject. "Do you eat here often?"

"Lately I have been. Whenever I get stuck late at the clinic and haven't stocked my refrigerator in a while."

Sounded like a lonely bachelor problem. My hopes rose.

"In situations like that, I tend to mooch off Dawn," I admitted. "Her shop has a freezer full of health foods, and she also can whip up a nutritious, politically correct, and tasty meal in record time. She really came through for me the night after I found DeLeuw's body, when I was too shaky to even boil water."

Mark's straight dark brows drew together in sympathy. "I can't imagine what that must have been like. I guess you were questioned by the cops and everything?"

Our appetizer came, and while we scooped up the garlicky hummus with our pita wedges, I recounted the whole ordeal.

"The weird thing is," I said, "when I went to the viewing, people there seemed almost cold about George's death. His ex-wife . . . well, maybe that's not so surprising. But also his sister, his assistant, his coworkers. I didn't see anyone cry except his housekeeper! Makes me wonder if any of them hated him enough to have killed him . . . or arranged for him to be killed."

"I guess it's possible. Someone could have disliked him *and* thought they had a lot to gain from an inheritance. On the other hand, it might just have been a stranger looking for something to steal."

"Have to be pretty desperate and stupid, though, wouldn't he? In the middle of the day, with the owner and two of his staff on the property?"

Mark shrugged. "Drug addicts do some crazy things. At veterinary school, we had people try to steal ketamine, morphine . . . sometimes while a vet was right in the next room!"

"Yes, I've heard of that too." By way of explanation, I quickly added, "I worked as a vet tech for a couple of years."

"No kidding." His eyes sparked, as if he might consider hiring me. "Why did you stop?"

Before I could respond, the perky waitress brought our dinners. We'd just started on them when a man of about seventy, in a plaid shirt and well-worn jeans, stopped by our table. His face appeared creased with worry as he stooped to address Mark.

"Dr. Coccia . . . really sorry to bother you while you're eating."

"That's all right, Pete. What's up?"

"I was gonna call your clinic, but it's closed now, and then I saw you here. . . . My dog, Honey, ain't doing so good."

"She's the retriever, right? What's wrong?"

Pete went into a recital of the elderly dog's past visits to the clinic for various ailments. "Now she wants to go out—y'know—all the time. Like, almost every hour. If nobody's home, she has an accident 'cause she can't hold it. An' this afternoon my wife got upset 'cause the pee was kinda bloody. She thought maybe we should take her to that twenty-four-hour emergency clinic on the highway, but it's so expensive. . . ."

Mark nodded. "It's probably not that kind of an emergency. Knowing Honey's history, it could be just a urinary tract infection. Can you bring her in tomorrow around eleven? We're pretty booked, but I can fit you in then. Okay?"

"Yeah, sure. Thanks." The lines of Pete's face lifted a bit in relief, and for the first time he glanced at me. "Didn't mean to interrupt."

"No problem," I told him, appreciating Mark's patience. When the man had left, I told Mark, "And I thought only human doctors got asked for medical advice while they were out to dinner."

Mark shook his head. "That doesn't happen often, but it does happen. His dog is nine—old for a big breed—but he and his wife are very attached to her. Not the most pleasant subject for dinner-time, though."

"Luckily, I'm also used to dealing with animals who sometimes have 'accidents.' " We went back to our meals, and I picked up the former thread of our conversation. "You asked me why I quit being a tech. The truth is, I burnt out fast. So many of the animals we saw were beyond saving—too badly neglected or abused. It felt good when we could actually help one or two, but I was losing my faith in human nature." I tried to lighten the mood. "I always got compliments on my grooming skills, though, so I decided to concentrate on those. At least these days most of my customers really care about their pets, and giving a cat a bad haircut doesn't have life-or-death consequences. With short-term boarding, too, I don't have to handle a lot of health crises."

Mark focused on me again. "So the next natural question is, why just cats?"

I laughed. "I love all animals, but cats have special needs. Often, they don't do well in a place that also boards dogs. The odors and barking can make them nervous."

"True. We have that problem at the clinic, even with the ones that just have to stay a few days for observation."

"I'm sure you also know that cats are harder to groom. Some really hate being restrained and can put up a heck of a fight. When I learned that a lot of groomers refuse to deal with cats at all, I knew I'd found my niche."

"Cats are tougher than most people realize," Mark agreed, with a smile. "They may be small, but they move fast and those little claws can slash like razors. I give you credit—you're a brave woman!"

Though he said it in a half-teasing way, the compliment almost embarrassed me. "You're the brave one. You hung in there, where I couldn't." I told him about the sad old man I'd seen on my last visit to the clinic, the little collar sticking out of his pocket as he settled up his bill. "You deal with the really hard stuff."

Ashley took away our empty plates, and since

Mark and I were on a conversational roll, we both ordered coffee. I heard my cell phone vibrate faintly in my purse, but doubted it was anything that couldn't wait. After our coffees came, along with the check, I asked Mark how he'd decided to become a veterinarian.

"My dad was an orthopedic surgeon," he said. "When I started bringing home injured birds, and stray cats and dogs with various problems, my folks indulged me. They figured someday I'd go into medicine too. But even after I grew up, I liked doctoring animals more than people. They don't argue with you or lie to you or make excuses . . . even though their owners sometimes do."

I twisted my mouth at the memories. "Yeah, that's the part that always got to me."

"Though I have to say, most people are really grateful when you're able to help their pets. And even the animals seem to appreciate it."

Dr. Coccia was far more than just a pretty face, I decided. He was smart, funny, and kind. And it was a rare experience for me to be able to talk shop with someone who really understood my unusual line of work.

I might have been wearing some type of moony expression, because he dropped his gaze to the check and pulled it toward him.

"Really, I should treat," I volunteered, "since I suggested dinner."

"Did you? I thought we both came up with the idea at about the same time." He pulled out his wallet and counted out a few bills for the tip. "How about I take care of this, and maybe you can get the next one?"

Next one, eh? I liked the sound of that. "Fair enough."

Mark clasped his hands on the table and shifted to a more serious tone. "I should tell you, Cassie, that I'm just out of a long relationship. As in, we broke up a couple of weeks ago. And I don't know your situation—maybe you're involved with somebody. . . ."

"Not at the moment," I told him smoothly. He didn't have to know that "the moment" encompassed the past six months since I'd call it quits with Andy.

Mark nodded once in acknowledgment. "I had a great time talking with you tonight, and I really like you. But I'm still a little shell-shocked right now, so I'd rather keep it light for a while."

Uh-oh, I thought. *This doesn't sound so good. Did I screw things up somehow?*

But aloud I said, "Absolutely. I went through a rough breakup myself not so long ago, so I'm kind of in the same place."

"Glad you understand," Mark said. "'Cause I would like to see you again."

My sense of dread eased. "I'd like that too."

On our way out, Mark paid the cashier, and we agreed to check back with each other after I moved Harpo into my shop. He walked me to my car and pecked me on the cheek, probably as conscious as I was that passersby might see us and start the rumor mill spinning. (Not that Pete couldn't get one started all by himself if he cared to.)

As I slid behind the wheel of my Honda, I told myself I was fine with the idea of "keeping it light for a while," as long as it wasn't just a brush-off.

Mark Coccia seemed like a guy worth waiting for.

I was about to turn the ignition key when I remembered the muted phone call and wondered if I might have a message. I did, from an unfamiliar number.

The recorded voice was unfamiliar too—male and probably young, but with an oddly formal speaking style. I also could hear occasional, muffled PA-type announcements in the background.

"Cassie McGlone, this is Dion Janos, son of Nicholas Janos. He asked me to tell you that he finished the post for your back stairs, but he won't be able to come by tomorrow to install it, as he planned to. I had to take him to Saint Catherine's tonight, and he's there now in intensive care. He may have had a heart attack."

Chapter 10

St. Catherine's Medical Center, on the highway just outside Chadwick, was one of several small hospitals in a county network. Around eight p.m. on a weeknight, the ICU was busy but not overwhelmed, and only half a dozen visitors sat in the gray molded-plastic chairs of the waiting area, most on their cell phones.

It didn't take me long to spot Dion, even though I'd never met him before. About thirty, he sported collar-length dirty-blond hair and chin stubble at least two days old. He wore black sweatpants, a gray hoodie, and sneakers that no longer resembled whatever color they originally might have been.

He sat hunched with his elbows on his knees and gripped his smartphone with both hands, although he stared off in the general direction of the glass-walled nurses' station. He might have sounded almost robotic on the phone, but his posture conveyed how worried he really was.

I had to touch his shoulder to get his attention. "Dion?"

He startled like a deer and looked up in confusion. I might have been the Grim Reaper, checking in with him before I went to take his father away.

"I'm Cassie McGlone. You left me a phone message about your dad's condition."

"Yes. And you . . . *came* here?"

Was he grateful or annoyed? I didn't meant to intrude, but knowing he and his father had only each other, Mrs. Janos having passed a few years back, I thought he might need the support.

To make it sound more casual, I told him, "I was already in my car, and I wanted to see how Nick was doing. Have you had any news?"

Dion relaxed just a little at my explanation. His pale gray eyes and blond lashes gave him the look of a creature that rarely saw the sun. The black T-shirt that peeked through the gap in his hoodie bore a bright green mandala-like design of electronic circuitry. "Pop's awake and talking, and I guess the pain has eased up. They sent me out because they're running tests on him. Electrocardiogram and bloodwork."

I nodded, remembering that routine from a couple of close calls my own father had survived. Turned out his heart was fine. That didn't make any difference, unfortunately, when a hit-and-run driver ended his life three years ago.

I'm sure my mother and I were still affected by that event in ways we might not even realize. At least back then we could turn to each other to help us survive the loss of Dad. But Dion seemed to have no one to lean on but Nick. Maybe that was why, even though I hardly knew him, I felt moved to offer some support, at least until his father was out of the woods.

In case Dion didn't understand medical terminology as well as he did electronics, I explained, "Those tests will tell them if it was really a heart attack, or something less serious."

"Really?" The idea that it might be a false alarm seemed to calm Dion a bit, and he loosened the death grip on his phone.

Sitting next to him, I asked what had happened. He said his father had been complaining since the early afternoon about pains in his left arm, and thought he'd strained it lifting some lumber. But while they were eating dinner, the discomfort had turned into chest pains and finally he'd allowed Dion to drive him to the medical center.

"He's had problems like this before, hasn't he?" I asked.

"Yes, but not for a while. He was watching his diet, taking an aspirin every night, and trying to avoid stress." Abruptly, Dion broke off eye contact and swallowed hard. "This is probably my fault."

"What is? You mean, because you were questioned by the police?"

"I guess he told you about all that. She called me back in this morning, that Detective Bonelli. She thinks George DeLeuw was killed because of something to do with my invention. Now the FBI is getting involved!"

Wow, I thought, *who'd have expected things to go that far?* "Why would they be interested?"

Dion sighed as if he wished he'd never heard of DeLeuw and maybe even wished he'd never come up with whatever it was he'd invented. "They were going over the guy's personal files and found a lot of material they think was encrypted using my method. The FBI has code breakers, but even they couldn't decrypt it." A brief smile of pride brightened his scruffy features. "Anyhow, Detective Bonelli kept browbeating me to give them the key. She kept coming back to that, even though I told her I have no idea what the key might be. DeLeuw would have programmed that himself. And he can't tell anyone now, can he? Because he's dead."

Dion stated this in a flat, almost callous tone. Because he'd killed George himself, or just because George's murder was turning out to be a major pain in the neck for him and his dad?

Maybe the guy was just irritable from fatigue and worry. I noticed a sign forbidding any food or drink in the waiting room, and made a suggestion. "Nick's probably going to be tied up with those tests for a while, and you may have a long night ahead. Want to step out for a minute and get some coffee?"

"That's a good idea." He stood up, started for the hall, and looked almost surprised when I came along with him. No wonder Nick kept trying to fix this guy up. Dion acted as if his only social life took place in virtual reality.

Because he didn't think of it, I told the ICU nurse where we would be, and asked if Dion could be notified in case of any news. She promised to call the cafeteria.

A few minutes later Dion and I both drank sludgy coffee and nibbled prepackaged muffins at a wobbly laminate-topped table. I felt as if I were on the worst blind date ever as I tried to draw him out. "So, Dion, what do you actually do? I mean, for a living? Your father mentioned that you have clients coming to the house."

His air of depression briefly fell away. "I'm a games tester and a freelance programmer. Companies that design new video games send them to people like me for testing before they put them on the market. I find obvious glitches, and I also give them tips sometimes on how to make the game more challenging. That's the part I enjoy the most, but it's not steady. So I also do programming of all kinds for small businesses."

At least he did have a real job, I thought, even though the spotty income probably explained why he still lived with his dad. Of course, maybe he just preferred to, for company. "And I guess that's how you came up with your invention? What does it involve, exactly?"

Dion sized me up for a second and obviously concluded I was not very high-tech savvy. I sensed he was translating his explanation into the simplest possible terms. "It's a new process for performing more rapid public key encryption and decryption." He kept his voice low, probably so no one sitting around us in the coffee shop would hijack his idea. "See, right now public key encryption involves two separate keys—a public one and a private one—to encrypt or decrypt messages and files. Because of . . . well, their mathematical properties . . . the private key can't be determined from the public key."

He scrutinized my face for some sign of comprehension. I humored him with a nod so he would continue.

"The main problem is, this method takes a long time to encrypt and decrypt material, so it's not very useful for long messages or larger files. My method speeds up the process. It lets the user encrypt large messages or files with a public key, but only someone with the private key can decrypt them."

Though I still didn't grasp the technicalities, I began to see why his innovation could be valuable. "With all the emphasis today on cybersecurity, I guess that would be a big improvement, right? Assuming, of course, that it works."

He sat taller in his molded-plastic chair, looking almost offended. "Oh, it *works.* To use it on a commercial computer, you just have to embed the process in a hardware chip. I asked DeLeuw to see if the guys at Encyte would create a prototype chip. We could use that to demonstrate the system to big tech companies, maybe even government security agencies."

"So you gave him . . . what? A copy of the software program?"

Dion nodded. "More than a month ago. He acted really interested at first. But time went by, and whenever I called to ask if Encyte had responded yet, he kept putting me off and making excuses. Finally he just stopped answering my phone calls and my texts."

I could understand Dion's frustration, but I also imagined that he could make a major nuisance of himself when he got locked on to an idea.

He chewed and swallowed another mouthful of bran muffin, then continued. "So a couple of weeks ago, I dropped by DeLeuw's house again. He was in a meeting with his assistant, that guy Ross. They both acted totally pissed off that I came by without an appointment. But what else was I supposed to do?"

It was the first time I'd ever heard of someone being stalked over a computer program, but I could see that, in some ways, Dion still had the prickly temperament of a teenager. "Your dad said you saw a news item, that another company was coming out with the same kind of system."

He finished his coffee, then crushed the paper cup in one hand. "One of the big Chinese firms. I can't even pronounce the name. But from the description, it sounded almost exactly like my concept."

I felt pretty safe in the hospital coffee shop, even if he lost his temper, so I pushed further. "The police seem to think you got so mad that you went to DeLeuw's house and killed him. Because you thought he made a deal with the Chinese and cut you out."

Dion shook his head miserably. "I can't even say for sure that he double-crossed me. Maybe it was a coincidence—maybe the Chinese already had a similar idea in the works. Could even be that

Encyte knew something similar was in progress, and that's why they were stalling me. All I know is, somebody beat me to the punch!"

Poor choice of words, I thought, *even though DeLeuw hadn't been hit with a fist.*

Nick's son leaned forward and lowered his voice again. "Yeah, I blew off some steam to Pop, and we both called DeLeuw a few names. But I never even went back over to the guy's house again. By then I was thinking more about suing him, not that we have the money to do that. I hadn't figured out *what* I was going to do about it, if anything. But going to his place in the middle of the day and killing the guy? Really?"

It did seem like a radical departure for someone who lived in a world of abstract thought rather than action. On the other hand, he did seem possessive about his invention and angry at DeLeuw's dismissive treatment. And while Dion might not be in peak shape, at about six feet he was tall enough to have swung that lethal chunk of stone.

Even if he hadn't committed the murder, could his invention possibly have been a factor in some way?

"You said George would have programmed the key himself, and might be the only one who had access to it," I remembered, "and you told Detective Bonelli that. Did the police search for it? Could George have had it on him when he died?"

"She said they went through his clothes, his study, practically the whole house, and didn't find anything like what I'd described. But that doesn't mean much." Dion shrugged. "The chip would be really small, so if it's hidden, it could be almost anywhere."

A food-service lady approached our table. "Mr. Janos?" she asked in a quiet tone. "They have your father's test results in the ICU, anytime you want to go back."

We thanked her, and Dion dashed from the cafeteria. I took the time to empty both of our trays into the garbage before following.

By the time I reached the ICU waiting room again, Dion was talking to a middle-aged Asian woman in green scrubs. She spoke softly, but I could just overhear her telling him that his father had not suffered any damage to his heart.

"It appears to have been just serious angina," she said. "We've given him some medication, and we'll keep him here overnight to make sure he's stable."

"Can I see him?" Dion asked.

"For a few minutes, but then he really ought to rest. He shouldn't have too many visitors tonight." Because I stood close behind Dion, the doctor glanced at me. "Are you family too?"

"No," I admitted, "just a friend, and I don't need to crowd in on this. Dion, please tell your dad I wish him a speedy recovery. I'll check in with you tomorrow to see how he's doing."

The young man's shoulders sagged in relief. "Thanks for coming, Cassie."

On my drive home, I felt drained from the day's highs and lows. I was glad Nick's prognosis was better than expected, and that I'd made the effort to support Dion. In talking to him, I also might have learned some helpful things about his conflict with DeLeuw. Not that I had any business trying to solve the murder.

Only now did I have a chance to reflect on my date with Mark, which was great until the very end. Did he like me as much as I did him, or not? Another mystery . . .

My life sure had become a roller-coaster ride lately. And tomorrow I had to revisit the murder scene to pick up Harpo.

At least we should be able to rule him out as a suspect!

A charcoal-gray Dodge Charger sat parked across the street from George DeLeuw's house, with a young man in dark sunglasses relaxing behind the wheel. This told me that while the place was no longer an official crime scene, the Chadwick police still kept it under surveillance.

I parked up the driveway, just outside the closed garage and next to Anita's older-model blue Toyota sedan. Even with a cop across the street, I felt a shadow of fear as I raised my hand to press the front doorbell. When that glossy oak door with its beveled window swung open, might I walk in on another scene of carnage? Maybe with Anita lying dead this time?

My post-traumatic-stress fantasies evaporated when the housekeeper peered briefly out through one of the sidelights, then opened the door with a smile. "Hello, hello, Cassie!" she greeted me like a long-lost sister. "Come on in. I'm sure somebody else is gonna be very glad to see you too!"

She'd certainly been keeping the place spotless, as if still trying to live up to George's exacting standards. On the other hand, she had a lot less to dust and vacuum these days. Only the major pieces of furniture remained. Even in the front hall, nails jutting from the walls and empty niches and pedestals showed where DeLeuw's beloved artworks had been confiscated. I tried to avoid looking into the study, but even passing by I noticed that the bloodstained Oriental rug had been removed from that room too.

"He's upstairs," Anita told me, and it took me a second to remember that she meant Harpo. "I already put him in the carrier so he wouldn't give you no trouble."

The Persian had never given me any trouble in the past when I was grooming him, but I guess being shut up for a week alone in a bedroom could make any cat irritable. "Thanks, Anita," I said.

We climbed the steep, curving front stairs, the same as on my visits to the grooming studio. Faint halos on some walls told of more missing artworks. The big, modern credenza remained on the second-floor landing, but I missed the huge, abstract painting, with slashes of sunset rose and gold, that used to hang above it, and the hand-thrown ceramic bowl with the wavy edge that had rested on top of it.

The FBI had really moved all those pieces into storage in a warehouse? Because something might have been used as a weapon, or because DeLeuw might have hidden the key chip in one of them? Dion said it could be made small enough to stash almost anywhere. I guessed they had already checked the furniture thoroughly before leaving it in the house.

Tempted to do a search of my own, I reminded myself that this was not my job. *I'm just here to get the cat, not to solve DeLeuw's murder.*

But . . . what if I found evidence that might acquit Dion? I hated to see poor Nick driven to the verge of a heart attack with worry, especially if his son really was innocent.

A throaty wail of distress from behind one of the doors helped me refocus on my immediate goal.

"It's okay, kitty!" the housekeeper called back in a lilting voice. "Your friend Cassie is here. She's gonna take you home with her!" Anita pushed down the polished-brass latch and swung the door open.

George's spacious bedroom followed the same theme as the rest of the house—beige tones and clean-lined furniture meant to emphasize the artworks. The décor looked bland now that everything colorful and creative had been removed. Anita gestured toward the bed, where Harpo paced as well as he could inside a big, soft-sided pet carrier. The mesh panels all around gave me a good view of him, and vice versa.

I sat down next to the carrier and unzipped the front far enough to stroke his fluffy blond fur. "Hi, handsome! Been having a rough time, haven't you? Sorry about what happened to your person— that sucks. I'm sure you miss him."

Starved for attention, the Persian rubbed his cheek against my hand so hard that he shed meringue-like fur inside the carrier. Anita also must have noticed his desperation, because she smiled sadly.

"I fed him this morning," she said, "and he used the litter pan right before you came. I cleaned it out so you can take that, too, if you want."

"Might as well. His routine will be disrupted enough, so he should have familiar things around him."

While I continued to pet the restless cat, Anita and I also discussed what kind of food he was used to eating and a few kinds that didn't agree with him.

"Do you have his medical records in case of any emergency?" I asked.

She blanked for a second as if she hadn't thought about that. But after a quick trip to George's home office, she came back with vet records for all of Harpo's vaccinations, his neutering, and other medical procedures. She even handed over his official papers from the breeder who'd sold him to DeLeuw.

"That's great," I told her. "Whoever he ends up with will appreciate having all of this background."

I zipped the carrier shut again and we all went back down the long front staircase.

Just as we reached the landing, I saw someone outside walk swiftly past the great room window. I stopped short and caught Anita's arm.

She jumped a little too, but mainly because of my reaction. "It's okay," she chuckled. "It's only Louis. He was coming by to mulch today."

I remembered Marjorie's suspicions that one of George's household employees had been pock-

eting some of his smaller artworks in the past.
Whether or not that was true, no harm in giving
both Anita and Louis the run of the property, I
guessed, now that so much had been confiscated.
Louis wasn't likely to sneak a sectional sofa into
the back of his landscaping truck, especially with a
cop posted across the street.

But if Anita or Louis had been stealing, could
that explain the missing computer key? What if
one of them had taken home, say, a small antique
box or a Chinese snuff bottle that George had
used as a hiding place for the chip? The thief
would now possess an even more valuable treasure
. . . maybe without being aware of it.

As the housekeeper and I continued on to the
entry hall, I asked, "Does it make you nervous,
working here now by yourself?"

"It does sometimes," she admitted. "'Specially
since they never caught whoever killed Mr. DeLeuw.
I figure that person probably doesn't have any reason to hurt me, but who can be sure? What if he
thinks I know more about it than I do?"

I set Harpo's carrier down for a second on the
marble tile floor. "At least you have a cop watching
the house. Is he here all day?"

"Seems to be, at least for the few hours that
I'm here. And sometimes, like today, Louis works
outside at the same time."

*Let's just hope she doesn't have anything to fear from
him,* I thought. Unless they'd been conspiring . . .
something I found hard to believe.

"But when I'm all by myself, it does get lonely,"
Anita went on. "Mr. DeLeuw was a quiet, serious
man, so he didn't make a lot of noise. Still, just

having him around was company." She scanned the high-ceilinged entry hall. "And now that all the art is gone, it's so empty . . . sometimes I feel like I'm working in a *mausoleo*."

A tomb, I thought. "I suppose the police checked everything for fingerprints?"

"They left that messy dust over everything." She flapped her hands to indicate the front rooms. "If they found the killer's prints, wouldn't they arrest somebody by now?"

"You'd think so." I glanced toward one particular empty pedestal. "At the funeral home, you said you thought they were looking at this stone sculpture as the murder weapon."

"*Sí!* I heard two of them talking about how it could have made the mark on the back of his head." Anita hugged herself. "I never liked that stone thing—it just looked like it was made to hurt somebody. It even had a bad name!"

The pedestal still bore a small bronze plate, so I stepped closer to read the artist's name and the title of the work. Both seemed to be in Italian. "*Timore?* What does that—"

"I asked Mr. DeLeuw once, because we have almost the same word in Spanish." With an obvious shudder, Anita translated, "It means 'fear.' "

Chapter 11

"Goodness, Cassie," said Sarah. "That's the most beautiful cat I've ever seen!"

I scratched Harpo under the chin. "Pretty impressive, isn't he? He'll look even better after we give him a good combing."

I had just eased the Persian out of his carrier and onto my grooming table, where he shook out his fur to its full glory. His "imperfect" tail curled in a jaunty plume over his back. Unfortunately, in just a week with only minimal brushing by Anita, it all had gotten a bit matted. He'd need some tidying up before we put him into his boarding condo.

Meanwhile, Harpo's round, copper eyes seemed to be asking, *What's going on? Why aren't I home? And where's George?*

Sarah steadied him while I started untangling his thick undercoat with a wide-toothed comb. I dropped puffs of fur, the texture of cotton candy, into a step-on garbage can near my feet. Anytime I hit resistance, I braced the area with my fingers and used the comb as a pick to loosen and remove the mat. Though this had to be done carefully, I knew Harpo's coat well enough by now to make good progress. If anything slowed me and Sarah down, it was the cat's attempts to rub his head or hip against our hands.

Even when Sarah stretched him on his side as I'd taught her to, so I could work on his belly and legs, Harpo didn't resist. Maybe he was grateful to us, and not just for the grooming.

"What a sweetie." She beamed at him.

"You see why I couldn't let this nice guy go to a shelter. Or even to somebody in DeLeuw's circle who might not treat him decently." I paused to spritz the cat's fur with an antistatic moisturizer to help with the dematting. "So, did anything important happen here while I was out?"

"Not much. The Burmese was acting restless this morning, so I let her out to climb around on the shelves for a while. And a Mrs. Reynolds called to ask if you could do a Maine Coon for her. I took a message, up at the desk."

I mulled this prospect. "Coons can be a challenge—they're so big, with so much hair. I just hope he's not in too bad shape, or too cranky."

"If he is, charge extra," Sarah suggested. "Other than that, it's been quiet. One guy did stop to look in our window, but he didn't come inside."

"Oh?" I gently loosened another clump of blond fluff.

"Too bad you weren't here. He was young and good-looking. Probably disappointed to see an old lady like me behind the counter!"

My comb caught in the mat and I froze it there for a second. "What did he look like?"

"Medium tall. Brown hair that kind of came down over his forehead. And he was wearing a blue blazer with some kind of badge on the lapel."

Damn. I didn't say it out loud, but Sarah's sharp instincts picked up on my reaction anyway.

"What? You think he was some kind of health inspector?"

"If he was, I think he would have come in, don't you?" I went back to my grooming. "I'm just worried it might be my ex."

"Oh dear. Not the one who knocked you around?"

I nodded. "Mom said he just got a job as a security guard in Morristown. That would explain the blazer. Could be he drove out here on his lunch hour, trying to track me down."

"I didn't think of that. Then maybe it was lucky you *weren't* at the desk this morning, eh? If he thinks I'm 'Cassie,' maybe he won't be back."

Silently, I regretted the brilliant idea to include my nickname as part of the name of the shop. Too late to do much about that now, though. I told Sarah, "If he ever does come in, and introduces himself as Andy, feel free to chase him off with the pepper spray."

Once we'd restored Harpo to his full handsomeness, I buckled his powder-blue collar around his neck again. Its rolled design let his neck ruff lie smoothly—DeLeuw obviously had chosen the collar with care. It held the cat's license tag plus a tiny silver heart stamped with his name and George's home phone number. I reflected sadly that the number was obsolete now and Harpo's next owner, whoever that might be, would have to change it.

"Speaking of boyfriends, how did your date go last night with Dr. Coccia?" Sarah asked.

Her question revived mixed feelings of elation and frustration as I remembered how vaguely the evening had ended. I carried our new boarder to an extra-tall cage with a perch that gave him a view of the whole room before I answered. "It went well, I think. As you can imagine, Mark and I have a lot in common, and the more we talked the better I liked him. He did warn me, though, that he just came out of a long-term relationship and wants to take things slow. I told him I was pretty much in the same place."

Peeling off her vinyl gloves, my assistant nodded. "That's fine. You're both young; you've got time."

"As long as it's not his way of letting me down easy. Could be code for saying he's just not that into me."

"Not necessarily. Some people find it hard to jump from one relationship right into another one. Didn't you feel that way yourself, after the problems you had with . . . what's his name, Andy?"

That was true, I thought. And I'd certainly prefer to be with someone who took his relationships seriously rather than hopping from partner to partner. With a shrug, I concluded, "I guess I'll know better if he actually calls me again." Pulling off my own gloves and tossing them into the trash can, I changed the subject. "It was a weird night all

around. As I was ready to leave the diner, I saw I
had a phone message from Nick's son, Dion, saying his dad was in the hospital."

Sarah and I took a lunch break while I told her
about that crisis. "When I left Saint Catherine's,
everyone there seemed to feel Nick would be all
right. So far I haven't heard anything different,
but I'll check with Dion today."

We were just about to get back to work when
the front-desk phone rang. Though I'd given Mark
my cell number, I still hoped it might be him. Or
possibly Dion, with an update on his father.

A less welcome thought struck me. *Or, God for-
bid, Andy!*

With all of those possibilities looming, the last
voice I expected to hear on the line was Detective
Angela Bonelli's.

"Cassie McGlone?" she said. "You and I need to
talk."

At least I didn't have to go back down to Chadwick's depressingly sterile police station. It was a
warm day, so Bonelli suggested we meet in the recently upgraded Riverside Park. To get on the detective's good side, I offered to bring coffee from
Starbucks. When she requested nothing fancier in
hers than cream and sugar, it did not surprise me,
and I got the same.

We sat on one of the wrought-iron-and-oak
benches—Victorian in style but only a couple of
years old—facing the river. A running path crossed
behind us, but in midafternoon few passersby
came near enough to eavesdrop on our conversa-

tion. The flock of Canada geese browsing on the shore, a few yards away, couldn't have cared less.

Bonelli wore tailored pants and an L.L.Bean rain jacket that made me wonder if she owned anything that wasn't navy blue. Her sunglasses hid her eyes as she sipped her coffee and faced the serene glittering river. "I understand you went to DeLeuw's house this morning."

"That's right. I got permission from his lawyer to board his cat. Anita told me Harpo was going crazy, closed up all alone in that house. I figured if the investigation dragged on much longer, he might end up in a shelter."

"And this is your concern because?"

"Hey, I'm an animal lover. Besides, from what I could see, George doted on his Harpo. If only for his sake, I didn't want to see his cat come to a bad end. At least now he'll have a safe home, until someone else volunteers to take him or until George's will is made public." I was tempted to ask if the police had any inside knowledge about the terms of the will, but that probably also fell into the range of things that were not my concern. So I tried a more roundabout approach. "How much longer do you think that will take?"

"We're working on it. I guess that's why you attended the viewing at the funeral home? I heard you asked a lot of questions of the other mourners there. Did you discuss anything with them besides the cat?"

"I didn't ask them about the murder, but a lot of them give me their opinions anyway. George's sister from California, Danielle, suspects the landscaper, Louis. The ex-wife, Marjorie, thinks it was an art thief or an enemy he made through his business. Jerry Ross, the assistant, thinks Dion Janos did it. All of this without me asking any questions on the subject, swear to God!"

Bonelli slipped me a grudging smile. "I guessed that any possible suspects might talk more freely to a civilian than to a police officer."

I remembered what Nick had said about Bonelli being new on the force. Was she hinting that I might be able to help her? "I figure, either they were angry about George's murder and looking for someone to blame, or at least one of them is guilty and trying to throw suspicion onto somebody else."

A cloud passed over the river, and the detective removed her sunglasses—all the better to pin me with her stern, heavy-lidded gaze. "This is what I was afraid of, Cassie. You're getting too involved."

"Sorry. I majored in psychology in college. And I read a lot of murder mysteries."

"A dangerous habit."

I noted that, behind her intimidating façade, Detective Bonelli at least had a sense of humor. "Since George's cat will be taking up condo space at my shop until this case is solved, I'd like to ask if you guys are making any progress. But I figure you probably won't tell me."

She took another swallow of the coffee. "You figure right."

"On the other hand, I imagine your forensics team went through all of DeLeuw's stuff before it was put into storage. If they found any fingerprints that didn't belong, you'd probably be closing in on somebody by now."

Bonelli's eyes narrowed as if she was losing patience with my prying. "Who says we aren't?"

"You questioned Dion, but let him go, so I'm betting you didn't find his prints. Of course the killer might've worn gloves . . . but on a warm spring day, that would mean premeditation. More likely, he wiped off the fingerprints—"

"Enough!" Bonelli snapped. "Keep on like this, Cassie, and you'll convince me that you did it."

"Except I had absolutely no motive." I chuckled weakly. "Grooming George's cat was helping to keep my business afloat. Now that he's gone, I need to find more clients, fast. And if you think I wanted to steal his cat, George already explained to me that Harpo isn't show quality—he's worth a few hundred dollars, at most. Hardly enough to make me murder my best client."

"Is someone paying you now to board the cat?"

"Only because the lawyer insisted, and at a reduced rate. I'd still rather have George as a live customer."

The detective leaned back on the bench and crumpled her empty cup with an amused expression. "Maybe I should ask who you think murdered DeLeuw."

"Sorry, I have no idea. I'd rule out Anita, because she seemed totally horrified when she saw him lying dead. She told me he was a good boss, so like me, she probably was better off when he was alive. And I don't want to suspect Dion, because his father is a really nice guy and my handyman."

Bonelli looked alert. "You know Dion Janos?"

"I know his dad well, but I only met Dion for the first time last night." I explained about Nick's angina attack, and what Dion had told me about his encryption system. "Is it true that George's electronic files included some that were encrypted using that method?" When Bonelli's lips thinned as if she wouldn't confirm this, I simply pressed on. "If it is, your guys probably looked for the key already. But if DeLeuw hid it before he died, it could be anywhere. You'd have to go through all of those artworks in the storage unit with a fine-tooth comb."

"More like a handheld scanner," the detective said. "The FBI found one in DeLeuw's office that looks like it was specially designed to read the chip. At least, that's what Dion told them, if he can be trusted."

That was interesting news, I thought. If both a key and a chip existed, they must have been manu-factured somewhere. By Encyte? If DeLeuw al-ready had prototypes created, why hadn't he told Dion that? Could it be true that he was shopping the product around behind its inventor's back?

"Did George have a bank safe-deposit box?" I asked.

She nodded. "The FBI has checked that, and all the other obvious places such as locked desk drawers, file cabinets, and a wall safe. After they found nothing resembling the chip in any of those places, they moved the rest of his stuff out of the house so they could take their time searching it.

And to reduce the chances that someone else might find the key before they do."

I could see the wisdom of this approach. "I still have my doubts, though, about Dion as a killer. If you questioned him, you must have noticed that he's a serious nerd. I can picture him maybe getting worked up during a *World of Warcraft* game, but not clobbering someone in real life."

"No telling what someone will do if he thinks he's been cheated out of a fortune," the detective said.

True, I supposed, since Nick and his son lived a very modest, working-class lifestyle. Still, I hoped to deflect suspicion from them. "Of all the people I met at the viewing, only Marjorie seemed really hostile toward George. Did you know their only daughter died of a heroin overdose about four years ago?"

"We questioned his ex about that. As you say, she didn't speak very kindly about DeLeuw. But she can prove she was in New York at the time of the murder."

"She might've paid someone to do it."

"But a hit would be premeditated, wouldn't it?" Bonelli reminded me. She sounded as if, against her better judgment, she was enjoying our brainstorming session. "Besides, the woman had been divorced from George for years and was getting alimony. So why kill him now?"

With no answer for that, I fell to watching the action at the small playground a few hundred feet away. A young mother mediated between a couple of toddlers, no doubt brother and sister, who squabbled over the swings.

"Is Danielle his only living relative?" I asked Bonelli. "If so, she'll probably inherit everything. Though, at the viewing, she acted as if she couldn't imagine anyone killing George over something as petty as an inheritance."

The detective scoffed. "I have a feeling DeLeuw's inheritance will be anything but petty. Those artworks alone have to be worth . . . Well, I'm no expert, but—"

"A whole lot," I finished. "Speaking of his collection, Anita and I have a theory about the murder weapon. Was it that abstract stone sculpture from the front hall?"

Bonelli locked those dark eyes on me until I suspected handcuffs would come next.

"I'm interested in art, so I noticed it before," I explained. "Dion said you questioned him about that piece. And I saw that strange, ragged wound on George's head. The stone had a kind of sharp edge."

"Cassie . . ." She shook her head, maybe at the futility of keeping any police information confidential in a small town. "Yes, we found traces of his blood on that piece."

"Just traces? Any fingerprints?"

"It had been wiped down with some kind of cloth."

Ah, I thought. *So the killer did act on impulse, but took enough time afterward to try to erase the evidence.* "Fibers?"

"A few. They didn't match any items that we could find in the house."

Finishing my lukewarm coffee, I reflected on that for a minute. "Did anyone see a visitor come to DeLeuw's house around that time? One of the suspects, or even a stranger? After all, it was the middle of the day."

"The middle of a workday, when his nearest neighbors weren't home. The landscaper claims to have been working at the back of the property, with noisy equipment and ear protection, all afternoon. The maid says she was cleaning upstairs. She did hear DeLeuw talking now and then, but assumed he was on his speakerphone. She said she'd been told not to eavesdrop, so she deliberately tuned that out."

I put all this together. "So it sounds as if someone parked on the street—instead of in the driveway—and came up the front walk. George willingly let him or her in. They talked but didn't get into an obvious shouting match. That person killed him, then left the same way, without being seen."

Bonelli nodded. "That's the most likely scenario. So you see why we're looking at people he knew well."

The sunlight slanted lower through the park's trees now. Three teenage boys with backpacks approached down the path, ribbing one another and guffawing loudly. If the high school had let out, I thought, it must be after three o'clock.

The same idea probably occurred to Bonelli, because she uncrossed her legs and leaned forward on the bench.

"You're pretty good at this, Cassie, but you need to back off now."

"Was any of the stuff I heard from the people at the viewing helpful to you?"

"Not really. I interviewed all the same people you talked to. The difference is, I didn't take what they said at face value. I dug a little deeper."

"And?"

"Nick Janos probably didn't tell you that he went over to DeLeuw's house himself, the day before the murder, and accused George of cheating Dion."

That threw me. "No, he didn't."

"And no matter how blasé Danielle acted about her possible inheritance, she needs money very much right now. She's invested more in her line of shops than she can ever hope to make back. She admitted that last month she asked George for a loan, to help keep the business afloat, but he turned her down."

I had to appreciate the detective's investigative skills. Of course, she must have resources far beyond my puny Internet access.

"Anything else?" I asked.

"Louis Monroe, the landscaper, has a juvenile record for shoplifting. Nothing violent and no arrests since then. Still, he could have been pocketing some valuable knickknack when DeLeuw walked in. If George threatened to call the cops, maybe Louis panicked."

I remembered Marjorie saying she suspected Louis. Could she have known about his record, or was it just her knee-jerk reaction to suspect "the help"?

Bonelli handed me her card. "If you do hear or see anything genuinely suspicious, let me know." She stood up then, and zipped her rain jacket higher against the late-afternoon breeze. "But as for the folks you've talked to so far, take it from me. Every one of them probably lied to you . . . about something."

Chapter 12

Sarah greeted my return with a worried frown, as if she'd expected Bonelli to haul me away in the back of a squad car.

"Everything's fine," I reassured my assistant. "She just wanted to know why I was questioning people at the funeral home. And after I explained, she wanted to know what I found out."

"That's a relief!" Sarah pressed a hand to her chest.

"Bet you thought you might be stuck running this place by yourself, eh?" I teased.

"Where I come from, people do get put in jail for crimes they didn't commit," she said soberly. "Especially in something like a high-profile murder, when the cops are in a hurry to make an arrest."

I'd never pried into Sarah's personal background, and from her mailing address I knew she lived in a nice enough area these days. But she'd mentioned having taught in a couple of inner-city schools, so this hint that she'd also grown up in a tough neighborhood didn't surprise me.

"And of course, they always look hard at the person who reported finding the body," I added. "Guess I managed to convince Bonelli that of all the possible suspects, I had the least to gain. Plus, they know I wasn't trying to make off with any artworks—at least, not that day—because they searched my pockets, my duffle bag, and my car."

"Glad you're in the clear." Sarah shouldered her satchel-style purse. "Well, if you don't need me for anything else tonight, I have a committee meeting at my church. . . ."

I glanced at the clock. It was already past five, so she was legitimately done for the day. "No problem. Thanks again for staffing the counter while I was gone. I'll do my level best to spend more time here in the shop from now on!"

"Not exactly your fault, when a policewoman takes you off for questioning." She smiled and wiggled her fingers in good-bye. "Have a nice, uneventful evening."

"I'll try."

Left alone, I checked on the boarder cats again. Satisfaction warmed me when I saw that Harpo had eaten all of his supper—his regular food, supplied by Anita—and now settled in on the perch of his condo to groom himself. For a creature who had been through so much—and downsized from a McMansion to a closet-sized enclosure—he looked fairly serene. *Everyone should roll with life's changes so well.*

Upstairs, I fed my own cats and nuked a frozen

dinner for myself. While the microwave was counting down, I called Nick's home phone to check on his status. Foolishly, I hadn't gotten a cell number for Dion, and absentmindedly he hadn't offered it, so I got an answering machine. I left a message to say I hoped his dad was on the mend and asked Dion to keep me posted.

After dinner, I sank down on the slipcovered sofa. It was only around seven, but once again I felt exhausted too early by all of the tense situations I'd navigated that day. And I'd thought boarding and grooming cats would be an easy, no-drama way to make a living! Of course, I'd never expected to get involved in a client's murder.

You're not involved, Cassie. Bonelli warned you to stay out of it, and you should listen to her. All you need to do now is wait and see if anyone wants to adopt Harpo.

Of course, it will have to be someone who's sincerely interested in his well-being, not someone who'll abuse him or neglect him. I realized that, from what I knew of DeLeuw's inner circle, I didn't really trust any of them to have the cat's best interests at heart. That could complicate the issue for me if one or more of them did come forward.

If George actually left the cat to one of them in his will, though, I may just have to hand Harpo over. That would be tough, but I don't have any legal right to refuse.

I stretched out on the living room sofa, my head propped on a throw pillow at one end, and tried in vain to find something worth watching via my very economical cable TV subscription. Cole (full name Cat King Cole) stretched like a black mini-sphinx across the back of the sofa. The quietly affectionate Madame Matisse curled up against my bare feet, while Mango perched on the armrest behind my pillow to noisily chew on my hair. He would always be the joker in the pack.

Was it weird of me to feel so contented, surrounded by my little feline family? Was I on the fast track to Crazy Cat Lady status? Most women my age would be out hitting the bars and clubs every night, desperately searching for Mr. Right.

I knew, because I'd done enough of that myself when I lived in Morristown.

And the one time I thought I'd found Mr. Right, he'd turned out to be Mr. Very Wrong.

Probably that had soured me on the whole idea, even prompted me to move to Chadwick. Yes, I loved the old-fashioned charm of the town, but I couldn't deny the lack of hot spots to meet other singles. Right now that didn't bother me much, but would I feel differently a few years down the line? If someday I yearned for a more-than-feline family?

The local TV news, though happily free of any more murders, bored me so much that I dozed off for a few minutes. In a mildly erotic dream, Mark Coccia, wearing his blue medical scrubs, gently massaged my scalp. Ahh, those skillful veterinarian hands . . .

A sharp yank on my hair brought me back to reality. "Mango!"

The tabby leaped off the arm of the sofa, and I could swear I heard snickering.

Before I could relax again, the jazzy guitar intro of "Stray Cat Strut" beckoned me to check my cell phone. The call was from Dawn.

"Cassie, you've got to help me!" she pleaded. "He's driving me crazy."

I doubted that she was complaining about her laid-back boyfriend, Keith. "Okay, what's Tigger the Terrible up to now?"

"I turned my back for a second, and he got into the loose herbal tea that I keep behind the counter. . . ."

"Was it mint?"

"How'd you know?"

"Never mind. Anything else?"

"Oh God, what didn't he do? Chewed up a few bundles of sage. Made off with a thirty-dollar amethyst crystal on a silver chain—which later turned up in his water dish. Clawed the corner of my antique oak display cabinet. Kept batting at my ankles while I was trying to wait on customers . . ."

Good thing Dawn couldn't see my wide grin. "Is that all?"

"No! The worst thing is, every time the front door opens, he bolts for it. I'll think he's safely across the room, but as soon as he hears the string of bells ring, he's there in a flash. Today he actually got out once! Luckily, he was so confused about what to do next that I had a chance to scoop him up and bring him back inside."

"You could try taking the bells off the door," I suggested.

But Dawn was so frustrated, she hardly heard me. "I swear, if the little beast likes living on the street so much, maybe I should let him do it. I'd still feed him, but—"

That kind of talk wiped the smirk from my face. "Now, now. Even if I were okay with letting him roam, you still have to wait until he's neutered." While stroking Cole's satiny black head, I got an idea. "Maybe you can clicker-train him."

"Huh?" Dawn paused for a moment. "I think Keith did that with his dog once . . . but would it work on a cat?"

"I got Cole to use a scratching post that way. Where are you, still at the store?"

"Yeah." She sighed. "Doing some inventory. And I guess I'm afraid to shut Tigger up in the supply room for the night, not knowing what he might get into."

"Hold on. I'll be right over."

It took me only a few minutes to find the small blue plastic clicker that I'd used with Cole, plus a bag of cat treats and a fishing-pole toy. I put on my jacket and set out for the short walk to Nature's Way.

Even in the brief time since I'd purchased my shop, Chadwick had developed more of a nightlife. The galleries and other specialty shops occasionally stayed open until nine, and more little restaurants had opened up, catering to those who wanted something more elegant than the diner. They seemed to be doing a brisk business, too, because more people roamed the streets tonight than I remembered, even from last year.

A few windows had letter-sized posters for the Small Business Sunday event that Dawn had told me about. It was taking place in the high school gym that coming weekend. With so much on my mind lately, I hadn't had time to give it much thought. Or maybe I'd put it out of my mind because, since I stayed open half a day on Saturdays,

Sunday really was my only day to rest. Marketing my business was still work.

I also passed a couple of Dawn's handbills, taped in the window of a shoe-repair shop and to the post of one vintage-style streetlamp. As I'd advised, she kept the message ultra simple: *Did you lose a kitten? Contact Dawn at Nature's Way.*

I approached Kin Khao, the Thai place that she and I kept meaning to try, just as a well-dressed couple came out the front door and strolled down the block ahead of me. The woman, in heels, was maybe an inch taller than the man. Something about them seemed familiar, but not until they reached their car and he helped her into the passenger side did I recognize Marjorie DeLeuw and Jerry Ross. That was part of what threw me—I wouldn't have expected to see them together!

What's going on there? I wondered as they drove away. *First of all, why are they still hanging around town? The police only asked that I not leave the state.* I wasn't sure where Ross lived—close enough, I supposed, to meet regularly with DeLeuw when he was alive. But Marjorie supposedly had an apartment in Manhattan, and I thought she'd have been allowed to return there by now.

She'd talked so negatively about DeLeuw being "all business," and even implied he might have been killed because he "got his hands dirty" in the Wall Street game. Now that I thought about it, she'd even thrown a shrewd look in the direction of Schroeder and Ross, who'd been talking together, when she'd said that.

Could it all have been an act? Could DeLeuw's

hated ex have been involved with his trusted assistant?

Bonelli said everyone at the funeral home probably lied to me about something. Maybe she knew what she was talking about!

"Okay, Dawn, now you try it."

Looking unsure, my friend pointed to the braided rug in front of her wood-burning stove, which fortunately burned nothing at the moment. "Tigger, rug! Rug!"

The kitten chirruped and bounded sideways, tail puffed and back arched. He just wanted to play.

Dawn sighed, with a droop of her slim shoulders. I'd never seen my friend look so beaten down. Still, I couldn't help smiling.

"It's okay. Keep at it," I said. "And show him the treat."

"Rug." She pointed with the tidbit this time. "Rug!"

Wide eyes focused on the food, Tigger approached until he was standing on the rug.

"Good," I said. "Now bring the treat down just above his head until he sits."

Naturally, he tried to stand on his hind legs and snatch the tidbit from her. Dawn said, "Nah-ah-ah!" and hid it in her fist. Finally the kitten sat.

"Now click," I directed her. "Wait a second, and then give it to him."

She followed my instructions and finally opened her palm. Tigger gobbled the food.

"The clicker gets his attention and tells him he's done something right," I explained.

"Okay." She smiled wearily. "But how is that going to keep him from running out the door?"

I leaned against her antique oak sales counter. "Practice this routine whenever you have free time during the day. It'll take some repetition, because he's a kitten, so he has no attention span. Eventually you should be able to say, 'Rug,' and he'll go to the rug and wait for his treat. Then, when someone comes to the door and you see him about to sprint, you can tell him to go to the rug instead."

She shook her head. "I don't know. . . . I guess it's worth a try. I sometimes forget, you actually went to school for this stuff."

"Strange as it may seem, I did." I scooped the kitten up in a hug and then looked him straight in the eye. "You listen to Dawn, okay? And no more stealing jewelry or getting high on her mint tea!"

"Was he really?"

"Probably not, but it is a little like catnip."

"Eeeep!" Tigger agreed.

My friend sank down in one of her throw-covered easy chairs. "I'm bushed. Running after a baby all day really wears you out."

"I brought you something for that, too." I grabbed the plastic fishing rod with a bunch of colorful feathers on the end from her sales counter. Tigger was instantly riveted, and leaped a foot in the air to catch this elusive "prey." I showed Dawn how to make it move stealthily along the floor, "climb" the counter, and dart through the air like a real mouse or bird so he couldn't resist chasing it.

"When you're ready to close at night, before you shut him up, give him a good workout with this thing," I told her. "Then feed him, and he should sleep through the night. Maybe give him another play session in the morning before you open."

"I can manage that." She looked a little more optimistic now; maybe it was the irresistible charm of watching a kitten at play. "Cassie, when he's trying to get out . . . you don't suppose he wants to go home?"

I thought that over as I wrapped the cord around the pole and put it aside, much to Tigger's disappointment. "Possibly, but it's usually older cats that really have a sense of home. And he was already camping out in your storeroom, so he mustn't have been that attached to any other place." I sat in the other armchair. "Guess you haven't had any responses to your posters."

"No one actually saying that they lost him. Of course, most people think he's *adorable*—like I did, once." She rolled her eyes to dramatize her agony. "They joke that they'll take him if I don't want him. So if things get too bad, I do have options."

"Well, be sure you still check the person out first. At any rate, since nobody's claimed him, you've got an appointment in a week to have him neutered. Promise me you'll at least keep him that long."

"I will." She picked up the kitten and cupped her hands over his tiny ears. "Shhh! You'll just give him more of a reason to run away."

"True—maybe he's figured that out."

Dawn tried to mask a yawn, and I knew it was time for me to leave so all of us could get some sleep.

"I really appreciate your coming over," she said. "And for the clicker and the toy, and all your tips."

"No problem." On my way to the door, I noticed the fresh marks on her oak cabinet. "I'll bring you a scratching post tomorrow too. I've got a kitten-sized one that all my guys have outgrown."

"Jeez, I'm so selfish, I forgot to even ask you how your date with Dr. Dolittle went!"

I smiled, not having the energy to get into that topic at the moment. "We'll talk about that tomorrow. Good night, you two."

"Bye, Cassie." This time Dawn took no chances and held on to the kitten until I'd left, waving his paw at me.

My phone had rung during our practice session, so on the way back home, I checked for messages. I was happy to hear Nick's voice sounding hale and hearty. He thanked me warmly for coming to the hospital and said he was sorry he hadn't been in any shape for me to visit with him.

"*But I'm much better now,*" he added. "*They gave me new medicine and said I could go back to work as along as I don't overdo. So I'm working on your post, and I should be able to bring it over by the end of the week. No charge, because you been such a good friend to me and to Dion.*"

I let out my breath in relief. I hoped Nick wasn't rushing his recovery, but I was glad he felt well enough work again. And it would be good to finally have that back post secured, for nights like this when I came home late.

When he came to install it, that would be the time to ask him about his lie of omission. Why he'd never told me that he went to DeLeuw's house, and threatened him, the day before George was murdered.

Chapter 13

Saturday morning, when I opened the front of the shop to let Sarah in, she had a piece of paper in her hand. "This was under the door," she said.

I unfolded the good-quality notepaper. Felt a chill when I saw the heading for Morris Plaza in bold blue capital letters and recognized the handwriting.

> *Your mom told me about your new shop, so I stopped by to see it. Sorry I missed you. So you're still working with animals? I've got a new job too, guess she told you. The hours are regular and it pays more than up at the mall, so my head's in a better place these days. We really need to talk, Cassie. Our breakup was a terrible mistake—maybe by now you realize that too. I don't know if my calls or e-mails are getting through, but you*

know where to reach me. Or maybe the next
time I stop by, I'll get lucky.
   —Andy

My hands began to perspire in spite of—or
maybe because of—the breezy wording of the note.
It must have been Andy, then, that Sarah had seen
looking through the shop window. Now that he'd
found the place, he could come back anytime . . .
even after dark.

Had he cased the building, and did he suspect
that I lived upstairs? My CR-V had been in the
parking lot . . . but I'd bought it since we'd broken
up, so he might not realize it was mine. He might
even think someone else rented the second floor.

Good. Let him go on thinking that.

"Our breakup was a terrible mistake"? Like hell! My
not telling the cops what he did to me was the terrible mis-
take.

"Cassie?" Sarah had set down her bag and
taken off her jacket, and now stared at me in concern.

"My ex." With shaking hands, I refolded the
note. I wanted to tear it up, but maybe because I'd
been thinking in terms of crimes and evidence
lately, I decided not to. Instead I tucked it away in
the shallow drawer below the counter.

"Then the guy I saw scoping the place out was
him?"

I nodded. "Apparently he plans to keep drop-
ping by until I relent and take him back."

Sarah's pursed mouth slipped to one side.
"Maybe you should *carry* that pepper spray."

Putting on my apron and gloves to empty the

litter pans, I calmed a little. "At least if I run into him out in the street, I can make a fuss and probably get people to help me."

"You said he's working as a security guard. Could he have a permit for a gun?"

So much for calming down. "Jeez, I don't know. He didn't on his last job, but—"

Sarah also suited up for litter detail. "What did the note say? Did he threaten you?"

"No, nothing like that. He just sounded like he had no clue that I moved here to get away from him. But that's what creeps me out—he's *got* to know. It's like he's saying, 'I found you now, and I can get to you anytime I want to.'"

"You should tell the police," Sarah insisted.

Bonelli's face floated into my mind, and for once its no-nonsense demeanor comforted me. "I just might do that. First, though, I'm going to have a talk with Mom."

We cleaned out all the litter pans and fed our boarders. After that we had no appointments right away, so I let Harpo out to romp on the cat trees for half an hour. Sarah had a great time dragging a toy over the wall shelves for him to chase, while I stole the chance to make a call.

I caught my mother at a slow time at her job too and told her about Andy's note. "He's stalking me, Mom. If you see him at work, tell him to stop, or so help me, I'll report him to the police."

"Honestly, Cassie, are you overreacting? If he's gone so far out of his way to look you up, he probably still has feelings for you. Would it be so bad to just have coffee with him, and see—"

Remembering Sarah's wise advice gave me to courage to finally come clean. "Mom, Andy and I didn't just argue a lot. He was abusive. He twisted my wrist once and threatened to hurt my cats. I finally broke up with him because he shoved me into a steel bookcase and nearly broke my shoulder."

The silence on the line made me feel a bit guilty for shocking her. Finally she said, "Honey, I'm so sorry. I had no idea. . . ."

"I know. I should have told you before, but you liked him so much that I figured you wouldn't want to believe it." The few brief times that they'd met, I remembered, Andy had turned on his considerable charm and Mom had fallen for it—the same way I had. "Then when I broke up with him and moved away, I thought that would be the end of it. But the way you kept on about how I should get back together with him, I figured you finally needed to know the truth."

"I never imagined . . . but you're right, Cassie. I should have trusted your judgment." I couldn't believe she was finally acknowledging that. "It's just that I worried about you being alone. When your father died, it was the worst time of my life. After you went back to college, being all by myself in that house . . . During the day I'd go to work and see friends, of course, but the nights were so lonely."

Seems like I had to learn to be sensitive to my mother's feelings too. "I didn't realize that, Mom. I knew you missed Dad, of course—I sure did too.

But when I called from school, you always sounded upbeat and like you were keeping busy. I didn't realize it affected you so badly."

"Maybe we've been shielding each other too much," she commented with a sad little laugh. "Trying to be strong."

"I guess so."

A catnip mouse that Sarah had tossed for Harpo landed almost under my feet. While he dashed for it, she put a hand over her mouth in a mute apology. I smiled and bounced the toy in the other direction.

"Anyway, I'm not isolated here," I insisted. "I have my new assistant, Sarah; my friend Dawn; my handyman, Nick, and his son, Dion. . . ." Okay, including Dion among my best pals was a bit of a stretch. "*And* it might surprise you to know that I actually was on a date last week."

"Really?" My mother sounded dubious. "I didn't think . . . I mean, really, what kind of man are you going to meet out there?"

"He's about my age, good-looking, intelligent, kind"—I couldn't resist a slight exaggeration—"and a doctor."

It was a good thing Sarah had retreated halfway across the room with Harpo. When she overhead this, she muffled a squeak worthy of one of the cats.

Mom tried to pump me for more information, but I stonewalled her. "The point is, if you see Andy again, you can tell him that I'm dating someone. You can even say you didn't know, and you're sorry if you misled him."

"I can do that," she said thoughtfully. "And then I can kick him in the shin."

"Even better!" I laughed, relieved that she finally had the proper attitude.

The shop door opened then, and when I recognized the visitor, I shifted focus sharply. "I've got a customer now, Mom. Gotta go. You take care."

Marjorie DeLeuw glanced around at the scratching posts, cat toys, and other merchandise of the sales area with a faint smile that could have been approval or amusement. She looked like she'd be far more comfortable in a Madison Avenue boutique, although at least today she'd traded the hourglassy black suit—her merry widow funeral garb—for a peach silk sweater and brown capris. Her auburn hair still waved back from her face in a movie-star style, an effect that was enhanced by her oversized sunglasses.

"This place is so *cute*," she cooed. "A spa for cats! Do you do mudpacks?"

"Those don't go over so well with our clients," I told her, "but they do get a free mani-pedi with every visit." When she looked blank, I mimed clipping claws.

She responded with a tepid laugh, took her off her sunglasses, and tucked them into a pocket of her Gucci shoulder bag. Her eyes looked like they'd "had some work done," as the saying goes, but at least they didn't have that perpetually astonished slant. "I just stopped in to see how our boy Harpo is doing."

Huh? Suddenly someone actually cared about

the cat? And of all people, Marjorie? My spidey sense went on full alert.

"He's fine. Been eating well and had a long play session with Sarah today." I glanced toward my assistant, who had just returned the Persian to his condo.

"Jerry Ross, my ex-husband's assistant, told me that you were asking around at the funeral home to see if anyone there wanted to take the cat. You never asked me."

Oh boy, this could get awkward. "To be honest, I didn't think you would want him. Mr. DeLeuw gave me the impression that you weren't fond of cats."

She turned frosty. "He discussed me with you?"

"Just that detail. He usually stayed in the studio while I was grooming, and we had some feline-related conversations."

Sarah had wisely retreated to the back of the shop by now. She probably suspected that, at any minute, it was the humans who might start hissing and spitting.

"Well, it so happens I am very interested in giving Harpo a good home. I have plenty of room in my New York apartment, and I'll be heading back there today. So I'd appreciate it if you'd pack the cat up and bring him out."

It was the kind of confrontation I'd antici-pated, though not this soon, and I was somewhat prepared. "I'm sorry, but I don't feel comfortable doing that."

"Excuse me?"

"Under the arrangement I made with Mr. DeLeuw's lawyer, I'm to keep the cat until the terms of his will are made public. He may have left Harpo to a family member or a friend, so it's best to wait and see. We'd want to respect his wishes."

"That's ridiculous. I might as well keep him in the meantime as you. At least I won't charge for the privilege."

She had some kind of hidden agenda going here, and I suspected the cost for my services was just an excuse. "I was willing to do it for free. Mr. DeLeuw's lawyer insisted on paying me—at a reduced rate—because of some legality. My only concern is that Harpo should have a safe home until the will is read."

"And I can't give him a safe home?"

Maybe it was my overactive imagination, but I suddenly felt like I was fending off Cruella de Vil. Might as well use my strongest ammo. "Mr. DeLeuw told me that his other cat, Groucho, went to you in the divorce. And you had him put to sleep."

Her jaw sagged, countering the effects of all that careful makeup. "Of all the insane . . . That cat was sick! It started throwing up all over my apartment two or three times a week!"

"Did you ever brush him?" I asked quietly. "Or take him to a groomer?"

"Of course not. I was working then. I didn't have time."

"When he got sick, did you at least take him to a vet?"

"Yes, and she said he had some kind of blockage in his abdomen. So of course I had him put down! Should I have let the poor thing suffer?"

Hairballs, I thought. Left to groom himself, the Persian had probably swallowed too much of his own long fur. Surgery would have fixed the problem, but I doubted that Marjorie even investigated that far.

"I'm sorry," I repeated, though at that point I wasn't at all. "The agreement says I'm to keep Harpo until we find out if he was left to someone in George's will. From what you've told me, I think it's best I stick to that plan."

Marjorie must have been very used to getting her way, because now her cheeks turned a deeper shade that had nothing to do with makeup. "Think you're smart, don't you? You've played this pretty well. But I know what you're up to, honey, and you won't get away with it. I've got a lawyer of my own, and he'll put a stop to this!"

She strode out the door in heels that would have tripped me up after three steps. They made her exit even more dramatic.

Sarah reemerged from hiding. In a daze, I asked her, "What am I up to?"

She shook her head. "All I can say is, if she's that mad about not getting the cat—even though she doesn't much like cats—it's got to be about money. Is she dumb enough to think he's really valuable?"

"Doesn't seem likely, after how quickly she got rid of his brother."

My assistant considered. "Then maybe she knows something about the will . . . or thinks she does."

The more I contemplated this, the more it made sense. "DeLeuw had no surviving children, he apparently had no serious woman in his life when he died, and his relationship with his sister seemed kind of cool. I got the impression he was pretty lonely. He told me once that Harpo was his buddy and his 'confidante.' "

"Like he was closer to the cat than to any of the people in his life."

"Exactly. So what if he left his estate to Harpo? Then maybe whoever has the cat when the will is read . . . gets the whole kit'n'caboodle!"

"That would explain why the ex-wife thinks you're up to something." Hands on her hips, my assistant shook her head at me, bemused. "Good thing your mother works with lawyers, Cassie. You're liable to need one!"

As it turned out, though, I wasn't the one in need of a lawyer just then. Nick was.

Sarah only worked a half day on Saturday, and I had just seen her off when I got another call from a distraught Dion. This time, his father had been taken down to the police station for questioning.

After finding out that Nick had visited DeLeuw the day before the murder, the cops had searched his panel truck. They'd found a rag with some faded pink stains that turned out to be blood—the same type as George DeLeuw's. It would take further DNA tests to confirm that it was a match, but the fibers also were the same as those found on the granite sculpture.

"Pop says he never saw the rag before," Dion told me, "and I believe him. It was kind of a funny, thin material—more like a big handkerchief with one corner torn off. I don't think he's ever owned a handkerchief like that, and I sure never did either. Though I guess if they decide Pop couldn't have done it, they'll probably be looking at me again."

"Is it possible somebody planted it?" I asked. At the funeral home, there certainly seemed to be enough people ready to blame Dion, or George's household staff, for the crime. They could have been trying to deflect suspicion from themselves.

"I was wondering about that too. Pop usually keeps the truck locked up at night, or if he leaves it anywhere for long, because people can steal his tools. But if he's in a good neighborhood and he's going back and forth to get stuff out, he doesn't lock it. And the night he wasn't feeling well and went to the hospital . . . I'm not sure he locked it then. It was parked in our driveway, so he probably wasn't worried about it."

"You spent all that time at the hospital," I reminded him. "If anybody deliberately wanted to implicate him, or you, they could haven driven by your house, seen the truck there, and tossed the rag inside."

"That is so twisted, though!" Dion sounded incredulous. "Why would anybody go to so much trouble just to make us look guilty?"

I had to state the obvious. "Because if you look guilty, they don't. I doubt that anybody has a particular grudge against you or your father. You're just the easiest people to frame, because you both accused DeLeuw of stealing the computer program."

Dion blew out a long breath. "I wish I'd never come up with that encryption system, or at least that I'd never brought it to DeLeuw. Bad enough when the police thought I murdered him, but Pop . . . This could give him a heart attack for real!"

"The evidence may not hold up," I tried to reassure him. "It's all what they call *circumstantial.* That means it looks bad, but there could be some other explanation for it. I've talked to Detective Bonelli a couple of times now, and I think she's pretty sharp. I'll go down to the station tomorrow and see what's up."

"Would you? Every time I talk to those cops, I probably just make things worse. I get too upset."

I offered to ask my mom to recommend a lawyer, but Dion said his father had a cousin who'd take the case if necessary. I sure hoped the guy had the background and skills to defend someone accused of murder.

Hanging up, I thought again about how absurd this all was. Why would Nick keep a ripped, bloodstained rag—even if he'd tried to wash it—in the back of his truck for anyone to find? It would have been easy to throw it away or even burn it. He'd certainly had enough time.

I called Detective Bonelli, who wasn't available, and left a brief message. She had to realize this was a setup.

Also, it seemed even less likely now that DeLeuw had been killed by a random assailant. A thief passing through town wouldn't return just to incriminate some local resident for his crime. Was the murderer worried about being caught? Did he or she feel the cops might be closing in?

Or maybe there was another reason, I thought. *As long as the crime remains unsolved, the terms of George's will might be kept under wraps. Maybe someone is getting impatient to cash in.*

Chapter 14

After dinner that night, I called Dawn to bring her up to speed. She sympathized with Nick's plight and also didn't believe he could have committed the murder. She agreed too that Marjorie's interest in Harpo could mean whoever took the cat in would benefit financially.

Still, Dawn's main curiosity at the moment seemed to involve my love life—such as it was. "We still haven't talked about your dinner date with Dr. Dolittle," she said. "How did it go?"

"Well, I think. We had a good time, though it turned out to be kind of a weird evening." I told her how one of Mark's clients had interrupted him during our date, which had been followed by Nick's health scare.

"Boy, Nick's been through the ringer lately, hasn't he?" Dawn noted. "But let's get back to Mark. Did he seem interested? Did you make another date?"

"Jeez, you sound like my mother. He said he's fresh out of a long relationship and wants to take it slow."

Dawn groaned. "Uh-oh. You know what that means."

"Something other than what it sounds like?"

"That's code for, 'I'm not quite over my last girlfriend, but I still want to keep my options open with you.' "

I hoped Mark was being more honest than that, but of course, I hadn't known him long enough to be sure. I didn't want to imagine him spending tonight with his ex, just to make *sure* he was ready to move on.

"Anyway," I told Dawn, "the upshot is, it's Saturday night and I'm home talking to you. And trying to figure out how to make ends meet next month without my usual check from George DeLeuw, may he rest in peace."

"Why not come to the expo I told you about? Chadwick Small Business Sunday?"

With all the craziness that had been going on, I'd totally forgotten. "That's tomorrow, isn't it? I'm probably too late to even get a space."

"Keith and I have spaces next to each other, and he doesn't need much because he mostly sits in a chair and draws people on the spot," Dawn persisted. "I have some products from the shop, but if you just brought a small table, we could fit you in."

I still didn't feel prepared for a full-out marketing effort. "What could I even display? I've got brochures, and that's about it."

"I shot a video of you grooming your first cat,

remember? What did you call it—a Himalayan? Do you still have that?"

"Yeah." I started to see where she was going with this. "I could play the video on my laptop. And I have still shots I took of my shop, right after Nick finished the condos and the playroom. I could do a slideshow of those."

"Now you're thinking!" Dawn laughed. "Too bad you can't use Harpo for a live demonstration. But with that witch Marjorie trying to get her claws into him, you probably shouldn't risk it."

"True . . . but maybe I can come up with a ringer." I glanced at my wall clock—it was past eight. Our brainstorming session had started my gears turning, as Mark would say. "Dawn, thanks for the motivation. I'll see you at the high school tomorrow. Right now I need to get out to the highway before the stores close."

School gyms don't hold the best associations for me. I never excelled at team sports, and attracted more than my share of scorn from gym teachers and coaches of all kinds.

Fortunately, by the time I arrived at the Chadwick Senior High School on Sunday, the institutional gymnasium walls had been camouflaged with spruce-green draperies that formed backdrops for the assorted vendor spots. A long banner stretched below the high windows announcing SMALL BUSINESS SUNDAY. Beneath it, people were busily and noisily setting up tables and erecting posters to promote their goods and services.

If nothing else, I thought, this should be a cool

opportunity to get to know some of the other professionals in town. And it certainly could give me exposure to a few new customers.

I found Dawn and Keith, who already had mounted displays for their totally unconnected businesses. She offered plates of goodies such as sunflower-seed-butter cookies (trust me, they're delicious) and sample bowls of a special granola mix, as well as brochures for the "healthy" brands of frozen meals and other packaged goods that she carried. Keith had propped open a photo album of his corporate illustrations on a book stand, next to a modest display board of his caricatures. Tall and lean, with curly auburn hair, a beard, and glasses, Keith held a sketch pad at the ready. He even wore a hokey but eye-catching black beret to brand himself as an "artist."

I didn't see Keith that often, but I always enjoyed his slightly warped sense of humor. He and I chatted for a few minutes about the DeLeuw murder and all the surrounding drama so far. He also helped me maneuver the prop I had brought instead of a table—a four-foot-tall cat tower. As Dawn had promised, there was plenty of room to fit that, and my folding chair, between their two booths. On top of the carpeted tower, I opened my wireless laptop and cued up the grooming video. Lastly, from a big shopping bag, I pulled out a life-sized stuffed Persian cat and set him on the middle perch of the tree.

"He's too cute!" Dawn cooed. "Be careful he doesn't walk off, though."

"Thought of that!" I tied a cord around one of

the cat's plush back legs and secured it to the center post of the perch.

I also donned my Kelly-green grooming apron with the name of my shop printed in white, the words stacked so the three big initial *C*s overlapped. That was all I had for signage, though. Some vendors sported preprinted name tags on lanyards, but I had to make do with a stick-on badge. I felt woefully unprepared next to most of the other exhibitors, and vowed to put in more effort next year.

As soon as the doors opened at ten o'clock, a fair number of browsers began to circulate. I had my speech prepared about the special boarding and grooming needs of cats and the amenities my shop could offer. I'd been worried about possible negative publicity from the newspaper story, which placed me at the scene of the DeLeuw murder. But of the first half dozen people I talked to, only one asked me about the crime. I simply said it was a terrible shock and I was sorry to lose him as a customer, and claimed to know no more about it than that. Maybe the story actually drew more people to my booth, from curiosity. At any rate, I passed out brochures and business cards to all of them and several said they'd be in touch.

When the foot traffic slowed down a little, I asked Dawn to keep an eye on my minimal display and took a stroll around to the other booths. A couple of agents were on hand from the insurance company in the building next to mine, and we had the first real conversation since I'd moved in. I weakened and picked up a red velvet cupcake from the Cottone's Bakery booth, and admired handmade ceramic jewelry from a boutique called Jaded.

I was delighted to come across a booth by a cat rescue group, the Fine Feral Friends. I could have spent hours talking with the two volunteers, Josie and Mike, about their work. They offered to display some of my brochures, and I took some of theirs to return the favor.

Browsing in this casual way, I spotted a familiar figure at one of the booths up ahead—DeLeuw's landscaper, Louis, had an impressive display board of garden photos for his company, Eden Landscaping.

I introduced myself, but he remembered me from that traumatic afternoon when he, Anita, and I had discovered George's body.

"That was a rough day," I commiserated. "I guess you got grilled by Detective Bonelli, too."

He frowned. "That first day, I got Officer Bassey, and his philosophy seemed to be 'guilty until proven innocent.' Bonelli called me down to the station later, and she seemed a little more reasonable."

I remembered her telling me that Louis had a juvenile record for shoplifting, and wondered if that had made her look at him more closely.

He gestured to the photos on the board behind him. "At last year's expo, I put a couple of shots of DeLeuw's property up here, because I'm proud of the work I did for him. But this time . . . I figured maybe it wasn't such a good idea. Pictures of his house have been in the paper, and I don't need any more people connecting me with his murder. Bad enough I lost a good client, without having that kind of suspicion hanging over me."

Louis didn't put it into words, but I wondered if he also felt that the more well-to-do white people in our suburban area didn't need another reason to be wary of hiring a young black man to work around their homes. I remembered that Danielle was all too ready to point the finger at him for killing George to cover up some theft.

"I know what you're saying," I told him. "I'm here trying to pick up new business too. And I was also worried that people might avoid me because I actually found the body. On cop shows, that always puts you high on the list of suspects."

He smiled widely for the first time. "Well, I don't suspect you, Cassie, and neither does Anita."

"Thanks." I leaned across his table and spoke quietly. "If it's any consolation, I don't think the cops are that suspicious anymore of people like us, who were just doing jobs around the house. I think they're looking at people George was connected with personally and professionally."

Louis nodded slowly, as if weighing how much he should reveal. "DeLeuw could've had some secrets. Years back I was in a bad situation, keeping the wrong company. But I pulled myself out and went legit. I sometimes got the feeling George was trying to do the same thing." He shook his close-cropped head. "Not as easy as it sounds, though. Sometimes your old friends, they don't like to let you go."

I was about to ask Louis what he meant when, out of the corner of my eye, I saw something that made my heart freeze. Across the gym, a brown-

haired man in jeans and a green argyle pullover
lingered by my display, watching the video on my
laptop. His face was half-turned away, but from the
sweater, the set of his broad shoulders, and the way
he stood with one hand in his pocket, I recognized
Andy.

"Excuse me." I started away from Louis's booth,
then paused. Every instinct told me to escape. If
Andy hadn't seen me yet, I could dodge him easily.
Run to the ladies' room or some other corner of
the big school. Even sneak out to the parking lot,
get in my car, and split. I could phone Dawn from
a gas station, explain the situation, and ask her to
call me back when Andy was gone.

"No contact." That was the advice I'd often
read for dealing with a stalker. *And he must be stalking me. He works in Morristown—what other reason
would he have to come, on a Sunday, to a local business
expo in Chadwick?* It scared me to realize how ob-
sessed he must be, to have found out about this
event and driven so far just to check it out.

And to have homed in so quickly on my booth.

But damn it, why should I skulk away as if I was
the one who'd done something wrong?

Dawn and Keith had never met Andy. Now he
appeared to be asking them about my display and
she seemed to be eagerly answering his questions.
My skin twitched just to see him talking with my
friends, but I stayed rooted near Louis's booth.

Chuckling at something Dawn had said, Andy
reached for the stuffed cat. He seemed confused
when he couldn't pick it up, and gave it a sharp
tug.

I flashed back to the threat he'd made against

my cats during one of our fights. The sleeping rage inside me woke with a roar, and I crossed the gymnasium toward him with long strides.

"Sir, that's not for sale," I called out in a sharp tone. "It's part of the display."

Dawn and Keith glanced up in surprise, but by the time Andy swung around, he wore the deceptively easygoing, confident smile that I'd once found so seductive. He might have had the face of an ogre, though, for all the appeal I found now in his handsome features.

"Cassie! I thought I might run into you here. How've you been?"

Nearer to him now, I dropped my voice to avoid startling any passersby. "A hell of a lot better since you've been out of my life." My fear vanished now that I felt surrounded by friends and potentially helpful strangers. I was more afraid that I'd lose control and hit *him*.

"What a thing to say!" Andy half joked. "Look, I know we didn't part on the best of terms, but we can at least talk about it. I'm willing to let bygones be bygones if—"

"Well, I'm not. Listen, Andy, we are *over*. Do not drop in at places because you think you might run into me. Do not come by my shop. Do not call me, text me, e-mail me, or write to me. Do not ask my mother about me."

"Oh, c'mon, Cassie. You make it awful hard for a guy to—"

"I have friends on the Chadwick police force. If you keep stalking me like this, I'll get a restraining order against you."

He made an incredulous face but did step away from me. "Jesus . . . you're crazy, you know that?"

"Sure, it's always my fault."

Keith, slimmer but taller than Andy, stepped in between us and glared at my ex. Even with the goofy beret, he managed to look intimidating. "I think Cassie's made herself clear. Are you leaving now, or are we calling a security guard?"

Andy paused for just a second, still fuming. In a last tantrum, he gave the cat tree an irritable push and almost sent my laptop crashing to the floor. Good thing years of dealing with cats had sharpened my reflexes—I caught it just in time. Finally Andy paced toward the exit.

Keith started to follow, but I caught his arm.

"Not worth it," I said. "But thanks for your help."

Dawn hugged me. "Are you all right? I had no idea that was . . . *him.*"

"I know you didn't. I'm glad you guys were here for backup, though. Otherwise, I might never have had the guts to yell at him like that."

Keith grinned. "You sure ripped into him. I don't know how psycho that guy is, but if it were me, I'd never dare come near you again! But if he ever does, at least I've already done the police sketch."

He showed me his pad, where he'd dashed off a darn good likeness of a scowling Andy Wade. I had to smile, but waved the drawing away.

Dawn pulled my chair over so I could sit. "I can't make you tea, but how about some coconut water?"

I wondered silently if the wine shop had a booth nearby, but meanwhile, I accepted the bottled drink. I was sipping it through a straw when I heard the muted strains of "Stray Cat Strut" from my pocket. Great—was Andy calling from the parking lot to curse me out?

But Mark's number showed on the screen.

"Hi, Cassie," he said. "Having a restful Sunday?"

"Not so much, actually." I wasn't going to tell him about Andy, but I explained that I'd decided at the last minute to take part in the expo.

"That's cool," he said. "I did that for the first couple of years after I opened the clinic, and it really helped make people aware of us." He paused on the line. "Runs until about five o'clock, doesn't it?"

"That's right." Provocatively, I added, "Why do you ask?"

He laughed. "Yes, I do have an ulterior motive. How do you feel about jazz?"

"I like it. My dad was a serious buff, so I heard a lot of jazz growing up."

"Terrific! Look, I know this is last-minute, but how'd you like to go to the Firehouse tonight? Y'know, that club they made out of the old fire station? Usually it's blues and rock, but I just found out they've got a jazz trio playing this eve. And it's so hard to find any music like that around here!"

That sounded good to me, too. I'd been to the Firehouse just once, with Dawn, but the rock band that night had been painfully loud for the intimate space. A jazz trio, though, should be just right.

"I'm in," I told Mark. "What time?"

"The music starts at eight, but if you want to eat first we can get there early. They just have light food."

"I'm sure it'll top whatever I've got defrosted."

"Pick you up about seven thirty, then? I'm really looking forward to this!"

After he hung up, I wondered whether it was the prospect of hearing some jazz or of seeing me again that he was looking forward to, but decided not to split hairs.

Dawn was smiling at me across her display table. "Dr. Dolittle?"

I nodded. "How's that for timing!"

"You're not kidding." Her expression turned wary. "Probably a good thing we got rid of Andy before you took that call!"

She was right, I realized. My ex was volatile enough already. I didn't want to imagine his reaction if he'd overheard me making a date with another man.

Chapter 15

In hopes of kicking things up a notch from my diner date with Mark, I paired my nicest jeans with a red-orange V-neck sweater, took a little time to style my hair with a curling iron, and put on boots with three-inch heels, the highest I'd go. I topped it all off with my well-worn brown leather jacket, and by quarter to seven felt I looked appropriately jazzy.

Suddenly I remembered my wobbly railing. I hadn't warned Mark about that—if he came to the back door, he might get a rude surprise. The evening was mild and clear, so I decided to wait for him out front.

At first I didn't feel too conspicuous standing in my shop doorway. Cassie's Comfy Cats was on a side street, after all, not the main drag. A block down, everything turned pretty residential. At seven twenty-five, it was still fairly light out, though too overcast to see the moon. Commuters arrived home from work; a teen girl on a bicycle whizzed by; an older man walked a small, fuzzy terrier.

It took me a minute to notice a shiny, dark sedan parked across the street and a little ways down, its headlights on. I was just thinking that the owner might end up with a dead battery when they snapped off. A nearby streetlamp showed the driver still in the car, in silhouette. Most likely a man—judging from the height, wide shoulders, and short hair—but in the twilight that was all I could make out. It was too far off for me to read the license plate, either.

I waited for the driver to step out of the car and go into one of the houses. He never did.

As the minutes dragged on, I glanced again and again toward Center Street, willing Mark to show up. Was I just imagining things, or was the parked driver watching me?

Had Mom done as I'd said and told Andy I was dating someone? Maybe he'd decided to spy on me to see if it was true. Damn, I thought that would discourage him—it hadn't occurred to me that it might make him jealous and even more dangerous! That sedan didn't look like Andy's car, but I'd changed vehicles since we'd broken up; no reason why he might not have done the same.

I sure as heck wasn't going over to check, though. If it was Andy, I just hoped he wouldn't get out and try to pick a fight when Mark arrived.

I checked my watch. Seven thirty-five now. Mark wasn't really late, though, at least not by my standards. His clinic was only a couple of blocks over, but he'd probably gone home to change, and I didn't know how far away he lived. Maybe, in the meantime I should wait around back, where I'd be less—

A cobalt-blue RAV4 turned in at the corner and slowed as it approached my shop. I exhaled, though I still kept one eye on the sedan. Mark cruised to a stop and started to get out—probably to open the door for me, like a gentleman—but I'd already hopped in the passenger side. When he paused in confusion, I laughed as if we'd just gotten our signals crossed.

"Guess you must be hungry!" He smiled and slid back in behind the wheel.

"I just waited out here because of the railing on my back steps." Sounding even to myself like a total ditz, I went into a long, tedious explanation. But meanwhile, my quick move helped get us safely under way before any confrontation with the guy in the parked car could take place.

Of course, there would only have been a confrontation if the guy was Andy, but I wasn't taking any chances.

As we drove across town, I moved from the topic of my shaky railing to the news that my handyman had been arrested for DeLeuw's murder, based on evidence as flimsy as a handkerchief. When I relayed Dion's description of the piece of cloth, Mark wrinkled his elegantly arched Italian nose in suspicion.

"He said the corner was torn off?"

"Yes. Why? Does that mean something?"

"Maybe, maybe not. But a good-quality handkerchief sometimes is monogrammed in one corner. Could be the killer was trying to hide his identity."

Because the monogram wouldn't be Dion's or Nick's.

Of course. "Mark, you're a genius! I didn't think of that. And I'm sure Dion didn't either, because I doubt that he and his dad are the type to carry monogrammed handkerchiefs."

"There you go." Mark drove on down Center Street. "All you need to do now is look for someone who *is* the type."

Mentally, I ran down the list of suspects. "I guess a woman could have a monogrammed handkerchief too."

"I guess." A glint of humor in his eye, he added, "If she was the type."

Unfortunately, that didn't narrow the field very much.

"Anyway, I am not going to spend this evening discussing the DeLeuw murder case," I promised. "There are too many other interesting things to talk about."

"I second that." He threw me a crooked grin that made my heart leap like Mango springing after a catnip mouse.

I loved the way many older buildings in Chadwick had been adapted for new uses, and the Firehouse was a prime example. The old brick two-story structure with limestone trim sprouted one corner turret, maybe where the firemen's pole had come down. Three large front bays, originally for the hook-and-ladder trucks, now featured tall double doors with windows. These could be opened in summer; even closed, as they were tonight, they still let in lots of natural light and offered a view of the street.

A chalkboard sign on the sidewalk in front advertised the Bobby Burke Trio with the welcome message, *Sunday—No Cover.*

The front section of the pub offered high, round tables and bentwood stools near the bar, but we opted for a booth a little farther back and closer to the music. The ceilings throughout were the original pressed tin, dotted with industrial-style fans and pendant lights. One wall of exposed brick ran all the way through to the rear stage area. It was a little bit of sophisticated Morristown—or even lower Manhattan—right here in Chadwick. I enjoyed the idea that our town could be quaint and trendy at the same time.

After Mark ordered a beer and I a white wine, we deliberately avoided any talk about either murder suspects or exes. Since he had drawn me out about myself on our first date, I determined this time to find out more about him. I learned that he'd grown up just outside Philadelphia and gotten his DVM degree at UPenn. He'd spent some time as part of a larger practice in South Jersey before deciding to start a clinic of his own in our small town.

"I looked around for an area that didn't seem to have that much in the way of veterinary services," he said, "and when I visited Chadwick, it just appealed to me. It's far enough into the country that I get to deal with some farm animals too, though they're not a big part of my practice."

By the time our shared appetizer of chicken tenders arrived, I also knew Mark had played jazz on the guitar when he was younger, and still owned one, but was out of practice these days.

"Any pets?" I had to ask.

"Growing up, I always had big dogs. In the condo complex where I live now, they only allow little ones." He shrugged. "I might consider a cat instead."

I laughed. "I may know of a kitten that's available—last time I visited Dawn, Tigger was driving her crazy. I gave her some tips on clicker-training him, but I haven't heard how that's going. You can ask her about it when she brings him in next week."

A curly-haired waiter brought Mark's Firehouse Burger and my blackened chicken over Spanish rice. (No more flirty waitresses, anyway!) Meanwhile, I glimpsed a party of three being seated in a booth across and slightly in back of us. Something about them made me turn, discreetly, for a better look.

It was Charles Schroeder, the stylish brunette who'd been with him at the funeral home, and Danielle DeLeuw.

"Huh!" I said to myself, drawing Mark's attention.

"You know those folks?" he asked.

I explained. "Chadwick really *must* be an up-and-coming hot spot. The beautiful people from Wall Street and the West Coast come here and never want to leave."

"Maybe they're still wrapping up some aspect of DeLeuw's business."

The Bobby Burke Trio started its first set then, and Mark and I concentrated on our meals and the music. The weathered brick walls and old spiral staircase of the firehouse formed a mellow backdrop for the guitarist, keyboard guy, and drummer as they played. Burke, the guitarist, sported a white beard and a battered fedora, and showed a dry sense of humor in his patter between numbers. They performed fresh versions of many songs I'd heard on my father's LPs, including "'Round Midnight," "Misty," and the bossa nova "Insensatez." Among these, they interspersed a few very listenable compositions of their own. They earned genuine applause for every number.

Along with appreciating the music myself, I enjoyed watching its effect on Mark, who often nodded along with a blissful expression in his deepblue eyes. Nothing about this date was fancy, I thought, but somehow it was perfect. Low-pressure, but still with a subtle touch of romance.

After about half an hour the trio took a short break. Mark and I ordered coffee, eager to stay and hear the second set. Meanwhile, maybe my colorful sweater had raised my visibility, because Danielle suddenly appeared at my side.

"Cassie, what a pleasant surprise!" she hailed me. Call me paranoid, but that warning bell in the back of my brain sounded again.

"Hi! I saw the three of you come in." I introduced her to Mark and vice versa; I didn't feel the need to point out Schroeder and his companion. "Are you enjoying the music?"

"Very much. I didn't expect to find such a fun little place here in Chadwick, but Chuck and his wife knew about it. They came here once or twice with George."

I nodded, glad to hear that DeLeuw had not been a total hermit, after all.

Tonight Danielle wore another long, knit dress—
taupe-gray this time, instead of mourning black—
with more makeup than at the funeral home.
Uninvited, she perched on the end of my booth
seat and tapped me on the arm with one French-
manicured finger. "Actually, you're just the person
I wanted to talk to, and maybe while there's a
break, we have time. I understand that you're
keeping George's cat at your shop until everything
is cleared up."

*Here we go. There had to be an explanation for the
sudden friendliness.*

"I know at the viewing I said I wouldn't be able
to take him because of my busy schedule,"
Danielle went on. "I assumed that someone else in
George's circle would step up, though, and I
gather no one else has. So rather than keep the
poor darling in a cage any longer than necessary,
I'm willing to take charge of him. I'm flying back
to California at the end of the week, and I can
make arrangements to bring him with me."

If she had told me this at the funeral home, I
probably would have agreed with no argument.
But her sudden change of heart, coming right
after Marjorie's, made me suspicious. "You said,
though, that you're hardly ever home to take care
of a pet."

"I do travel a lot; it's true. But I have a housekeeper who comes in while I'm away. Besides, you
can hire sitters for pets, can't you? My house isn't
as large as George's, but it's in a lovely location up
in the hills above San Jose. I know George didn't
let his cat out around here, probably because of

the busy roads. At my place, though, little Harpo could roam to his heart's content!"

I saw a flicker of alarm cross Mark's face, which probably mirrored my own. "Er . . . that might not be the best thing for him. You may not be close to roads, but in a place like that it sounds like there could still be stray dogs, or even wild animals, that could attack him." Jeez, even around Chadwick we saw the occasional coyote.

This insight made Danielle pause for a second. "I hadn't thought of that. Well, okay, maybe I won't let him out, but I can still give him a good home. And really"—she leaned closer—"I *am* George's nearest relative. So if he left the cat to anyone, most likely it would be to me."

You'd think that these people begrudged me what little money might be trickling out of DeLeuw's estate to cover Harpo's board. It had to be more than that, though. Maybe they really did think George had designated a large part of his inheritance to whoever was willing to take the cat. Maybe he'd even mentioned that to someone along the way, and now word had gotten around. At any rate, I sensed Danielle would not be much more conscientious than Marjorie about caring for Harpo. Especially not if she was just doing it for the money.

"To be honest, you're not the first person to approach me about taking him," I told her, "but for now his lawyer has said the cat should remain at my shop. I think it's better if we all wait and see if George made any special request. For example, there's no point in your taking the cat to California if it turns out he left Harpo to someone here on the East Coast. It's very stressful for an animal to fly cross-country once, never mind twice."

Danielle must not have heard that I'd already disappointed Marjorie, because she was just as astonished to be turned down. The news that someone else had put in a bid for Harpo seemed to make her even more anxious. "But if he *is* left to me, I'll have to fly all the way back here to get him! And who knows how much longer it's going to take for them to probate the will?"

I shrugged. "They tell me that even under normal circumstances, in New Jersey the process can drag on for months. And this does involve a murder investigation."

That set her back like a spray of cold water to a misbehaving cat. With a frown, she glanced from me to Mark and back again. "Well. Sorry to interrupt your evening."

I watched her return to her booth, where I figured she'd vent her frustration to her companions. Did Schroeder and his wife have any skin in the game of Who Gets Harpo?

"That was bizarre," said Mark.

"You don't know the half of it." The waiter had brought our coffees; while I added sweetener and milk to mine, I explained about the similar conversation I'd had with DeLeuw's ex-wife. I added my theory that both women might think whoever took in the Persian would inherit a windfall.

"I guess it's possible," Mark said. "DeLeuw doesn't seem to have been on the greatest terms even with the mourners who came to his funeral. Lonely people who become very attached to a pet *have* been known to leave all their money to the animal. Which of course means, to its caretaker, whoever that might be."

I took a sip of the rich, fresh brew. "Call me morbid, but this whole thing has made me think *I* should have a will. Even besides my business, I've got three cats of my own. I know my mother won't want them, and Dawn's already got her hands full with Tigger. I do have some other cat-loving friends, but . . . this just shows that maybe I shouldn't leave it up to chance."

"A lot of nice animals do end up in shelters just because their owners have died." Mark reached across, covered my hand with his own, and smiled. "Still, I think you've got at least a few years before you have to worry about that."

Surprised and warmed by his gesture, I still couldn't resist joking back. "Depends on how desperate these folks are to get Harpo . . . and if I'm the only thing standing in their way!"

The second set by the jazz trio was as satisfying as the first. Though we didn't hold hands the whole time, Mark did move over to my side of the booth, supposedly so he could see the stage better. A transparent excuse, but I wasn't about to protest. By the time we left the Firehouse, I definitely felt things heating up between us. Still, as we walked back to his car, his arm loosely around my shoulders, I felt the need to do a status check.

"The longtime relationship you mentioned before . . . what's happening with that?"

He sighed, which told me he had some regrets, but insisted, "That's over. She's seeing other people. She'd like to keep stringing me along, but I told her that doesn't work for me. So I'm ready to move on."

I just nodded, not bringing up my own unresolved issues—such as the possibility that my ex-boyfriend might have been spying on us when we'd left for our date. At any rate, when Mark drove me back to my place and parked, the mysterious dark sedan was nowhere in sight.

That was lucky. If it had been Andy, our lengthy good-night kiss in the car might have driven him to a homicidal rage.

"You know, I've never seen your shop," Mark commented afterward. "I thought we'd have time when I picked you up, but you seemed to be in a hurry."

"Sorry about that." Still conscious of the ex-girlfriend who was trying to hang on to him, I played it coy. "Maybe next time?"

His frown was good-natured, as if he remembered being the one who had asked to take things slow. "Absolutely. Need me to watch until you get inside?"

I opened the passenger door. "I think I'll be okay, but thanks."

A glance around my small backyard revealed no one lurking there, so I gave Mark an all-clear wave that sent him on his way.

Am I an idiot? I wondered. No, he had set the rules on our first date, and I was going to take them seriously. It wasn't as if we had to go far out of our way to see each other again.

Anything good was worth waiting for, I thought. And tonight had been really good. Especially that kiss.

I started up the back steps, triggering the motion-sensor light. Though tired and in a bit of a romantic daze, I was still conscious of the wobbly left banister and barely brushed it with my hand.

To my shock, the whole thing toppled off and crashed to the ground.

What the—

Nick just shored up that post with a bracket!

By the overhead light, I bent down to look at it more closely. Some of the screws had ripped completely out of their supports, splintering the old wood.

As if while I was out, someone bigger and heavier climbed the steps, leaned on it for support . . . and it gave way.

Chapter 16

A call to the police did bring out one officer in a patrol car, I suspected only because he had nothing better to do. He checked the banister but explained the old wood wasn't a good surface for lifting fingerprints; maybe he just didn't want to be bothered. My parking lot was gravel, so it would have been useless to look for footprints.

I checked the back door and found it still locked, and there was no sign of a break-in. But after I explained about the abusive ex-boyfriend, and the driver sitting in his car by the curb while I waited for my date, tall, crew-cut Officer Bassey walked through the whole place with me to make sure no one was lurking.

My car had been parked in back, but as far as I could tell, no one had messed with that. The tires looked okay, and when I turned the ignition key, it started up promptly.

On his way out again, Officer Bassey commented

that I ought to get a dead bolt for the back door. "A single lock, with this old wood—somebody strong could push right in."

I swallowed hard at that image. "When my handyman comes to fix the railing, I'll ask him to install one."

The whirling lights of the squad car alerted Mrs. Kryznansky, the plump gray-haired woman who lived over the insurance office next door. In a full-length winter coat that probably covered her nightgown, she stepped out into her yard to tell us she'd heard some kind of crash and then a man cursing.

"I turned on my light and came out there to see what was going on." She pointed to her second-floor rear porch. "Guess that scared the guy, 'cause he took off down the street."

"Can you describe him?" Bassey asked.

She shook her head of tight gray curls. "I mainly saw him from the back. Medium height, dark hair, dark sweatshirt, and jeans."

That could have been Andy, I thought . . . or maybe one-third of the male population of New Jersey. Mrs. Kryznansky went back home then, having done her good-neighborly deed. Bassey told me he was on duty all night and would cruise by a couple of times to make sure everything looked okay.

Knowing that did help me sleep better.

The next morning, Monday, Sarah brought freshly baked brownies to work—she'd made extra for an event at her church the day before. Just the way I liked them, not overly sweet and with a nice, earthy tang of cocoa. As I took a few minutes to enjoy one, I filled her in on the latest incident, just in case there might be another Andy sighting.

"Poor thing, you can't even enjoy a night out," she commiserated. "Not only does this guy seem to be lurking around and spying on you, but that Danielle woman interrupts your date. How rude!"

"I know. Mark was a good sport about it, but it *was* nervy of her."

When we fed the boarders, I realized I had only one can left of Harpo's special food. I'd never discussed with Jerry Ross how to get more of the stuff, and I hadn't seen it in any of the nearby pet stores. *Better give him a call.*

I reached Ross without a problem, and he offered to get a case for me. "I know a place on the highway that carries it," he said. "I used to pick it up for DeLeuw all the time."

So much for the glamour of an executive assistant's job, I thought. "That would be great, if you don't mind." It would also solve the problem of whether I'd be reimbursed, because the stuff was probably more expensive than what I usually bought.

"No problem. I'll bring it by later this afternoon." With a chuckle, he added, "I'll take an antihistamine first."

I'd forgotten about his cat allergy. "Yeah, you might want to. Though the front of the shop may not be as bad for you as the grooming and boarding areas."

For the next hour, Sarah and I worked on the new boarder, Bear, the Maine Coon. Fortunately, he seemed to have some show experience and did not use his considerable brawn against us, so we had him shaped up pretty quickly. As a reward for his good behavior, we then turned him loose in the playroom to explore for a while.

"I hate to leave you alone again," I told Sarah, "but I need to talk to Detective Bonelli at the police station."

"Good idea. You really should tell her about this guy stalking you."

"I will."

Among other things, I thought.

The detective actually invited me into her glass-walled office this time. It had few prestigious trappings, just a simple Formica-topped, L-shaped computer desk and a black multi-line phone with a cord. The only personal touch was a framed picture of a sturdy, middle-aged man and two preteen boys, the right ages to be Bonelli's husband and sons.

Maybe because I'd bought her a Starbucks the last time we'd talked, she offered me a hazelnut coffee courtesy of the neat little burgundy-colored Keurig unit on her console table. A Mother's Day gift, she said.

Holding a Styrofoam cup filled with the aromatic brew, I sat in the steel-framed visitor's chair and faced Bonelli across her desk. "Both DeLeuw's sister and his ex-wife approached me over the weekend about taking the cat."

The detective leaned back in her padded vinyl chair. "And that isn't good news?"

"No, because neither one of them seems to

know, or care, anything about cats. Marjorie put one of George's other cats to sleep for what sounded like a simple hairball issue. Danielle travels a lot, and sounded ready to turn Harpo loose in the hills of San Jose to get picked off by a coyote."

"I understand your concern, Cassie, but that really isn't your—"

"Yes, I know. If George has left the cat to one of them, I have no say about it. But here's the thing— why the sudden interest? Do they think Harpo comes attached with some big legacy, to keep him in the manner to which he's become accustomed? They were both pretty mad at me when I said we should wait to see what's in the will. Do they think I'm trying to cheat them out of big bucks?"

"They might be under that impression." The level way Bonelli said this gave me no insight as to whether she knew the actual terms of the will.

"But it could be a motive, don't you think? I doubt that George would leave anything to Marjorie otherwise, because he talked as if he hated her. You told me she was getting alimony when he was alive, but that will stop now. Maybe this is her way of making sure she gets what she thinks she deserves anyway."

"Could be. The most likely person to inherit, though, would be his sister. So why would Danielle need to manipulate you when all she has to do is sit back and wait?"

I pondered this for a minute. "She might have to wait a long while, and you told me her business is in trouble. Besides, if there was a separate amount set aside for Harpo, she still could lose out on that."

Bonelli frowned as if unconvinced. "Well, you've

told them everything's on hold, so stick to that. In the meantime, let's talk about something more pressing. You had a disturbance at your home last night?"

I told her what had happened while I was on my date with Mark, and gave her the full background on Andy. "I almost had myself convinced the guy sitting in the parked car was just a coincidence, until I came home and found that railing pulled loose." I also told her what my neighbor had heard and seen.

"Could have been a garden-variety burglar." The detective turned toward her desktop PC. "What's his full name? Your ex, I mean?"

I hesitated, realizing I hadn't spoken it out loud in a long time. "Andrew Wade."

Bonelli ran it through her computer, and after a minute her full lips curved into a faint smile. "Interesting. Looks like he was pulled over for a DUI last night around eleven, just outside of Morristown."

This evidence knocked the wind out of me. "Oh my God, so it really might have been him!" Andy wasn't a major alcoholic, but it was usually when he'd had one drink too many that he lost his temper. A video ran in my head of him stumbling when the rail pulled loose, then panicking when the light came on next door and dashing out of the yard.

"Well, even if it was, he shouldn't be spying on you again anytime soon—at least, not from the refuge of his car. His license was suspended for three months. They could give him jail time, too, though maybe they won't for a first offense."

I wondered how this would affect his new job as a security officer, then caught myself. "Now I'm actually feeling sorry for him. I've got to stop that."

"Yes, you do."

I liked Bonelli's plainspoken style, and breathed a little easier. Andy probably would not be bothering me for at least a few months. And if he'd gotten a good scare, maybe never again.

"Is that all?" The detective drummed her fingers on a closed manila file, obviously eager to move on to more pressing work.

"Just one more thing. While I'm here, could I see Nick Janos?"

"I'm afraid you can't. He was released on bail this morning."

"Oh. He was able to raise—"

"The judge didn't set it very high, and apparently Nick has a lawyer cousin who came through for him. He has got a court date, though."

"You told me Nick threatened DeLeuw. What did he actually do? Go to George's house and argue with him?"

"DeLeuw wasn't home, so he left a note in the mailbox. Unfortunately, it said, 'Cheat my son and you'll wish you were never born.' " Bonelli frowned. "Combined with the handkerchief we found, it doesn't look good."

"That handkerchief could have been planted," I pointed out.

"Probably what the judge thought. The lab said it was a nice material—Irish linen. No stores in town carry anything like that, but it might have come from a mall on the highway or a catalog. I found a similar type online, sold as a set of three. Monogrammed, too."

Mark nailed it! I told her about his theory, and she agreed.

"The fabric was pretty tough," she added. "It wouldn't have ripped easily. Our lab guy thinks the corner was actually cut off, then the edges were raveled to make them look torn."

That boggled my mind. Very clever—and pre-meditated.

"The bigger question is," Bonelli went on, "instead of just getting rid of it, why plant it in Janos's truck? If someone did that, they're sure trying hard to misdirect us."

I knew by "us" she meant the police department, but I liked to think I was also part of the investigative team by now. "There's something big at stake, whatever it is."

Her phone rang; someone reminded her about an appointment. She said she was on her way and stood up, taking the folder from her desk.

"Whether or not Dion or his father committed the murder," she said to me, "this all started when he told DeLeuw about the encryption system. So the FBI is still pursuing that angle."

I also got to my feet. "From what Dion told me, they're not going to get anywhere without George's key."

"Yeah, and they're searching for it in a warehouse full of art and other expensive knickknacks." The detective shook her head. "Talk about hunting for a needle in a haystack!"

* * *

Back at the shop, Jerry had arrived and was chatting with Sarah. Whatever his plans were for the day, he wore his usual business-casual turnout of a collared shirt, a navy blazer, and khakis. His short, dark hair looked freshly trimmed. He had stacked two cases of the special cat food on my sales counter, and joked that he figured Harpo was in for a long stay.

"I hope not," I admitted. "I'd like to see him settled in a good home where he can roam around instead of being confined all the time. At least he has it better here, though, than at animal control. We let him out for at least a half hour every day, and Sarah loves to play with him."

My helper beamed like a doting mother. "He was shy the first few days, but he's coming out of his shell now. He loves to chase toys and even play fetch with me!"

Jerry's smile was less enthusiastic. "I'll take your word for it. With my allergy, I probably shouldn't go past the front desk."

"Want me to bring him out and show him to you?" Sarah asked. "Just from a distance?" Before Jerry or I could respond, she darted into the back room.

Meanwhile, I recalled seeing George's assistant coming out of the Thai restaurant with Marjorie, and again wondered what that was about. Were they dating on the sly, or just thrown together by the circumstances of the funeral? Supposedly, Jerry knew all about George's business affairs. Could he have said anything to spark her interest in taking ownership of Harpo?

I offered the plate of brownies. "Have one of these—they're wonderful! Sarah is turning out to be a woman of many talents."

"Umm, don't mind if I do!" Jerry chose a corner square with ample chocolate icing.

"Can I offer you coffee? It's not Starbucks, but on the other hand, it's free."

He laughed and accepted that, too. I started pouring some into a spare mug until he said, "Just a half cup. I've got a couple more errands to run before noon."

I passed it to him, then leaned across the sales counter on my elbows. "So, Jerry, what's the scoop? Did DeLeuw make a will or not?"

The boyish assistant glanced toward the ceiling—invoking his deceased boss, maybe, or just expressing the madness of it all. "Apparently he had one, but that's all I know. He never discussed anything that personal with me. He got a private trust company to draft a will a few years back, and they're also serving as executor of his estate. As long as half of his possessions are impounded in a warehouse, though, everything's in limbo."

It seemed pretty crazy to me, too. "And after all this, they may never find that computer chip."

"Even if they do, what if it's a waste of time? I'm betting those encrypted files are just something routine, like an inventory of his artworks."

"So you have no inkling of what could be on there?"

He gave a palms-up shrug. "He told me he wanted to test Dion's system. I think he still intended to present it to Encyte. But then the kid got all worked up because things weren't moving fast enough."

"Dion told me a Chinese firm came out with the same idea, and he thought George had double-crossed him."

"Hey, I don't know whether or not the Chinese system is exactly the same—I'm no expert on these things. But even if it's close, they must have come up with it on their own. I can't imagine George selling the system to anyone except Encyte, where he's on the board."

Tempted beyond my ability to resist, I helped myself to a second brownie. "Detective Bonelli told me the cops found a special scanner among George's things that might have been designed to read the missing chip."

Jerry snapped his fingers. "See? Who else would have made that for him except Encyte? He probably was already talking to them about the deal."

"Did he tell Dion that?" I asked.

"I overheard him trying to explain to the kid a couple of times, but in the end Dion acted so paranoid that George gave up. Frankly, I think he felt insulted, with the son and even the father calling his house and accusing him. He probably figured, the hell with it. Why should he put up money for somebody who doesn't trust him? Who doesn't even know how the business works?"

That sounded more like the DeLeuw I had known. I could see that he might resent being pressured by someone like Dion, maybe even to the point of passing on a lucrative deal.

"How long did you work with George?" I asked.

"Let's see . . . about ten years. At Redmond & Fowler, I started as EA for a group of the MDs—that's managing directors. Then, as the business expanded, each MD got his own assistant and George asked for me."

"After he started working from home, I guess you only helped him part-time."

Jerry nodded. "And I went back to doing some work for another of the MDs."

"Charles Schroeder?" When he looked surprised by my guess, I explained, "You were talking with him at the viewing."

"Oh, right . . . when you introduced yourself," Jerry remembered.

Sarah returned then from the boarding area, with Harpo in her arms, and announced with a lilt, "Here he is!" She held the Persian the way I'd taught her to, firmly against her body, but the cat could still look over his shoulder at us. "I won't bring him too close."

Jerry responded with a kind of forced smile. "You've sure got him cleaned and fluffed up. Is that a new collar?"

"Oh, no," I said. "He's had that blue one all along."

"Funny . . . never noticed it before. But then, I was probably keeping my distance. What are those silver tags?"

This man really must never have owned a pet, I thought. "One's his license and the other has his name and George's phone number. In case he ever got lost. Which he could have the day that . . . that he got out."

Jerry turned pale. "Good ol' George," he said in a tight voice. "He thought of everything."

Maybe the sight of the cat brought it all back to him, I thought, even more than George's funeral had. The violent death of a man he'd worked with for ten years. Arriving at DeLeuw's house to find police everywhere, and being questioned by Bonelli, as we all were.

What would be Jerry's prospects now at Redmond & Fowler? If all the other partners already had assistants, would he become superfluous? Or would Schroeder find a spot for him?

"George did seem like a very careful and thorough guy," I agreed. "And he cared a lot about Harpo."

Sarah must have picked up on Jerry's discomfort, and possibly thought he was worried about his allergy. "I'll put him away now," she said, and took the cat back to his condo.

Seeing an opportunity, I added, "Actually, Danielle has developed an affection for Harpo too." I explained that I'd seen her at the Firehouse, with the Schroeders, and she'd tried her best to persuade me to let her take the cat back to San Jose.

Coolly, Jerry observed, "But you still have him."

"I said I'd been told to keep him until the will was probated and I intended to stick to that unless his lawyer advised me otherwise."

"Good for you," Jerry said, with a brisk nod. "This is the safest place for him." Checking his watch, he added, "Thanks for the brownie and the coffee. I gotta run! You need anything else for him, just call me."

"Will do."

As he closed the front door behind him, Sarah returned from the condo area. "Safest place? I guess he meant instead of the animal shelter."

I wondered too. "Yeah, that's probably what he meant."

Chapter 17

That evening, I actually had no plans and looked forward to the break—just me and my feline family again. Still, the DeLeuw murder was never far from my mind. I might have been willing to leave the investigation up to the professionals, but it was hard not to be curious—especially with George's sister and ex-wife bugging me about his cat.

Let's face it. As long as I still had Harpo in my care, I was enmeshed in the whole drama too.

Having been played with and fed, my own three cats now arranged themselves in decorative poses around my living room. This time shy Matisse had managed to beat the boys to the best seat in the house, cuddled up next to my thigh. Cole stretched out with his usual dignity along the sofa back, while Mango sat on one of the wall shelves to wash his face.

Meanwhile, I used my laptop to find out everything I could about DeLeuw's inner circle. I'm sure Bonelli had access to far more information through her law-enforcement channels. But she wasn't about to share everything that she knew with me, and maybe I'd make some connections that she'd missed.

She said everyone I talked to at the funeral home probably lied to me about something. So let's explore that theory. . . .

I started with Danielle. Whether or not she'd ever married, apparently she still did business under her maiden name, since her California boutiques were called DeLeuw Designs. They offered clothing and jewelry in the same minimalist, ultra-modern style that I'd seen her wearing—long, loose dresses, skirts, and pants in neutral tones, plus geometric metal and stone jewelry.

An online magazine for women entrepreneurs had done a profile on her a few years back, when she'd opened her second store. The interviewer took a feminist slant, asking if Danielle had encountered any particular obstacles as a business-woman.

"Well, I had a brilliant brother almost ten years older," she said, "so sometimes I got tagged as the ditzy little sister. My parents definitely took his accomplishments, in sports and in school, more seriously. He got an MBA from Columbia, which made my degree from the Fashion Institute of Technology look puny by comparison. But in the end, I think that just gave me more drive. I always felt I had something to prove."

A more recent financial story did indicate that Danielle's stores were in trouble, along with some other high-end boutiques in the San Jose area.

Maybe that was why she planned to expand farther south? I saw no mention of any dramatic downturn, such as filing for bankruptcy. But Bonelli said Danielle had asked George for a loan a month ago, to save her business, and he'd refused her. She also remained the most likely to inherit her brother's estate. Could her financial woes have been so serious, and maybe her childhood resentments still so strong, that she'd want to hasten his demise?

The only other place her name turned up was in a photo caption for a West Coast museum fundraiser. She glowed on the arm of a handsome darkskinned man in a tuxedo. The caption identified him as Deven Mehtar, chief technology officer for Encyte Cybersecurity.

That was interesting. Was Danielle dating someone from the same security firm that used her brother as a consultant? Of course, maybe that was how they'd met. This picture was the latest reference to her that I could find, from about six months back.

Not exactly a lie or a scandal. If they didn't object to a photographer taking their picture, I assumed both of them were single and free to date anyone they wanted. But now I wondered how savvy Danielle might be about her brother's business dealings with the high-tech firm. Had Mehtar known about the new encryption system that George intended to present to Encyte?

My phone rang, forcing me to jostle Matisse by reaching into the pocket of my yoga pants. I recognized the number. "Hey, Nick. How are you holding up?"

"I'm okay. No thanks to the cops in this town."

"I talked to Detective Bonelli today. If it's any consolation, she also thinks someone's trying to frame you. That's the person you should probably be mad at."

"Maybe. Anyhow, I didn't call to talk about that nonsense. I'm out of jail, feeling better, and I made the post for your steps. I can come over and replace it tomorrow morning if that's okay with you."

Matisse stood up, arched her back, and tickled my chin with her tail, trying to distract me from the call. I moved her to one side. "That's fine, Nick. Your timing couldn't be better—I already did the demo work for you." I didn't explain, for the moment, that an unknown intruder had caused the damage.

"That's weird," Nick said. "I thought I secured it pretty good."

"I thought so too. We'll talk about it when you come tomorrow, okay?"

"All right, Cassie. You have a good night."

Glad to hear my handyman had not suffered too badly from his brief incarceration, I returned to researching those near and not-so-dear to the late George DeLeuw.

Background on his ex-wife was harder to come by.

Marjorie seemed to have kept a low profile following the divorce. I found a brief interview with her from a different kind of charitable event, a Manhattan rally for a group called Mothers Against Drugs. The reporter noted that while most of those attending came from middle- or working-class backgrounds, Marjorie wanted to show that the scourge of hard drugs affected families in all strata of society.

"My daughter had every advantage in life," she was quoted as saying, "but we still lost her to this evil. There are people out there preying on our children. We have to band together and tell them, 'No more!'"

Again I wondered, did she still blame her ex-husband for making Renée feel unloved and driving her to seek comfort in heroin? From what I'd seen, DeLeuw was a restrained man but not a cold, unfeeling one. I might have preferred him as a parent, in fact, over Marjorie. But maybe I wasn't seeing her at her best these days, if she was still so angry about her daughter's death. Could she have been vengeful enough, after all this time, to have argued with George and killed him?

I found a fair amount of material on Charles Schroeder. Most revealing, though, was a short squib in an article about business leaders who had graduated from West Point. Apparently Schroeder had come from a military family, went to the Point, and did a stint in the navy. He then attended Harvard Business School, got his MBA, and joined Redmond & Fowler. Schroeder was quoted as saying, "My West Point training and naval service taught me the value of hard work, discipline, and survival under pressure that have served me well on Wall Street." This background fit well with what I remembered of him from our brief meeting at the funeral home—the athletic build, ramrod posture, and impression of stern control.

I'd left my front window open to catch the evening breeze, and now the loud slam of a car door startled me. On full alert, I stole over to the window and peered outside. Several cars were parked at the curb along my street, so I couldn't tell where the noise had come from.

What if Andy comes back now that I'm home? He might still find a way, even without his own car. I haven't gotten the lock on the back door replaced yet. If he pounds on that door in a drunken rage, he could break his way in. . . .

But minutes ticked by with no sight or sound of anyone approaching my house. I dared to relax again. *All this speculating about DeLeuw's murder is making me jumpy.*

My hypervigilant state even seemed to stir up the cats. I watched now as Mango oozed down the wall, from shelf to shelf, then trotted over to the sofa and stared up at Cole. The black cat took this as a challenge and sprang from the back of the sofa to chase the orange tabby. The two skirmished harmlessly underneath the kitchen table for a while, yowling now and then for effect. Matisse and I chose to ignore their boyish antics.

I turned to my last subject, Jerry Ross. It was easier to find information on him than on the other two. Not only was he listed on LinkedIn and other executive search sites, but he had a Facebook page. That was dominated by postings about his family, which included his wholesomely pretty wife, Chloe, and their preteen children Alice and Ethan. Mostly, Jerry seemed to be the one taking the photos as Ethan made a soccer goal or Alice rode her pony in a lesson. From some of the school teams and locations mentioned, I guessed they lived fairly close by, probably in the next county.

Funny. I'd have figured Ross for a workaholic, but it looks like he's had more of a balance between work and family than DeLeuw ever did. Of course, if he's seeing Marjorie on the side, maybe his suburban life isn't as rosy as it looks on Facebook.

From Jerry's executive profiles, I gleaned that he'd earned an MBA from the University of Pennsylvania and worked as an assistant at another financial firm before joining Redmond & Fowler. He'd mentioned to me that he'd worked for George for ten years and at R&F for a little longer.

My curiosity piqued, I read up on the job description for "executive assistant" at a large company. Online articles confirmed what I'd suspected—it was a fluid position that came with a lot of responsibility and not much prestige. Duties could range from developing and managing the executive's schedule and handling his calls and correspondence, to making his travel arrangements and accompanying him to conferences and high-level meetings. Most young people felt it was worthwhile, though, because there was always the chance of moving up, possibly even to fill the shoes of the person you'd been assisting.

But if Jerry took his present job when he was in his mid-twenties, he's been at it for twelve or thirteen years and still hasn't been promoted. That has to sting. He's probably well paid, but he's got two kids to put through school. Could he have thought that if George were gone, it would clear the way for him to move higher? Kind of a long shot, though . . .

Jerry had pooh-poohed the idea that the mystery files had anything to do with DeLeuw's murder. George must have encrypted them for some reason, though. More significantly, if the FBI was going to so much trouble to decipher the code, *they* must think the files held important information.

Matisse stretched a paw onto my lap and gave one of those extravagant yawns that cats execute so well. I got the message—time to turn off the laptop and hit the hay.

As usual, I did not let the furry threesome in the room while I slept, but felt oddly reassured that they stood guard outside. I also reminded myself that, at least for a few months, Andy should not have access to any wheels.

Tomorrow Nick would finally fix my railing. I'd ask him then about getting a dead bolt on that back door, too.

My handyman gave a low, drawn-out whistle when I showed him the remains of my banister. "The bracket I screwed on here last week is half torn out, and even the wood is splintered. Who leaned on this thing, Godzilla?"

"I don't know for sure," I told him, "but I suspect it was an ex-boyfriend. He isn't really that big or heavy, but he might have been drunk."

Kneeling by the steps, Nick peered up at me from beneath shaggy gray brows. "Guess that's why he's an ex, huh? And he's still coming around, when you're not here? Never mind, none of my business."

"He may be, in spite of all my attempts to discourage him. I'm afraid he's been stalking me." Briefly, I filled him in on my history with Andy. "The good news is, he got stopped for a DUI on his way home and lost his license for the next few months."

Nick set the banister aside. "Don't take too much for granted. Plenty of guys driving around with revoked licenses."

I hadn't thought about that. As long as no one actually took away Andy's car or even his keys, he might ignore his punishment. Still, if he got pulled over for anything else—speeding, or even a burnt-out taillight—the suspended license would show up and he might actually go to jail.

Nick also sized up the condition of my back door and agreed it needed a dead bolt lock. "And the gap in this windowsill is bad too. What's on the other side, again?"

"That downstairs bathroom that doubles as a utility closet. That's why I never bothered much about it."

"Before you were being stalked by the ex-boyfriend."

"Yeah, that's a new problem, since my mother very helpfully told him where I was living. Of course, I hadn't told her what a nut case he was."

Returning from his truck with the new post,

Nick wagged a thick finger at me. "That'll teach you. Shouldn't keep secrets from your parents."

Sounded like the pot calling the kettle black to me. "Speaking of keeping secrets, Mr. Janos . . . *you* never bothered to tell me that you went over to DeLeuw's house the day before he was murdered."

He dodged my eyes. "Pah. It doesn't matter; I didn't even see the man." He raised the new post, which he'd carved to match the other, undamaged one, into position. "Cassie, hold this in place for a minute, willya?"

I steadied the post while he reattached the handrail. "You left George a threatening note for the police to find. You told him if he tried to cheat Dion, he'd be sorry, or something to that effect."

"All right, I did do that. But I meant we might sue, and even that was a lame threat. I didn't say I'd physically hurt the guy. And I wouldn't have, even if he had been home."

"I believe you, but a jury of strangers could take the note seriously. All I can say is, those linen handkerchiefs come in sets of three, so you'd better not have any more lying around your house!"

Nick gave his balding head a wry shake. "Only handkerchiefs I ever had, my wife, Gloria, bought me one Christmas. Thought I'd use 'em for special occasions. She got 'em at some discount store, and they sure as heck weren't monogrammed."

After about fifteen minutes of his gluing the post into place and screwing the banister on more securely, I finally had a railing that would stand up to . . . well, maybe not the Hulk, but anyone who might actually be coming in my back door.

Sarah poked her head out to admire the improvement, and when she saw the beads of sweat on Nick's forehead, offered to get him a cold drink.

"Yes, come inside and rest for a second," I urged, not wanting him to work himself into another angina attack.

With a chilled bottle of iced tea, Nick strolled around the boarding area to see how well his earlier carpentry projects were holding up. Again, I considered how much I owed the success of my business so far to his designs for the wall shelves and my eight closet-sized cat condos.

He sized up the half dozen boarders, a few hiding behind their draperies but most choosing to lounge on their raised carpeted perches. "Which is the guy who's causing all the hoopla?"

"That would be Harpo, here." I laughed. "And he's in demand, all right."

I opened the condo door a little so Nick could stroke the cat's head, while I explained about the two women who were suddenly competing for the Persian.

"Do they know about the chip? Maybe they think Harpo's got it." Nick fingered the rectangular license hanging from the cat's collar. "Dion tried to describe it to me, but I'm not sure. . . . Would it look anything like this?"

"I dunno," I said. "Far as I can tell, that's a standard license. And from what Dion told me, the chip would be even smaller. . . ."

My eyes shifted to the little, heart-shaped tag stamped with Harpo's name and DeLeuw's phone number. It was thicker than the license. Could the chip possibly be . . . *inside*?

I remembered, too, the odd look on Jerry's face when he'd noticed the collar tags. A rush of adrenaline made me giddy.

"Nick, you may have cracked the case!" With hasty, shaking hands, I unbuckled the smooth leather collar and slipped it from beneath Harpo's blond ruff. "And maybe cleared yourself and Dion, too."

Chapter 18

Bonelli held the small baby-blue collar in her square palm and studied it as carefully as if it were a diamond necklace. Then she locked eyes with me. "Don't talk to *anyone* about this. Understand?"

I nodded, but apparently that wasn't enough to reassure her.

"Not your friends," she stressed, "not the Janoses, but especially not anyone connected with DeLeuw."

"Nick practically suggested the idea to me, so he already knows I'm giving the collar to you," I admitted. "And my assistant, Sarah, was nearby when I let out a 'eureka'-type shriek."

The detective frowned. "Well, then, that can't be helped. But warn Sarah not to tell anyone else, and I'll do the same with Nick." She dropped the collar into a clear plastic evidence bag.

"Aren't you going to scan it?"

"We don't have the scanner for this; the FBI

does. If you're right, I'm sure they'll be grateful to give up searching all that stuff in the warehouse."

I smiled to myself, muffling an inner thrill. What if Nick and I really had found the missing microchip? Of course, there was still George's murder to be solved, but the FBI seemed to think the two mysteries were connected. With any luck, they could take the investigation from here, and I could go back to running my business instead of playing detective.

"Glad to have been of help," I said.

"You have been, Cassie. As I suspected, several people who were on their guard around us tipped their hands when they were dealing with you."

"This could explain why Danielle and Marjorie were so persistent about trying to get Harpo," I added. "Easier to pretend they wanted the whole cat than to just ask me for his collar."

"It would suggest that they know what's on that chip," Bonelli agreed. "And if the FBI can read it, we may also have a better idea of who murdered DeLeuw."

Leaving the police station, I felt weightless. The blooming cherry trees along Center Street had never smelled so sweet, and the old-fashioned storefronts had never looked so charming. I strode down the weathered, uneven sidewalks with an extra swing to my step.

I'd solved a case even the FBI couldn't crack!

Maybe.

Only one fly in the ointment—I couldn't tell

anyone. I could talk to Sarah and Nick, probably, but not Dawn, Mark, or my mother.

Oh well, plenty of time for that after I was awarded a medal for outstanding citizenship by the FBI. Or at least an honorary detective's badge from the Chadwick PD.

Sarah greeted me breathlessly when I got back to the shop. "Well?"

I closed the door behind me and wished I had a shade to pull down too, like in those old suspense movies. "No way to know yet. Bonelli's going to give the collar to the feds to scan."

"This is so exciting!" Sarah grinned.

"We can't tell anybody. Nick knows, of course—Bonelli probably wishes he didn't—but beyond that, we're sworn to secrecy."

My assistant pretended to zip her lip. "I'll take it to my grave."

"Don't even joke about that. I have no idea how much is at stake here! Think about it—does the FBI always make this big a deal about the murder of a prominent businessman? One who's semi-retired, for Pete's sake? And Bonelli's taking it all very seriously. I'm sure she knows even more than she's telling me."

Sarah's eyes widened. "So . . . we've gone past exciting to scary."

I tried to wave away her fears. "At least if the chip's in the collar, it's literally out of our hands now. Anyone who wants can try to get it back from the FBI, and good luck with that. Meanwhile, speaking of scary . . . did you check on Stormy today? Has he adjusted to the lion cut yet?"

She answered with a lopsided smile. "It hasn't

improved his temperament any. When I stopped by his condo to say hello, he lunged at the door and spat at me."

"Ordinarily I'd let him out to burn off some of that energy, but I think we'll give him another day to settle down. Besides, I don't know if we could ever get him back in his condo." I sighed. "Remind me to draw up some stricter rules of behavior for the cats we'll accept as boarders. And then remind me to stick to them, okay?"

The afternoon went by quickly from there on. Near closing, Dawn called to tell me that Tigger had come through his neutering procedure with flying colors and would be recouping overnight at the clinic.

"Want to celebrate with me?" she asked. "You and I never did get to that Thai restaurant."

"Sounds great." I didn't add that I had something of my own to celebrate. It would take all my self-control to spend the evening with Dawn and not reveal the Secret of the Cat's Collar. But for the sake of that honorary detective's badge, I could be strong.

Kin Khao combined a Zen-like ambience with a dash of spice. Leaf-shaped iron sconces threw low lighting over the grass-textured walls. Deep red cloths covered the tables, and upon each one a narrow vase held a single spidery orchid. Fortunately, the prices weren't as steep as the elegant décor would suggest.

Avoiding the items flagged with a red-pepper icon, I opted for the pad Thai, a stir-fried dish with egg, rice noodles, and bean sprouts in a peanut sauce. Dawn, more adventurous, went for a red curry made with coconut milk, bamboo shoots, and bell peppers. To properly toast Tigger, we also ordered wine, the waitress recommending a Riesling to go with our dishes.

After we'd ordered, I took a minute to recall having seen Jerry Ross coming out of this restaurant just a week ago with Marjorie DeLeuw. They made an odd couple; though attractive, she had to be at least ten years older than Jerry. It seemed unlikely that he'd jeopardize his marriage to a cute young wife, with whom he had two children, for a fling with Marjorie. What other reason, if not romantic, might they have had to get together? True, they'd both attended George's viewing. But Jerry impressed me as loyal to both George and to Redmond & Fowler, while Marjorie didn't seem to think much of either one.

I didn't have any trouble avoiding the subject of the murder investigation with Dawn, because she was bubbling over with her own news. Over the last few days, she appeared to have fallen madly in love with her new kitten, partly because she'd had some success in training him.

"A couple of times I did keep him away from the shop door by distracting him with the fishing-pole toy," she reported. "And I think he might be getting the idea of the clicker-training. At least when I say, 'Rug,' now, he goes right to it. He's really smart!"

"He might be a little less eager to dash out the door now that you've had him fixed, too," I suggested.

She pouted in sympathy for the little brown tabby. "He was such a good boy at the vet today, not scared at all. I worried about him, but Dr. Coccia said by the time they closed tonight, he was already starting to come out of the anesthesia. They just want to keep him overnight to be on the safe side, because they did his procedure so late in the day."

"I'm sure he'll be fine," I said. "It's a pretty simple operation, and cats don't even seem to have much discomfort afterward. Tigger will be bouncing around again in no time."

Our dinners came and I promptly tucked into mine, not having had anything since lunch. My one previous experience with Thai food had made me a bit wary, but this dish had a delicious blend of seasonings and was mild enough even for my sensitive stomach. Meanwhile, Dawn happily dove into her dinner too, though from time to time I thought I detected wisps of steam coming out of her ears.

"Speaking of the dashing Dr. Dolittle," she said, "you two had another date on Sunday? This sounds promising!"

"I'd like to think so. Our evenings out so far have been kind of jinxed, though."

I told her how Danielle had interrupted our second date, after which I'd come home to find that someone had demolished my stair railing. By the time I'd finished, Dawn's long-lashed brown eyes were bugging out for reasons that had nothing to do with her spicy meal.

"That Andy seems like a real wack job," she

said, with a shake of her head. "You be careful, girl."

"I will. It's good to know the Morristown cops have clipped his wings for a while, but I'm also going to ask Nick to beef up my home security."

I refilled my wineglass, realizing this was the first time since DeLeuw's murder that I'd felt free to completely relax. If the microchip really was in Harpo's collar, and on its way to the FBI, maybe the whole case would soon be wrapped up, and the bad guy—or gal—would be in custody. At any rate, I wouldn't be stuck in the middle anymore.

Dawn paused a forkful on the way to her mouth. "Why the Mona Lisa smile? Because Andy got pulled over by the cops? Or because things are going well with Mark?"

"Um . . . neither, really." As I'd feared, she knew me so well by now that it was hard to keep anything from her. "I can't talk about it yet. Let's just say that this whole mess may be cleared up soon, and I was able to help."

"What mess? The murder?"

I flinched and glanced around at our fellow diners. "Not so loud! I shouldn't have said anything—I've had too much wine. Anyway, if I'm right, I'll know soon enough."

That Riesling went down a little too easily, so it was a good thing both Dawn and I lived within walking distance. After my scare stories about Andy, she went the extra two blocks and made sure I got into my building safely before heading home herself.

It had been a long time since I'd allowed myself to drink even a little too much, and my cats scolded me loudly—as if I hadn't fed them before going out. I gave them enough food to keep them quiet for the night, changed into a T-shirt and pajama bottoms, washed my face, brushed my teeth, and stumbled into bed. Sarah would arrive at nine or earlier, more cheerful and energetic than anyone her age had a right to be. It wouldn't be fair for me, as the supposed boss, to greet her bleary-eyed and hung over.

A couple of hours later, though, I was shocked out of my deep, sludgy sleep by a horrible electronic shrieking. I jerked upright with a pounding heart, but my mind took a bit longer to process the source.

Smoke alarm!

But not the one in my apartment. The sound was too muffled.

The shop.

I threw on a short robe over my pajamas, blindly scuffed my feet into slippers, and dashed into the hall. All three cats met me there. Their wide eyes begged for relief, while their ears cocked backward as if to block out the din.

"Easy, guys. It's okay, it's okay!"

But is it?

I wavered at the top of the stairs. What to do first? Check in case it was some kind of false alarm before I called 9-1-1? Scoop my own cats into carriers in case I had to get them out? Check the boarders first, in case the fire was closer to them?

I felt torn in half between saving my own pets and those of my customers.

I made the 9-1-1 call, then ran downstairs, shutting my guys in the apartment behind me. With any luck, they'd be safe up there until I figured out what was going on.

Maybe it's just a short in the wiring setting off the alarm. Some old damage? Once upon a time, this place did have mice. . . .

A few steps into the shop, though, I saw a haze in the air and smelled smoke. Down here, the screeching of the alarm was almost unbearable. I felt sorry for the boarders, whose tender ears must be suffering even worse than mine. I psyched myself up for the job of wrestling six frightened cats into carriers and hustling them outside to safety.

Could I even do that by myself? Just lifting Bear was a challenge under the best of circumstances, which these were not.

By the time I reached the condos, I was coughing from the smoke. One good sign—although the boarder cats were agitated, the fire hadn't spread to that area yet. The smoke spewed from the doorway of the grooming studio, the only room with electrical appliances. That was why I'd hung the sensor in there.

Damn, did I leave something plugged in? Did the hair dryer short out? And what's the weird hissing sound?

The sprinklers! I'd actually forgotten about them.

From the doorway, I could see that two of the ceiling units had popped open and were drenching everything beneath with a fine spray. They responded to extreme heat, and with the system

Nick had installed, only those closest to the fire would activate.

During the renovations, he'd nagged me about the need for sprinklers in any commercial space until I relented. Once again, I appreciated the amount of foresight and care Nick had put into renovating this old building for my shop.

Still coughing, I fought my way through the white haze toward the source of the fire. It seemed to be the first-floor powder room, which Nick had equipped with shelves so it could double as a closet for my grooming supplies. When I reached it, I got a shock—the door looked exploded open. Some plastic bottles on the shelves had melted, and flames still danced around a few stacks of towels.

I grabbed a towel that remained untouched and covered my mouth against the smoke. It had an especially nasty stink, I thought, searing my lungs and making my eyes water. Was that from the spilled soaps and lotions?

I found my fire extinguisher on the studio wall. Fumbled with the handle and shot some foam onto the parts that were still burning.

Only after the last sparks appeared smothered, and my pounding heart and coughing had eased a little, did I have time for questions.

The fire started in the powder room? Had I stored anything in there that could have combusted? In my shaken state, I couldn't remember.

The drawn-out wail of a siren approached outside. No longer in crisis mode, I grabbed a stool and climbed onto it to silence the alarm above the door. I pictured all of the cats, upstairs and down, breathing sighs of relief. If my ears were ringing, theirs must have been painful.

I let two firefighters in the front door and told them what I'd figured out so far about the source of the problem. A tall, thin older man went through the storage closet and hosed it down thoroughly to be sure no embers still smoldered. A stocky woman checked around the back of the building to be sure the flames had not spread out there.

As the male firefighter checked my wall of condos, I explained about my business. "These are all cats of paying customers. I'm glad the sprinklers controlled the fire, because I couldn't imagine how I was going to evacuate them—quickly—all by myself."

"You better work out a plan for the future," he advised. "At least these guys are caged. It's worse when pets are running loose in a house. They panic and hide under furniture, so it can be really tough to catch them." He sounded like he spoke from sad experience.

His partner called to us then through the rear door. "Odd thing back here, Carl . . . the window-sill is singed."

We joined her as she trained her flashlight on a gap below the powder room window—the same one Nick had called to my attention earlier. Although the rest of the siding was unmarked, that spot near the end of the sill was deeply scorched.

Carl examined the opening. "No wires running through there. Nothing inside that's resting against that spot either."

His partner leaned close enough to sniff the sill and drew back with a blink of repulsion. Even from a few feet away, I also could pick up a chemical stink.

"That's weird," I said. "What could cause that?"

"Something soaked in an accelerant. Pushed partway through the window, then set on fire." The uniformed woman scratched beneath her bulky helmet. "Ms. McGlone, you got any enemies?"

Chapter 19

"We've got to stop meeting like this," Detective Bonelli cracked—dryly, of course—when she arrived on the scene. The firefighters were wrapping up, and Officer Bassey was also back, interviewing Mrs. Kryznansky. From what I overheard, though, my neighbor had been asleep until the fire truck arrived, so this time she hadn't even seen the perp running away.

"I don't suppose you'd have any motive to set fire to your own shop while you were in it and while it was full of your customers' cats," Bonelli said.

"Not unless I was completely out of my mind." We stood outside in the chilly parking lot, but at least the fresh air had started to soothe my burning throat and eyes. "All I can figure is that someone believes I still have the chip. Maybe they thought I'd have to evacuate all the cats, and in the confusion they'd have a chance to snatch Harpo."

"But if it weren't for your sprinklers, the whole shop could have gone up." All right, sometimes Bonelli could be a little *too* blunt. "The cat and his collar tags would have been destroyed."

"Could be that's what the arsonist wanted," I reasoned slowly. "Maybe they already know what's in those files and just want to make sure nobody else finds out."

A second officer had been sifting through the ashes of the studio, and now called out to Bonelli. "Found something."

I trailed the detective as she went inside to investigate. We passed through the condo area, where I already had gathered every available floor and table fan to clear out the smoke and fumes.

The young cop who stood in the grooming studio had a respirator pushed down around his neck. Wearing latex gloves, he held up a scrap of a brown towel. "Looks like the rest of it burned away fast," he said, "but this part stayed stuck under the window frame."

"Bag it," Bonelli told him. "We'll get the fire marshal out here to give this place a thorough going-over."

"This is insane. . . ." It suddenly hit me full force, that if not for Nick's sprinkler system, I could have lost my whole business tonight. Even if the smoke alarm had awakened me, even if I'd managed to get my three cats into carriers and move them out safely—a mighty big "if"—all or most of the boarder cats could have died.

Tears rolled down my cheeks, and I started to tremble.

Who could hate me that much? Andy?

I remembered that he'd once threatened my pets during an argument, and I thought of the childish way he'd shoved the cat tower at the expo, nearly smashing my laptop. Still . . . I found it hard to believe that he would go this far.

Burning the shop was so extreme, I doubted it was a personal vendetta against me. The cats, and even I, would have been collateral damage.

Someone either desperately wanted the key to that encrypted file, or wanted it destroyed.

When we returned to my soggy grooming studio, I said to Bonelli, "You've got some idea what's in those files, or what the FBI thinks might be in them. Is it that big a deal?"

She started to give me one of her stern looks, then softened a bit. I must have been a pathetic figure in my pajamas and robe, my hair a rat's nest. My voice hoarse and my eyes tearing from smoke and exhaustion. My customers' terrified cats crying from the next room.

"I can't talk about that," she said. "But they have the collar, and we should know soon if the key is in either of the tags."

"If it is, will whoever wants it finally leave me the hell alone?"

"At that point, the investigation should narrow down to just a few people. Once they're called back in for questioning, I doubt they'll be bothering you anymore. They'll have much bigger things to worry about."

That promise was too vague to console me.

Maybe it was the smoky haze that lingered in the air or maybe it was a panic attack, but suddenly I couldn't get my breath. I leaned back against the steel grooming table and squeezed my eyes shut. I felt beaten, and this wasn't even my fight. I didn't even know who the enemy was or what was at stake.

Bonelli put a hand on my shoulder, a lavish emotional display for her. "I'd tell you to find another place to live for a while, but I guess that's not possible, with all your responsibilities here. Do you have a friend who can stay with you? At least for the rest of tonight?"

I thought of Dawn, who would come in a flash if I called her. "I do, but I'd hate to put her in danger too."

"Don't worry about that. We'll have a unit in front of the house all night." The detective started toward the back of the shop, where her men were wrapping up. "Meanwhile, the fire marshal will get his own team out here and analyze what we found in your supply closet. I'll try to put a rush on that, and maybe it'll help us catch who did this. Okay?"

I nodded and thanked her. Realistically, though, I didn't think they had much to go on.

After Bonelli and the two officers had left, I called Dawn. The sirens just a couple of blocks away had woken her, but she'd never dreamed that they were headed for my shop. She looked almost as haggard as me when she showed up at my door. Of course, she'd had even more of the Riesling at dinner, though she usually handled it better.

It was almost four by now and hardly worth either of us trying to sleep. Only the cats were delighted, because they could badger me into giving them an early breakfast. I didn't mind, because I was so grateful they hadn't been harmed.

Dawn brewed some chamomile tea to steady our nerves. Meanwhile, she asked me, "Are you sure this fire wasn't some revenge tactic on Andy's part?"

"I really don't think he's that much of a psychopath," I told her as I scooped dry kibble into three dishes. "I mean, he left me alone for a pretty long while before Mom naïvely put me back on his radar. He's a hothead, but I can't see him as a cold-blooded killer. Whoever did this had no way of knowing I wouldn't die in the fire."

"Wouldn't anyone who'd been in your shop know you had the sprinklers?"

"Not necessarily. They're very subtle, just a couple of white discs on the ceiling in every room." I brought out what was left of Sarah's brownies, to go with the tea, meanwhile thinking through the mechanics of the crime. "Someone pushed a towel through a gap beneath that bathroom window and set fire to it. It's a dark space—they might not have even have realized it was just a supply closet. Or they might have figured in a spot like that, I wouldn't notice the fire until it was too late."

Dawn poured the tea into mugs and we sat at my little table. "I walked you back here around ten. I heard the sirens about one. The fire must have been set close to midnight."

"It's funny the arsonist didn't do it earlier, while we were at the restaurant. But I never moved my car, and I left a light on upstairs, so they might have thought I was home and awake. At least it doesn't seem like they were spying on my every move." I sipped the tea slowly. "Maybe they thought I'd be dragging all the cats out to safety, by myself. Maybe this person was even lurking nearby, hoping to grab Harpo. When the firemen came, and I didn't need to move the cats, he or she might have realized the plan was a bust and took off."

"Could be." Dawn bit into a brownie, and her eyebrows gave it a five-star review. "Sarah baked these? She deserves a raise!"

"She really does, with everything she's had to put up with. And we'll probably have to groom every cat again now. Their coats must have absorbed the smoke."

My friend fell quiet for a beat. "Cassie, have you considered that someone could have been hired to do this?"

"Oh, I have. Especially since two of my prime suspects are women who probably wouldn't dirty their own beautifully manicured hands. Thank God I didn't turn George's poor cat over to either of them!" My eyes scratchy with fatigue, I turned my gaze out the kitchen window. The sky past Mrs. Kryznansky's upper porch was starting to lighten to a satiny rose. I pictured the mess left in the grooming studio, thought of the supplies I'd have to reorder. "I guess I'm going to have to close."

Dawn's spoon rattled against her mug. "What? No, Cassie, you can't—"

When I realized she'd misunderstood, I faced around with a half smile. "For today, I mean. Unless—Oh damn, Bear's owner is picking him up at two! I'll either have to groom him again this morning or call her and explain what happened." I felt my throat shutting down again. "Dawn, am I going to lose all my customers over this? Will they decide their cats aren't safe here? I might, if I were them."

"They'll understand. Why don't you tell them the firemen figured out what happened and you're making sure it doesn't happen again? It's an old building, after all. . . ."

"But the papers might report that it's being investigated as arson. Would you want to board your pet with someone who's under that kind of threat? If we can't find out who did this, maybe I *will* have to close."

Dawn clenched her delicate fists on the tabletop. "*When* they find out who did this to you, I hope I get a chance to work him over!"

I laughed. "Thanks, but Angela Bonelli will probably get the first shot, and I'm sure she's had more practice than you at pummeling bad guys." Despite my best intentions, my eyelids were closing. "Primo chamomile, Dawn. I think I might actually be able to catch a few winks now."

"Why don't you, while I'm here to keep an eye on things?"

I shuffled toward the bedroom. "My clock's already set, but just in case, don't let me sleep past eight. I have to pull myself together before Sarah comes."

"And before I can open, I'll have to bring poor neutered Tigger home from the vet's." She smiled sadly. "Even *he* probably had a better night than you did."

* * *

Naturally, my assistant was horrified when she heard what had transpired overnight and saw the ruined utility closet. "They're sure it was arson? Some of those cleaning supplies didn't just spill and . . . interact, or something?"

"Afraid not. I don't stock anything that flammable—nasty chemicals are bad for the kitties." I told her about the firefighters' theory that a towel had been jammed into a gap in the window.

Sarah looked thoughtful. "Didn't your handyman just point out that opening earlier yesterday?"

"Yes. But of course I don't suspect Nick! If he were going to set a fire that way, he sure wouldn't call my attention to it. Besides, he was the one who hinted that the chip might be in Harpo's collar, and by the time he left, he already knew I was giving it to the police."

She nodded. "So he, of all people, would have known there was nothing to gain by torching your shop."

"Exactly."

In the morning I found a few things in the studio moved or removed, but Bonelli had warned me that the fire marshal might take samples from my storeroom and the nearby area. Luckily, he'd still left me enough supplies to function for a while.

Sarah and l fed the clamoring boarders. As I had feared, all of them had absorbed the smoky smell into their fur. They'd have to be washed, and with a cat that always presented a special challenge. At least I had only three longhairs on board right now: Bear, Harpo, and . . .

Oh yeah, Stormy. Well, at least he wasn't that much of a longhair anymore.

By ten, all the cats had eaten and Sarah and I had cleaned out all their pans, so we started grooming. Bear, the only cat with an imminent departure time, got the first bath. We put him in the raised tub, cushioned with a soft bath mat. Sarah held him by the scruff while I wet him down with a sprayer held close to his body. The big cat complained a little when I tried to hurry through the process, so I was forced to slow down to keep him calm. I massaged a cat-safe soap into his abundant fur, which morphed into wavy, marbleized patterns as I rinsed him off. My phone rang twice during this whole time, but I had my hands more than full. Sarah raised Bear gently to stand on his hind feet so I could get all the soap off his belly and his britches, as groomers call the hind legs.

Finally I wrapped him in a towel to squeeze out most of the water, gave him a comb-through, and repeated the process with a second towel. We have a hair dryer, but since the sprinklers had drenched most of the studio, I thought I should wait a bit longer before trying to use it. If Bear was still damp by the time his owner came to pick him up, I'd just have to apologize and explain.

I thanked Sarah for her help, and while she took a rest, I checked my phone for messages. I found two. The first, from Bonelli, was typically efficient and to the point.

"*They analyzed the substance on the towel fragment,*" she said. "*The accelerant was acetone, a common solvent. It's used in paint thinner and nail polish remover, among other things. Unfortunately, those are so common and easy to come by that it doesn't narrow the field very much. As for the cat's collar, it's been turned over to the FBI. I assume they'll scan it, and I should have the results on that later this afternoon. Here's hoping!"*

Paint thinner or nail polish. I considered. Of course, Nick would have plenty of the first lying around, but it wasn't likely he'd set fire to the back of my shop right after having gone to the trouble of repairing my banister. Unless he was a split personality—handyman by day, arsonist by night! Nail polish remover suggested a woman, if only because a man might draw more attention if he purchased a jumbo container of the stuff. Also, a woman might be more likely to have read the label on the product, as even I had, warning that it was highly flammable.

The second call had come from an unfamiliar number. The way things had been going, I didn't dare ignore it. I just hoped it wasn't my arsonist, threatening worse to come.

When I heard Marjorie DeLeuw's voice, I thought it just might be. *"Ms. McGlone, you should be aware that by insisting on keeping that cat, and by your association with Dion Janos, you're putting yourself in grave danger. We need to talk, someplace private. I'll come to your shop at one o'clock. Don't tell any of the others—they can't be trusted."*

At first I assumed she was simply gearing up for an even more aggressive attempt to wrest Harpo away from me, and I was ready to call her back and tell her not to bother. But her last line gave the message a different spin.

She sounded as if she might actually know what was going on, and might be ready to tell me. If that was the case, you bet I'd meet with her!

Somewhere private but also public, though. And somewhere I couldn't be bludgeoned with any heavy objects.

Chapter 20

The Marjorie who sat a couple of feet away from me, in the shadows of the park gazebo, was a different woman from the one who had stormed into my shop days before.

Her makeup and clothes were more subdued, her manner less arrogant. I realized that she might have meant her phone message as more of a warning than a threat. But I still wondered if she was just hoping to make me a coconspirator in some new scheme.

She'd first suggested walking in the park, but lowering clouds made us retreat to the park's quaint shelter for what promised to be a long talk.

Hands folded in her lap, Marjorie began with an apology for her high-handed attitude when she'd last visited my shop. "You've probably suspected, by now, that my interest in Harpo had very little to do with the cat himself."

I nodded, playing my cards carefully. "You were hoping that whoever took the cat might also inherit some money from George's will."

Her alert reaction told me I'd guessed right. "That was my reasoning at first. The way George felt about me in recent years, I have no expectations of any inheritance. And maybe it's my own fault, because during our divorce I treated him pretty badly too. But it occurred to me that, the way he felt about his cat, he might have tied some bequest to whoever gave it a good home. I've been receiving a decent alimony check from George for years, and it will be hard to get by without it." She offered a thin smile. "If that sounds shallow and mercenary, at least you should see that I had no motive to kill him."

"None involving money, anyway," I said.

She sniffed. "What else? Jealousy? It's not as if I've kept tabs on his love life since we split. If there was another woman, which I doubt, she was welcome to him. We didn't break up over an infidelity."

"No. It was your daughter's death, I would imagine."

Her clear hazel eyes, rimmed in dark liner, locked on my face. "You know about Renée?"

"George once mentioned she had died young, and you commented on the lack of any photos of her in the slideshow at the funeral home. Later I searched online and found an article about her death in a Philadelphia newspaper. I know it was a drug overdose."

Sharply, Marjorie turned her gaze out across the park, where some Canada geese grazed in a peaceful herd. "I could never forgive him for that."

"You felt she got into drugs because he was so absorbed in his work and didn't pay her enough attention?"

Another sour smile. "If it were only that, I might have gotten past it . . . eventually. But then there was the FBI investigation of Redmond & Fowler."

I'd almost forgotten about that. Could there be a connection? "The firm was accused of laundering drug money. But they were cleared, right?"

"Because no hard evidence could be found. The FBI turned R&F's files inside out but couldn't find proof of any illegal transactions."

A high-pitched scream made us both jump. A light rain had begun, and a couple of giggling preteen girls sprinted across the playground with their sweaters pulled over their heads. Marjorie let out a long breath, as if feeling foolish. I guessed our secretive conversation was making us both paranoid.

She waited until the girls had moved on before she continued. "I'm sure any records R&F had of those transactions were whitewashed, hidden, or destroyed. Probably, the cash was moved around through wire transfers, loans, and other methods that looked totally legitimate. Some of the most damning files may just have been conveniently misplaced."

"George told you that?"

"Not in so many words, but from what he did say, I could read between the lines. I'll give him credit; he never wanted any part of that scheme. I think he got pressured, maybe even threatened, to go along. That's why, once the dust settled, he all but retired from the firm."

She didn't need to connect any more of the dots for me. Renée DeLeuw had died of a heroin overdose. Shortly afterward, George's own firm was accused of laundering drug money from Central Asia by way of European banks. Even if there might be no direct connection, Marjorie must have seen it as the height of hypocrisy, the ultimate betrayal of their daughter.

"I can understand why that destroyed your marriage." I wondered if the damage done had ended, though, with Renée's death. "Could the company still be laundering money? Did that have something to do with George's murder?"

Marjorie shook her head. "With the scrutiny they've been under since then, it's hard to believe they'd dare. Certainly, George put pressure on the other managing directors and even the CEOs to clean up their act. *But* . . . I think he might also have hung on to a little insurance." In case I wasn't keeping up, she sketched it out for me. "I think he copied the incriminating files before they were destroyed. And I think he at least told Chuck Schroeder—whom he thought he could trust— that if R&F ever dabbled in the drug business again, he'd send the 'missing' files to the FBI."

I sat back on my bench to absorb this news. "Then, when Dion Janos came along with his encryption system, George saw a way of protecting those files so no one else would have access to them. It was a way of 'testing' the security of the system, but it also gave him more leverage over the decision-makers at his company. Even if one of them hacked into his computer and found those files, they wouldn't be able to open them. Maybe they couldn't even destroy them!"

"That's probably what happened, yes. Of course, a lot of this is guesswork on my part, because nobody's talking. After the funeral, I had dinner with Jerry Ross and tried, subtly, to find out how much he knew. He claimed George told him nothing about the will, except that one existed. When I poked around the subject of the old scandal, he got nervous and evasive. Loyal to George to the end, I suppose—although these days he's working for Schroeder, too."

I nodded. "Jerry mentioned that when he came by the shop yesterday."

She stiffened her spine against the back of the wooden seat. "Trying to get Harpo?"

"No, just delivering more cat food. Though he made an odd comment, that my shop was the 'safest place' for Harpo right now." I paused. "Danielle did make a pitch for the cat, every bit as forceful as yours was." I told her how George's sister had approached me at the Firehouse.

Marjorie rolled her eyes toward the gazebo ceiling. "Of course *she* would have caught on by now. George introduced her to the people at Encyte years ago, and after the funeral she was palling around with the Schroeders. Danielle's no bubbleheaded California girl. I'll bet she knows more about what's going on than anyone. The legit stuff and the nonlegit—"

She broke off at the sound of feet running in our direction. A lean, elderly man jogged past in the drizzle, shooting us a friendly smile. We waited until he'd passed out of earshot. Even the park gazebo wasn't quite deserted enough today for our conversation.

Speaking softly, I picked up the thread again. "Danielle could be concerned about keeping everything under wraps to protect her brother's reputation . . . and the company's."

"Very likely. Maybe *she* set your shop on fire, or hired someone to do it."

"Well, until fifteen minutes ago, you and she were running neck and neck as my main suspects. But if you were behind it, I can't believe you'd go out of your way to explain this whole complicated mess to me." I scrutinized her face, the worry lines more visible today. "But why are you telling me all this? With what you know, you could have gone to the police as soon as George was murdered."

She shook her head. "I didn't want to believe there was any connection. It wasn't until word got out about those encrypted files that I put it all together. Even then I thought if I could find the key myself, I could use it the same way George must have done . . . to keep R&F from repeating its past mistakes."

"A dangerous game," I reminded her. "Look how he ended up."

"I see that now. The point is, if Danielle also wants Harpo, I must have been right—the cat has something to do with the key. If you want, I'll go with you to the police right now and tell them."

I finally admitted to Marjorie that the situation was under control. "My handyman, Dion's father, guessed that it might be hidden in one of the collar tags. I gave them to Detective Bonelli, and she's already handed them over to the FBI. So if somebody wanted to keep those files secret, just by chasing after the key, they've brought about their worst nightmare."

Only after the words were out of my mouth did I remember that Bonelli had said not to tell anyone else that the FBI was checking out the collar. But really, at this point, what harm could it do?

Marjorie sagged against the back of the bench, looking both defeated and relieved by this news. "Those files may contain all the evidence anyone needs to reopen the case against R&F. So if George *was* killed over this business, at least he'll have his revenge in the end. I can't wait to see those bastards get what's coming to them!"

I got back to my shop just before Bear's owner, Cindy Reynolds, arrived to pick him up. Figuring that the tall, outdoorsy-looking woman might have read or heard about last night's fire, I explained that our sprinkler system had kicked in to protect the cats. I added, "We gave Bear an extra grooming this morning—no charge—to get any leftover traces of the smoke out of his fur."

Cindy still looked disturbed by what had happened, so I assured her that the firefighters had discovered the cause and it was being taken care of. She thanked me for my honesty and for the extra grooming. By the time she left, I had reason to hope that I would keep her as a customer.

"The cause of the fire 'is being taken care of'?" Sarah asked me slyly after the customer had gone.

"In the sense that Bonelli is trying to track

down the arsonist and throw his or her ass in jail."
Silently, I hoped I wasn't being overconfident by
staying open for business. Was I risking not just the
safety of all the cats, but possibly my life and
Sarah's?

My assistant took her usual seat behind the
sales counter. "Speaking of suspects, what did the
former Mrs. DeLeuw have to say?"

I let out a long breath. "What *didn't* she have to
say? She pretty much explained everything to
me—not who killed George; she doesn't know
that—but the probable motive. It turns out, she's
sort of on our side now and was very glad to hear
that Harpo's collar and tags are with the feds." I
grabbed the last brownie and poured myself a half
cup of coffee to wash it down. "This is a lot more
complicated than any of us thought, except possibly Bonelli. I'll tell you later—it's too much to go
into now. We still have four other cats to clean up
before the end of the day. And don't forget, one of
them is the infamous Stormy!"

"Oh Lord, that's right." My assistant winced.
"Good thing my medical insurance is paid up."

Giving the pale-gray creature a bath proved to
be such an ordeal that several times I wanted to literally throw in the towel and let the little monster
just lick himself clean. But even though he wasn't
very sooty, I knew there might have been unhealthy substances in the smoke that could make
him sick. At least his mostly shaved coat made our
job easier.

Sarah and I wrestled him into a harness and secured its leash to a metal arm above the tub. While
she squeezed liquid soap all over him, I massaged

it into his fur; then I held him as she used the sprayer to rinse him off, staying close to his skin so the water wouldn't strike him too forcefully. Still, from his wails, growls, and hisses, you'd have thought we were tearing him limb from limb. We both tried to stay cool and talk to him in soft, reassuring voices, but at that same time I kept a firm grip. Neither of us got too close to his face, and while I always held his front paws, Sarah kept an eye out for slashes from his powerful hind legs.

After a while he quieted a little and seemed resigned to his undignified fate. But when I tried to stretch him on his back so Sarah could rinse his belly, he convulsed in a suddenly howling frenzy and slashed me across the wrist. I didn't often curse at my clients' cats—or in front of my church-going assistant—but that was enough to break my resolution.

Sarah's jaw sagged. "Cassie, are you all right? You're bleeding!"

"I'll be okay." I grabbed Stormy by the scruff of his neck and stood him up on his hind legs in the tub. "Just rinse him off as quick as you can."

After that we wrapped our miniature lion in a bath towel, which at least kept him from using his claws on us, and blotted him dry. By now I trusted the hair dryer again, and Sarah turned it on low while I brushed and fluffed the fur around Stormy's face and paws and at the tip of his tail. I then deposited him in the drying cage, with a low-heat blower mounted outside but aimed in toward him, to finish the job.

Meanwhile, I noticed the towel from around his body was streaked with blood—mine. The inside of my lower right arm looked like someone had been playing tic-tac-toe with a razor blade.

"Gosh, you should see a doctor for that!" Sarah told me. "You might need stitches, or even a shot."

It stung like hell, but I could see the scratches didn't go very deep. "Looks worse than it is, I think. I'll just rinse it with peroxide and stick a gauze patch on it. At least it's not a bite!"

We continued with our grooming assembly line for a couple more hours, and I wore long gloves for protection. Most of the other boarders were short-hairs, which had pros and cons. They weren't as accustomed to being bathed and groomed, so they complained a lot, but with less fur to wash and dry, the whole process went quicker. Sarah and I got a rhythm going, and by five o'clock we had almost finished.

Both of us brushed airborne tufts of damp, wispy fur from our noses and lips. Our aprons and slacks of course, were covered with the stuff.

"You go on home," I told my assistant. "I can't thank you enough for your help today. I never imagined we'd ever have a marathon session like this one."

"It was kind of fun," she insisted, with a tired grin. "Of course, I wasn't the one who got slashed. You take care of that arm, and go to a doctor if it starts to look infected."

"I promise." Sarah had a tendency to mother me, but in a way that annoyed me less than my own mother's nagging.

I saw her out and locked the front door of the shop. Passing the coffeemaker, I decided I could use another cup before I started on Harpo. I'd left him for last, because unlike the others, he probably wasn't going anywhere too soon.

As I settled on a stool near the front counter with my mug, my phone rang.

Bonelli! That gave me a jolt of hopeful energy.

"Hi," I said brightly. "What's up?"

She sighed on the line. "Bad news, I'm afraid. They used DeLeuw's special scanner on both tags and even X-rayed them. They're solid tin. Nothing inside either one that could possibly be a chip."

"Damn." I slumped over the counter. "That's so weird, though. Marjorie was here this afternoon, and even she thought we were on the right track." I filled the detective in on what George's ex-wife had to say. Though Bonelli didn't comment much, I got the sense none of it surprised her. Probably the FBI had suspected all along that the encrypted files might relate to R&F's money-laundering shenanigans.

I didn't admit that I'd blabbed to Marjorie about turning over the collar to the authorities, but what did that matter now? It had been a false lead anyway.

"Guess it's back to square one," said Bonelli. "If there's anybody more disappointed than you or me, it'll be those guys who are still combing through all that stuff in the warehouse."

"I bet. Thanks for the call anyway."

Now I felt not only exhausted, but deflated. I'd been so sure we'd found the answer! There was no guarantee, of course, but it did seem likely that unlocking those files would help solve George's murder.

I recalled what Marjorie had said about Danielle. What was her interest in this? Did she want to bring her brother's killer to justice? Or was she his killer? She was most likely to inherit everything from him, but for that very reason it would be stupid of her to commit the crime herself. And from what Marjorie had said, Danielle didn't seem like a stupid woman.

On the other hand, for her to try to recover Harpo and the chip made more sense. She might just want to cover up anything that could tarnish George's memory and his company's reputation. I could see her forming an alliance with his colleague Chuck Schroeder to accomplish that. How far would she go, though? Douse a towel in nail polish remover, push it through my back window, and set it on fire? Or hire somebody to do that for her?

My right arm throbbed beneath the gauze bandage, my lungs still tickled from smoke and cat dander, and I felt a headache coming on. I decided I'd racked my brain and body enough for one day. I'd clean up Harpo before he ingested too much smoke from his fur, then call it quits. At least I knew I could handle him all by myself.

I went through the same routine as with Stormy, but far more peacefully. The cream-colored Persian was so starved for attention by now that he even purred during my quick pre-bath combing. I bathed and rinsed him off at a brisk pace, eager to be finished for the day. Unfortunately, now that his collar was off, the area around his neck had more of a tendency to mat. While I was drying him, I used thinning scissors on one spot and worked carefully to loosen the knot.

And felt something that I shouldn't have felt.

I ran my hands beneath his thick undercoat again, searching the nape of his neck and between his shoulder blades. There it was, all right—like an extra-large grain of rice under the skin. I'd felt microchips in pets before and had even watched vets implant them. They were tiny cylinders and transmitted a registration number to identify an animal, so if lost, it could be returned to its proper owner.

But Harpo had all that stuff printed on his collar tag.

From my studio filing cabinet, I pulled the medical records Anita had given me for the Persian and riffled through them. There was no mention anywhere of the cat's former veterinarian having implanted him with an ID chip. Could it have been done off the record?

As I smoothed Harpo's champagne-colored fur back over the raised spot, I remembered Bonelli's comment about looking for a needle in a haystack. This probably was a much smaller haystack than she'd imagined.

I thought of calling her, but hesitated. What if this turned out to be another false alarm? Would Harpo be whisked off by the FBI to be scanned? Hadn't the poor animal gone through enough already?

I gave him a hug. "I'll bet you've been a pawn in this nasty game all along and never even knew it." If the chip he carried was the one everyone was hunting for, by now it had become an unhealthy thing, like a tumor, threatening Harpo's life.

Time to get it out of him.

A glance at the wall clock told me it was almost six. Still worth a try, though.

I parked Harpo in the drying cage, pulled out my phone, and dialed. A female voice on the other end mustered the energy to sound cheerful. "Chadwick Veterinary Clinic."

"Hi, is Dr. Coccia still there?"

She paused. "Yesss, but I think he's just getting ready to—"

"Would you please put him on? Tell him it's Cassie McGlone . . . and it's an emergency."

Chapter 21

Mark Coccia passed his scanner over the base of Harpo's neck for a third time. From his frown, I could tell he wasn't getting the results he'd expected.

"There's definitely something under the skin," he said. "I can feel it too. But I'm not picking up the usual coding, just gibberish."

This was, however, the result I'd expected. "Then I'm right—it's not a normal pet chip. DeLeuw had it made by a cybersecurity company, out on the West Coast, to work with Dion's encryption system. The company admits that, but said they have no way of knowing what key he would have programmed into it. They also gave George a special scanner to read the chip. The cops found one among his things, and the FBI has it now."

Mark stared at me as if I'd told him aliens had landed on Center Street and we needed to make tinfoil hats so they couldn't read our minds. "For real?"

"I swear. That's why so many people are suddenly hell-bent on getting ahold of this cat. Can you take the chip out of him?"

That question stymied him even further. "I mean . . . I'm sure I could, physically. Some chips in animals can be hard to find, because they're meant to stay in, but this one seems close to the surface."

"Great! Then it should be easy, right?"

"Trouble is, ethically, it's more of a problem. He's not your cat, Cassie. If DeLeuw willed him to somebody, he intended Harpo to go to that person, chip and all. We could get in trouble if we tampered with it."

He was probably right, but the legalities didn't matter to me right now. It made me frantic just to know that Mark and I were the only ones in the clinic right now, standing between this tiny object and the bad guys who wanted it so desperately.

I reminded him, "People who don't give a damn about Harpo for any other reason are desperate to get this chip. They want to either decode George's files or destroy the chip so the files can never be decoded. If they get their hands on this cat, they won't have your ethics—or your skills—when they try to take the thing out."

Mark rested the scanner on the surgical table and studied Harpo as he pondered our dilemma. "Have you told your detective friend about this?"

"Not yet. I got her all psyched up for nothing about the tags on his collar, so I didn't want to go to her with this until I was sure."

"Well, we know it isn't a conventional ID chip." Mark managed a tired smile, having also put in a long day. "I'll take an X-ray, just to get a better look."

"I can help you with that, and hold him still," I volunteered. "I've done it before."

He nodded. "We'll show the pictures to Bonelli. If she thinks the chip might be evidence in a criminal investigation and wants me to remove it, I will. Then she can take it with her."

I grinned, glad to have someone so level-headed on my side. "Sounds like a plan."

Half an hour later Bonelli and I sat together in the clinic's waiting room while Mark wrapped up the minor surgery. The square-jawed young officer who had accompanied her stood casually on guard by the front door, just in case.

"I feel like an idiot," the detective admitted. "My dog, Sarge, has one of those chips, but it still never occurred to me that DeLeuw might have hidden the electronic key *in* his cat."

"I should have guessed too. I was fooled by the fact that Harpo had a license on his collar—I don't know of many pets that have both. If I thought about it at all, I figured for some reason George just didn't want to chip him." I noticed that Bonelli looked as exhausted as the rest of us, having fit the Secret of the Cat's Collar into whatever else her busy schedule entailed that day. "I sure hope this doesn't turn out to be another false alarm. You'll never forgive me!"

"I don't see it that way," she insisted. "There's a

good chance you're right, Cassie, and even if you're not, I give you points for thinking of it. At this stage we'll take any lead we can get."

Mark finally came out of the surgical suite carrying a small stoppered vial. Using a magnifying glass, he showed us the contents—a tiny, clear cylinder rounded at each end, with mysterious electronic bits stuffed inside it.

"Looks like a regulation pet implant," I said.

"Yeah, DeLeuw must have gone to a lot of trouble. Maybe he got the California company to make the chip, program it, and put it in this casing. Then he must've had a vet—or someone with similar skills—insert it into the cat." He handed the artifact to Bonelli. "Since this may have been the cause of one murder and one arson fire so far, I'm turning it over to the person with the gun."

"Thank you, Dr. Coccia." With a smile, she tucked it into the breast pocket of her button-down shirt. "I appreciate your help . . . both of you. Officer Jacoby will be cruising the neighborhood periodically tonight, just to make sure there are no more problems."

After she and the young officer left, and the burden of our discovery had passed into their hands, I became more aware than before of being alone in the clinic after hours with Mark. He cleared his throat as if also self-conscious.

"I just sedated Harpo, but he's still groggy," he said. "I should keep him here overnight to sleep it off."

"Good idea." I shouldered the strap of my purse. "I'll come pick him up tomorrow?"

"Please do." He regarded me with a worried frown. "Are you going to be all right over there by yourself? There might still be people out there who think you have the cat, and the chip."

Tempted as I was to suggest he keep me company, it felt too soon to take that step. "I should be fine, as long as that squad car is on patrol," I told him. "But thanks, Mark. For the concern, for believing me, and for going to all of this trouble."

"No problem—it livened up a dull evening." His hair mussed and his scrubs wrinkled from his long day, he still managed a crooked, flirtatious smile. "Is it always like this around you, Cassie? Nonstop excitement?"

I knew a good exit line when I heard one, and winked on my way out the door. "Guess you'll just have to stick around and find out!"

Because I'd been in a hurry and toting Harpo, I'd driven the three and a half blocks to the veterinary clinic. It was past eight now, Halloweenish clouds hid the moon, and the air carried a scent of rain.

I badly wanted to indulge in some optimism again and believe that *this* time we'd finally found the key to DeLeuw's files. But I'd been wrong before, so maybe I shouldn't have been getting my hopes up. Plus, I'd had so many nasty surprises at my place on recent evenings that I stayed alert as I turned onto my block.

A new-looking dark sedan sat across the street in the same spot as on Sunday evening, though this time it was unoccupied. Probably a coincidence, though. Andy wouldn't dare show up here again, would he?

Plenty of guys driving around with revoked licenses, Nick had said.

Or it could be an entirely different car. Not as if I'd been able to tell either the make or the license plate the first time.

Playing it safe, I parked in front of the shop instead of in my rear lot and got out the keys to the front door. I opened it quietly—no string of bells, like at Dawn's store—and looked around for signs of anything amiss.

I also sniffed the air. No smoke, that was good!

I postponed turning on the overheard lights as a precaution. A streetlamp that shone through my display window gave me enough light to creep back toward the boarders' area. But by the time I reached the playroom, with its many wall shelves and cat trees, I had just about decided all was well and I had nothing to fear.

Then I heard a series of sounds that stopped my heart.

The squeak of a condo door opening. The hiss of a cat—probably Stormy.

Sounds of a tussle. A man's muffled curses.

The little gray lion streaked out of the boarding area and past me. He paused for a split second in the playroom to get his bearings. In a quicksilver movement, he leaped to the top of a carpeted tower and then to one of the high wall shelves. From there, he glowered down at me and hissed again.

Startled, I lost a second before pulling out my cell phone. I had just dialed 9-1-1 when a man in burglar clothes—black sweater and jeans—came lurching around the corner and stopped dead.

He also looked surprised to see me. At least, as far as I could tell.

The lower half of his face was covered with a mask. Not the bandana type that bank robbers wear in old movies, though. This was a specialized, honeycombed design that hooked over his ears. The kind you might see on a doctor, or a worker handling toxic materials.

I'd guessed wrong, at least this evening. I could recognize from his hair and build that the intruder was not Andy. But he might prove to be even more dangerous.

Maybe I was just fed up. Or maybe I fell back on what I'd been taught about facing down a threatening animal. Whatever the reason, I went on the offense.

"Jerry, what the hell are you doing here?"

Unfortunately, he'd come prepared to be even more offensive. He pulled out a gun with an unusually long barrel. From watching TV crime shows, I knew a silencer when I saw one.

Jerry had come prepared tonight to shoot somebody, if necessary.

And the face mask wasn't a disguise, I realized, but a barrier against his cat allergy. Since I'd already recognized him, he tugged it down to enhance the impact of his threat.

My cocky attitude dissolved, along with the cartilage in my knees. I'd survived getting pushed

around by Andy, but I'd never faced down a fire-
arm before. Now my brain found it hard to focus
on anything else. It was just a small pistol, probably, but with that long black tube attached it loomed
like a cannon.

Then I noticed the gun was quivering a little,
because the hand that held it was shaking. Jerry
looked almost as scared as I felt.

*Maybe he doesn't have the nerve to shoot me. Maybe
it's all a bluff.*

His first words bolstered that slim hope.
"Cassie, I just want that cat. Help me catch him
and I won't hurt you."

"That cat? Why would you want Stormy?"

Jerry blinked. I guessed that, hunting through
the boarding cages in dim lighting, he'd seized
upon the only pale-colored longhair. After all, Jerry
had never handled Harpo or even gotten very
close to him.

"Don't screw around!" he warned me now. "You
thought you'd disguise him, I guess, by shaving off
his fur. But I know that's George's cat! You're the
expert, so you're gonna get him down from that
shelf and put him in a carrier."

For a second I thought about actually doing
that. But as mean as Stormy was, I still couldn't put
him in danger, and I certainly couldn't betray a
customer that way. "Jerry, that's not Harpo. This
cat is gray, not cream. Let me turn on the lights."

Taking a risk, I slid my hand along the wall toward the light switch and flipped it. My intruder
flinched at the sudden glare, but at least he didn't
fire. I realized that Stormy's lion cut left him with

long fur only around his face, his paws, and the tip of his tail. Maybe that wasn't enough for Jerry to be able to tell the difference.

"And Harpo has copper eyes," I added. "This cat's eyes are greenish-gold."

Like Ross would be able to see that from where he stood. But when he glanced up at the animal, I reached into my pocket and pressed Send on my phone.

Or hoped I did.

Jerry's eyes flashed back to me. "Damn it. If that's not Harpo, where is he?"

"He's not here. He's somewhere safe."

"*Where?*" He leveled the gun at me again.

No way was I going to tell him the cat was at the veterinary clinic. If he happened to know that was only a few blocks away, he'd probably break in there next. Mark might still be closing up, and I didn't want Jerry turning that gun on him.

Forcing down my fear, I shook my head and played dumb. "I swear, I have no idea why all of you people are so hell-bent on stealing him. Danielle, Marjorie, and now you? How much do you think he's worth? He can't be shown and he can't be bred. You'd go through all this for a few hundreds dollars?"

"Of course not," Jerry spat the words.

"You figure George might've left a pile of money to whoever gives him a home? Marjorie and Danielle seemed to think so." I turned up my palms in surrender. "Hey, I'm not looking to keep him. If the will says he goes to somebody else, I'll gladly hand him over. . . ."

"At this point, he's worth my life! And . . . my family—"

That got my attention. "What do you mean?"

Before he could answer, Jerry sneezed, hard. If I'd been a trained CIA agent, I might have darted forward and grabbed his gun. But I didn't have that kind of skill . . . or nerve.

I just froze, heart thudding. Hoped one of those sneezes didn't make him accidentally pull the trigger.

If Officer Jacoby is still cruising the neighborhood, please, please let him wonder why my store lights are still on!

Unfortunately, Jerry noticed my sidelong glance toward the front window. He gestured with the gun for me to move farther back, into the boarding area. Meanwhile, he used his free hand to pull a handkerchief from his pocket and wipe his nose.

A big, expensive-looking handkerchief. I couldn't see a monogram, but I still bet it would match the one found in Nick's truck. Jerry saw me checking it out and stuffed it back into his pants pocket.

"You should have taken an antihistamine," I told him.

He responded with a glare. "I did."

And, of course, he'd taken the extra precaution of wearing the mask. But then he'd pulled that down, the better to snarl at me.

In the boarding area, I stopped in front of the empty condo that had held Stormy. "You said Harpo was worth your life. Why?"

"There are people who will kill me if I don't get him back. If you're hiding him, they'll be after you, too. So one way or the other, you'd better tell me where he is."

Maybe if I pretended to see things Jerry's way, I could reason with him. "You killed George, didn't you? Probably over the hidden files. But that wasn't exactly cold-blooded, was it? You didn't bring a gun that time."

A series of emotions flickered across the assistant's face. "I didn't plan to. I was told to make sure he'd destroyed those files, but he told me he'd encrypted them instead. That was crazy! It was like he was blackmailing the company . . . but even beyond R&F, blackmailing some very dangerous people." Jerry bottled up another powerful sneeze, and I thought brain matter might shoot out of his ears. In a stuffy, de-nasalized voice, he went on. "I asked him, what if somebody breaks the code? George said they'd need his personal key, and he'd put that in a very safe place." Jerry swallowed hard, Adam's apple flexing, in what might have been sadness or anger. "Then he bent down to pet the cat. Damn, I should've guessed then!"

"And while he was bent over, you grabbed the stone sculpture and hit him."

"*They* made me do it. They said to destroy the file, and if I couldn't do that . . ."

Sharply, he pulled himself together. "We're wasting time! If this cat isn't Harpo, where is he? In one of these other cages?"

"No. And you'll never find out if you shoot me."

"That's probably true." He glanced around, and a sick smile spread across his face. "But I can start shooting cats. How many do I have to kill before you tell me what I want to know?"

Call me crazy, but this upset me even more than Jerry's threat against my life. It was something I could easily picture him doing—in graphic images that horrified me.

"Harpo's not here at all!" I blurted out. "He's with the police."

"I don't believe you. Why would they take him?"

"They know about the chip, and they took him away to remove it. The FBI has George's scanner, so they'll be able to read the key and open the files. By tomorrow they'll probably know everything." I edged back toward the playroom to lead Jerry away from the condos. "So you see? It's no use! Even if you shoot me, you'll only make things worse for yourself."

"That can't be true. You're making it up!" He was red in the face by now, and I suspected not just from frustration. His eyes looked puffy too. Obviously, his antihistamine was not up to spending time in close quarters with half a dozen cats.

When he let out another violent sneeze, I sprinted through the playroom. Maybe I could make it to the front door . . . or at least the sales counter, and my pepper spray.

A bullet ricocheted off the counter ahead of me—Jerry wasn't a bad shot. The silencer made a strange *ptew* sound that probably couldn't be heard outside.

Cut off, I dodged behind one of our tallest cat trees, about six feet tall with lots of perches. But even though I'm slim, it still left plenty of me exposed.

A strangled yowl spiraled down from above our heads. Stormy still crouched on the highest wall shelf. All the commotion below had him switching his tail and growling.

Jerry stalked me for real now. "If Harpo was with the police, you'd have told me in the beginning and saved yourself a lot of trouble. If he's not in any of the cages, I bet he's upstairs in your apartment. Let's go up together and have a look, eh?"

No! When he found no Harpo up there, either, he might start shooting my own cats! Call me crazy, but I'd defend them the same as I would my children . . . if I had any.

Jerry had planted himself directly across from where I still crouched behind the cat tree. Whether I ran for the front door or the back, he could fire to stop me.

Why the hell hasn't Officer Jacoby dropped by to ask why I'm working so late? Or why hasn't somebody responded to my damn 9-1-1 call?

But I was punching my phone buttons blind. Maybe I touched something else instead of Send?

"How do you get to the second floor? Through that door?" Jerry demanded now. "Let's go!"

When I didn't move, he lunged forward to grab my arm. Convulsed in another sneeze.

With a shove that took all my strength, I toppled the cat tower onto him.

I figured the piece weighed about sixty pounds. It might not hurt him badly, but it ought to slow him up. I dashed for the front door.

Though the weight of the tower knocked him to his knees, Jerry got off another wild shot. It went through the front window.

Mid-escape, I screeched to a halt.

He let out a burst of X-rated language as he struggled out from under the cat tree. Seeing him hampered for a second, I backed toward the rear doorway. . . .

And found myself caught in arms like bands of cold steel.

Chapter 22

I tried to scream. With the squeeze on my diaphragm, though, it came out like one of Tigger's mewling sounds.

My terrified mind ticked off the possibilities. *Mark? No, he wouldn't scare me like this.*

Andy?

A deep voice dripped with scorn. "For God's sake, Ross, get up. Can't you do anything right?"

Schroeder. I should have guessed he wouldn't leave his reluctant hit man unsupervised.

Jerry staggered to his feet, sniffling, eyes almost swollen shut. But he still held the gun.

"You've made a mess of this job, just like you did that last one," Schroeder told him with an icy calm. "Now that you've spilled your guts to this girl, you'll have to shoot her. Can you at least handle that?"

"I—I don't know," Jerry stammered. "I can hardly see—"

"You can see well enough, idiot." Holding me by the back of the neck with one hand, Schroeder snatched up a fishing-pole toy from the top of a cat tree. He tried to force my wrists together, but I realized what he was up to. Not so worried about Jerry anymore, I tried to twist free, even brought my sneakered foot down hard on Schroeder's instep.

Without a word, he slapped me hard across the face.

I felt shock even more than pain. Andy had shoved me against the bookcase in the heat of anger. This blow was emotionless. It let me know I mattered to Schroeder as little as one of those cats in the condos.

Stunned, tasting blood in my mouth, I finally stood still. He forced my hands behind my back and wound the long, thin cord of the fishing pole tightly around my wrists. Holding the wand of the cat toy to keep the string taut, he stepped to one side of me.

"There," he said to Jerry, in a patronizing tone. "Does that make it easier?"

The assistant threw his shoulders back and set his jaw, pulling himself together physically if not mentally. He lifted the gun again.

Is this how I'm going to die? Tied up and shot point-blank, execution style? In the playroom of my shop, designed to be such a happy place?

"Don't worry, Ross," Schroeder encouraged him. "No one will know it was you. They'll figure it was a robber, or maybe some ex-boyfriend she ticked off."

That random comment made my already racing heart stutter. Did this guy somehow know about Andy? Even if he'd just taken a lucky guess, he was right. If I was found in my shop shot dead and with a bruised face, everyone would think my ex had done it. They might never suspect either of these guys.

Ross seemed like the weak link here, though. If Schroeder could use psychology on him, so could I.

"Sure, Jerry, shoot me," I told him. "Then he'll have you killed! And in your obituary, he'll say what a loyal employee you always were. Like he said DeLeuw had 'high standards.' "

I heard Schroeder catch his breath, and braced for him to hit me again, but he resisted. In my side vision, I finally could see the taller man clearly. Even for this job, he wore a pale blue button-down shirt and dark slacks, as if he'd come from the office. Disposing of me was just another inconvenient wrinkle in his overall agenda.

Meanwhile, Ross appeared to consider my words. He held out the gun toward his boss, handle first. "You want her dead so much, you shoot her."

Would Schroeder do it? He'd gone to West Point, so he probably could handle a gun.

He gave his head, with its silver sideburns, a weary shake. "See, Ross, that's why you'll always be an assistant, never a leader. You can't handle the responsibility. Can't make the tough decisions." Still holding me by the makeshift leash, Schroeder reached for the pistol.

Jerry had changed his mind, though, and held it back. He looked his boss hard in the eye and nodded. "Y'know, Chuck, you're right. It's time I took charge."

He raised the gun and aimed . . . about a foot to my left.

With a gasp, Schroeder dropped the wand of the fishing pole and ducked. Jerry's shot just missed him and ricocheted toward the wall shelves.

I heard a high shriek from Stormy. Was he hit?

No, just outraged. But even an alpha cat like him knew it was time to bail. He leaped sideways from his shelf, trying to reach the floor . . .

Just as Schroeder backed underneath.

Stormy landed on his head, a one-cat SWAT team.

They went down together as Schroeder flailed with both hands, trying to fend off a demonic assault of teeth and claws. Growls and hisses mixed with his screams of pain.

Tough guy. Completely undone by a pussycat.

With the fishing pole's string gone slack, I worked my hands free. Meanwhile, Stormy split for the grooming studio. Schroeder—still reeling from the cat's attack, blood from his scalp dripping into his eyes—groped his way toward the back door.

I rolled one of the smaller cat trees into his path, and he went sprawling.

Jerry laughed until he bent double. He didn't even notice the whirling red and blue lights that suddenly filled my front window.

At last, the cavalry to the rescue! Officer Jacoby burst through the door, gun drawn. Guess the shot fired through the window had finally gotten his attention.

His command, "Drop your weapon!" wiped the smile from Jerry's face, but the assistant readily obeyed.

Back on his feet, Schroeder tried again to sneak out the back way, but a second officer met him there.

Jacoby took one look at the three of us and called for an ambulance. While we waited, he took my statement. It hurt to talk, but I managed to give him the whole story. He shook his head in wonder at some points and chuckled at others. Then he read Ross and Schroeder their rights and cuffed them.

The EMTs arrived. One checked me over and decided that, aside from a couple of loose teeth and a swelling jaw, I seemed to be all right. Chuck and Jerry got a ride to the hospital, though, under police guard.

Leaving my shop, they made a pathetic pair. One short, one tall. One bruised, puffy-eyed, and sneezing, the other half-scalped and bleeding.

I almost felt sorry for them. But they really should have known better than to threaten a cat lady on her own turf.

Chapter 23

My mother stood on the sidewalk to admire my shop's new front window. "Very nice. Not to hurt your feelings, Cassie, but the professional lettering looks better than when you stenciled it yourself."

"I'd be the first to admit that. Guess the chamber of commerce spared no expense." I held the door open for her. "Come inside and meet everyone."

It was a Friday, exactly two weeks after the cops had arrested Ross and Schroeder in my shop. The chamber guys had installed my new window that afternoon, to replace the one with the bullet hole. It was my thank-you gift for having caught DeLeuw's killer and suffered so much damage to my humble establishment in the process. More practical, I supposed, than a medal or even an honorary detective's badge.

Tonight, in addition to Mom, I'd invited friends who'd helped me survive the DeLeuw drama for a belated "window-raising." Making do with the resources at hand, I was serving cold cuts and side dishes off the sales counter and beverages from my coffee bar. Everyone congregated mainly in the playroom. Sarah and I had vacuumed everything in there, so our guests could rest their plates and glasses on the perches and shelves and could sit on some of the lower cubes and cylinders.

My mother had come right from work, and so looked a little overdressed in her khaki slacks and pastel tweed blazer. But they give her an air of authority, which I supposed she needed among all of those lawyers, since she was only five foot three. Her hair was wavier than mine, but there was enough of a facial resemblance that everyone guessed our relationship immediately.

Mom had set foot in the shop only once before, when I'd first opened. I introduced her to the early birds who had arrived promptly at five. Louis couldn't make it, but Nick, Dion, Anita, and Hector were all on hand.

"Dawn you already know," I added.

"Hi, Barbara!" With a plastic cup of iced tea in one hand, Dawn caught her in a brief hug.

In the weeks since Jerry's arrest, the full story behind DeLeuw's murder had gradually come to light in our regional and local news. It received lots of coverage, as one of the more colorful crimes Chadwick had seen in a long while.

Just for the offenses they committed at my place that night, Jerry Ross faced charges of breaking and entering (my old back door with the single lock had been pushed in), attempted theft (of Harpo), and aggravated assault for pulling a gun on me. That was even before they nailed him for killing George and then trying to frame Nick Janos.

Schroeder also got charged with assault for hitting me, and with unlawful restraint. But those accusations might soon be the least of his problems.

Once decrypted, DeLeuw's secret files turned out to be as incriminating as everyone had feared—or hoped, depending on your point of view. They documented how the drug money had been filtered through a series of complex transactions to conceal its true source. George had even included an addendum to explain the convoluted process. It seemed clear that he expected, at some point, to expose R&F's involvement to the authorities.

So far, that background information had only been hinted at in the newspapers. I knew about it from Bonelli, but I imagined more details would come out as various people were questioned and maybe prosecuted. Right now I was just happy that the right suspects had been fingered and the wrong ones cleared of all suspicion.

I led a quick tour of the cat condos, now fully occupied with a dozen boarders. Ironically, my decision to face down a gunman rather than put the cats' lives in jeopardy had boosted my credibility and attracted more customers. When my guests remarked on the layout of the playroom and construction of the condos, I quickly passed the praise along to Nick. I also credited his sprinkler system with saving my shop during the arson incident.

In return, he ragged me about putting off installing the rear dead bolt until *after* Jerry had broken in. "Isn't there some expression," he teased, "about locking the barn door after the horse has run away?"

A few guests were disappointed that Stormy, now known as the cat who nearly scalped Charles Schroeder, had already been collected by his owner.

"Why does anyone keep a vicious animal like that?" my mother asked, with a shudder.

"Home security?" Nick wisecracked.

"His owners swear he's a total 'mush' with them," I said. "Go figure."

Peering into the screened enclosures, Mom asked, "Which cat is DeLeuw's, the one everyone was after?"

"He's not here anymore," Dawn told her.

"Yeah," I said. "Quite a story behind that."

One of the biggest surprises was a letter George had left with his trust company for Marjorie. He'd requested that it be passed along to her in the event of his "death or mental incapacitation."

"Turned out the FBI knew about the letter but had never opened it," I explained. "They figured it was just about some personal matter between George and his ex-wife. If they'd been a bit snoopier, they could have saved themselves a lot of time and trouble."

In the letter, George left Harpo to Marjorie and explained the cat's connection to the secret files. He provided for her to continue receiving alimony payments from his estate, on the condition that she either give Harpo the best of care or find him a good home with someone else. George added

that he was entrusting Marjorie with this responsibility because he knew that, like him, she wanted
justice for Renée.

As our group drifted back out to the playroom,
my mother remembered my concerns about
DeLeuw's ex-wife. "So the woman who put his first
cat to sleep has the other one now?"

I shook my head. "She didn't really want the
responsibility and left it up to me to give him a
good home. Unfortunately, my apartment's already at full cat capacity." I glanced over my shoulder at my assistant, who was chatting with Anita
and Hector. "Sarah adores playing with Harpo,
though, and she's got the grooming skills to keep
him in good shape. So I officially signed him over
to her."

"Sounds like a happy ending," Mom concluded.

Dawn laughed. "Your daughter keeps convert-
ing more people every day to the joys of cat ownership!" She launched into an explanation of the
clicker-training method I'd taught her and how
well it had worked with Tigger. I let her keep my
mother occupied while I brought more snacks and
bottles of wine and soda down from my apartment.

To my surprise, though, on my second trip
down, Mom met me at the bottom of the stairs.
She took me aside and pulled a long envelope out
of her purse. "I don't want to upset you, Cassie,
but I promised to give you this. I haven't looked at
it and I don't know what it says. But I figure if it's
anything . . . bad . . . you can always hand it over to
the police."

I recognized the official Morris Plaza return
address in the corner and my name in Andy's

rather childish scrawl. Since my mother no longer expected me to reconcile with him, and was now thinking in terms of collecting evidence against him, I just nodded.

Returning to the front of the store, I tucked the envelope out of sight beneath the sales counter. Then I finished replenishing the snacks and drinks.

Dion approached me, dressed up for the party in faded but nontattered jeans and a gray T-shirt that read, in digitized letters, LET ME DROP EVERY-THING AND WORK ON *YOUR* PROBLEM. From his plate, I noticed he'd been one of the few people, besides me, brave enough to sample Dawn's excellent quinoa casserole.

In his oddly formal way, he told me the Encyte people had reached out to him directly about developing his system. "After what happened with DeLeuw," he said, "I guess I should find a lawyer this time, to protect my interests. I asked my cousin, but he says that's outside his area. He told me I needed to find someone who deals with intellectual property."

"I know just the person to help you with that!" I steered Dion toward my mother, who seemed happy to talk shop with someone.

Mark arrived a little late, having had to close up the clinic. His business had gotten a publicity boost too because of his role in finding and removing the implanted chip. As he headed in our direction, I remembered the unopened envelope. I intercepted Dawn and asked her not to mention Andy in front of Mark.

After the three of us made small talk about Tigger's latest checkup, Mark told me, "I still feel terrible that I didn't know that Ross guy was holding you at gunpoint that night, just a few blocks away! I might've been able to help you somehow."

"I said the same thing," Dawn told him. "Sounds like Cassie did okay on her own, though."

While building himself a sandwich with sliced turkey and cheese, Mark asked me, "I guess you never really suspected Ross?"

"Not at first. When he came to the house after the murder, he acted genuinely surprised and upset. Only after I did a little research on him, and his history with Redmond & Fowler, did I start to wonder if Jerry could have had a motive."

With our plastic plates and cups, we settled on various pieces of low cat furniture. I explained to them what I'd pieced together, with input from Bonelli and Marjorie. "When Jerry first joined R&F as an executive assistant, about twelve years ago, he hoped to eventually become an associate and then maybe a vice president. But apparently, that's a tricky move to pull off at an investment-banking firm. The higher-ups were more impressed with his skills at organization and problem-solving than at finances. So even though he made good money, and worked with the top managing directors, he never could break out of the 'assistant' category. That drove him a little nuts."

"After twelve years?" Mark raised an eyebrow. "I can see why."

"The way Bonelli explained it to me, when the top R&F guys got wind of the encrypted files, they leaned on Ross as the person most likely to know DeLeuw's secrets. He had more access than anyone else, and he was, after all, their 'problem-solver.' Schroeder promised Ross that if he found and destroyed the files, he'd get that promotion. If he didn't, though, he might become expendable . . . in more ways than one."

Mark grimaced. "Sounds like they really squeezed the guy."

"From something he said to me that night, I think the drug cartel maybe even have threatened his family," I added. "He had all these Facebook posts of his wife and two kids, looking totally happy and carefree. I can't help wondering, did his wife know about any of this? If not, what a terrible shock it must have been!"

"No kidding," Dawn agreed. "Successful young businessman . . . clean-cut, suburban husband and father . . . and ruthless murderer! She must feel like she's been living with Jekyll and Hyde."

"She also might have been nagging him all these years to try harder to move up the corporate ladder," Mark suggested. "But unless she's Lady Macbeth, she probably didn't expect him to resort to murder!"

I remembered how Jerry's hand had trembled, holding that gun. "I don't think he ever expected to either. Killing DeLeuw was a desperation move— he just grabbed whatever weapon was handy. He did come armed to my shop, but I don't think he expected to run into me that night. He saw my car was gone and probably hoped I'd be out for the whole evening."

In front of Mark, I didn't voice the rest of my thoughts. That maybe Jerry had made a few unsuccessful attempts to break in before. That maybe he was the driver lurking across the street the time Mark and I went on our date and I came home to find the stair rail broken.

That maybe I'd been wrong to blame Andy.

I thought again about the unopened letter stashed beneath the sales counter, but pushed it out of my mind once more. Whatever it might say, for now I was going to relax and enjoy the party.

A single tap on my arm snapped me back to the present. Mark asked, "What happened with DeLeuw's sister, the one who was so intent on getting Harpo?"

"Bonelli said she might have been conspiring with Schroeder and the other managing directors to protect R&F's reputation. Danielle apparently tried to find out details about the encryption system from Encyte, but George hadn't told them much. So in the end, she might have tried to destroy the chip by more low-tech methods."

Dawn guessed my meaning first. "She set fire to your shop? Didn't we both say that, because of the nail polish remover, it was probably a woman?"

"Bonelli thinks Danielle did it, or at least hired the arsonist. At least any money she might stand to inherit will still be tied up while they investigate."

"Think Danielle and Jerry were working together?" Mark speculated.

"Probably not, but both of them were trying to curry favor with Schroeder." It left a bad taste in my mouth to even say the man's name. Closing my eyes for a second, I felt again that tooth-rattling slap across my face, and was overcome with the same sense of helpless rage. "That's the guy I really want to see convicted! If there's a diabolical mastermind in this plot, it's him."

Now that my guests had finished most of the cold cuts and salads, Sarah and I put out her divine brownies and a selection of cupcakes from Cottone's. Anita and Hector were the first to gravitate toward the desserts, and I caught up with them there.

"I gotta say, I never liked that Mr. Ross," she recalled. "He always kind of looked *through* me, instead of *at* me. Even Mr. DeLeuw never did that! But still, I never thought Mr. Ross could be a violent person."

"The drug people made him do it," Hector explained to her, lifting a brownie onto his plastic plate. "That's what the papers said. They made him kill Mr. DeLeuw to cover up what the company was doing."

"Is that right?" Anita asked me.

Though it was an oversimplification of the whole complex scheme, I agreed. "Pretty much, yeah."

She frowned and clucked her tongue. "Those drugs! They're behind so much of the bad stuff that goes on, aren't they?" She turned to Sarah. "Cassie told me you got Harpo now! How's he getting along at your place?"

"I think he's really happy to have a whole house to run around in again," my assistant said. "Though I'm sure mine is nowhere near the size of his last home!"

Anita chuckled. "Not many people's are. But I can't complain—the lawyers are still paying me to clean it once a week!"

Then we noticed the front of the shop had gone quiet, with all conversation stopped and all heads turned toward the window facing the street.

A police car had just pulled up outside.

Chapter 24

My guests remained silent and tense as Angela Bonelli stepped through the door. After all, the last time most of them had spoken to her, they'd been under suspicion for murder.

She paused just beyond the sales counter, folded her arms, and swept the gathering with a baleful gaze. "We got a complaint about a rowdy party," she said. "Might've known it would be this crowd!"

Finally people broke into smiles and nervous titters. I could have warned them that Bonelli's stealth sense of humor took some getting used to.

I only had to introduce her to Dawn and my mother, since everyone else present already had met her in some capacity. I persuaded her to grab a plate of food and a glass of wine. She made conversation with everyone for a few minutes, then stepped to the front of the room and tapped a spoon against her plastic "glass" for attention.

"I'm not comfortable making speeches, so this will be brief," she said. "There are several people here tonight whom I'd like to thank for helping me solve my first murder case in Chadwick. I've dealt with homicides before, but big-city crime is different. With this case, in particular, it helped to know background on the suspects—more than they were willing to tell a police detective." Her penetrating gaze swept the room. "Anita, Dion, Nick . . . in your official statements and afterward, you provided valuable information that helped us piece things together. Dr. Coccia, your expertise and willingness to go the extra mile helped us find the chip and remove it from the cat before the bad guys could."

Mark waved a modest hand. "It was nothing, really. The Chadwick PD will be getting my bill."

When the chuckles died down, Bonelli went on. "As for Cassie . . . I admit, I was annoyed at first when I heard she was questioning all my potential suspects. But after I saw her intentions were good, I realized she might be in a position to hear and see things that I couldn't. What I didn't expect was that she'd be putting herself at risk simply by keeping the cat in her shop. Fortunately, she didn't suffer any serious consequences, and even ended up capturing the killer."

Everyone else applauded. I wanted to hide, but made a mock bow instead.

"You sure did a number on Ross and Schroeder." Bonelli grinned. "Those guys were a mess when they showed up in the ER!"

"I can't take credit for Jerry's allergy," I reminded her. "Or for Stormy attacking Schroeder."

"Still," the detective said, "if you ever want to apply to the police academy, I'll vouch for you."

Some egged me on to accept this challenge, though above their voices I could hear Mom's frantic protests.

"Thanks," I said, "but I'm like Batman—I work on the fringes of the law."

"Don't you mean Catwoman?" Dawn teased.

Bonelli laughed and pointed at her. "Hey, that's good!"

The detective left shortly afterward, and I wondered if I should have given her the letter from Andy. But I wanted to read it myself first, and I'd had no chance so far to do that.

By nine thirty, the party began to break up. Almost all of the guests happened to be self-employed and needed to get up for work in the morning, even on Saturday. Mom was one of the few exceptions, but she had a long drive home. Anyway, after having had a chance to talk with Mark, she seemed eager to leave me alone with him.

With a knowing squint, she asked in a hushed tone, "I suppose that's the 'doctor' you've been dating?"

"Don't start," I warned her. "We've only been out twice. But he's a great guy! He runs his own clinic and he was amazing during all the Harpo craziness. Stayed late to remove the chip, kept the cat safe at his place—"

"You don't need to sell me." She smiled. "He spent ten minutes of our conversation singing *your* praises."

I felt my cheeks redden. "He did?"

"He said when you believe in something, you don't give up. I assume he was talking about this murder case. Just make sure you don't give up on him!"

I gave her a one-armed hug. "It'll be more fun if you don't pressure me. Okay?"

As the party wound down, Sarah and I excused ourselves for a few minutes to check on the boarders. Meanwhile, I heard scratching and Mango's distinctive wail from the door that led to the second-floor staircase.

"I'm going to run up and check on my cats too," I told Sarah. First, though, I stopped by the sales counter and stuck the envelope from Andy in my pocket.

Alone, upstairs, I had a chance to really absorb the impact of the day's celebration. It brought sudden tears to my eyes. DeLeuw's murder had been a shock and a tragedy, but it also had drawn new friends into my life and deepened some of the relationships I already had. With their backup, I'd even grown more of a spine than I'd ever had before.

I felt suddenly moved by the way we'd all helped one another and made sacrifices to help solve the case and bring George's killer—or killers—to justice. I even felt a greater appreciation for the three graceful companions who wound around my ankles now, even though they were simply trying to charm a late supper out of me.

In this positive frame of mind, I felt strong enough to face the unknown content of Andy's letter. I waited until all three cats were happily chomping away at their food before I sat down with the unsealed envelope at my yellow kitchen table. My stomach still knotted as I opened the sheet of official-looking stationery:

> *Cassie—*
>
> *I know you told me never to contact you again, even in writing, but I had to make one last attempt. When I tried to talk to you at the business expo and you wouldn't even listen to me, told me to never come around again, and threatened to tell the cops, it finally opened my eyes. I realized I could lose my new job or even go to jail—all because of my temper. That was partly why I got fired from my last job at the mall, you know. I got mad one day, cursed at the boss, and he told me to get out. Guess I did that kind of thing once too often with you, too.*
>
> *Anyway, I'm going to one of those anger-management groups, and I think it's going to help. I'm not saying this to get you back, because I've probably screwed up too bad to ever make things right again between us. So I won't bother you again, or ask your mother to give you any more messages from me.*
>
> *I'm making progress, but I've got a long way to go. Meanwhile, hope you find somebody who treats you the way I should have. Have a good life.*
> *—Andy*

Briefly, I suffered one of those pangs of sympathy to which I was far too prone where Andy was concerned. But I'd nipped it in the bud. If he'd learned his lesson, wonderful! I hoped anger management worked for him. With any luck, he'd never inflict on another woman the physical pain and mental anxiety that he'd put me through.

Andy was right about one thing. I did deserve someone better. I even had someone in mind.

When I went back downstairs, only Mark and Sarah remained. He was helping her collect the remnants of the party—almost-finished trays of cold cuts, half-empty bottles of soda and wine— and dispose of the dirty plates in the trash.

"I'll bring the leftover food up to my kitchen," I told Sarah. "As long as the front rooms are straightened, we can let the rest of this go until tomorrow."

"You sure?" Then she saw Mark slip an arm around my waist and stammered, "R-right . . . no problem! See you tomorrow, then." Even better at reading people than animals, Sarah beat a hasty retreat.

Finally left alone, the good doctor and I kissed for a long while.

"Well, it is getting late." He glanced toward the new window, which showed darkness except for a solitary streetlight. "Are you *sure* you'll be safe here now, Catwoman?"

"Pretty sure." I smiled. "All of my archenemies seem to have been defeated . . . for the moment." He didn't know yet about Andy, and I felt a bit guilty about that. If my ex really had reformed, though, I should have plenty of time to explain. No need to lift the lid of that Pandora's box tonight.

Mark smoothed my hair, sending tingles down my spine. "Isn't Catwoman a villain, though? As far as I've seen, you always fight for truth and justice, as they say in the comics."

I shrugged. "I don't read comics, but I've seen a couple of the movies. Seems to me that Catwoman isn't all bad. Just like I wouldn't claim to be all good."

"Oh no?" Mark pulled me close again. "We didn't get much time to talk tonight, just you and me. It so happens I don't have any early patients tomorrow. Maybe you could open up a little later too?"

Only one good response for that: "Mr-r-row!"

Everyone knows a leopard can't change its spots. But can a thief hide the spots on a catnapped Bengal? Groomer Cassie McGlone is about to find out . . .

With no ID for his pet, an agitated young man shows up at Cassie's Comfy Cats claiming his house has burned down and he needs to board his big, brown cat, Ayesha. But after a bath washes dye out of the cat's coat and reveals beautiful spots, Cassie suspects the exotic-looking feline may in fact be a valuable Bengal show cat, possibly stolen. At the same time, there are rumored sightings of a "wild cat" in the hills of Chadwick, New Jersey. Could there be a connection?

When Ayesha's alleged owner turns up dead, it looks like whoever wants the beautiful Bengal is not pussyfooting around. Working with the police, Cassie and her staff need to be careful not to reveal the purloined purebred's whereabouts while they discreetly make inquiries to cat breeders to find her real owners. But after a break-in attempt rattles Cassie's cage, it's clear someone let the cat out of the bag. And when a second body is found, it's up to Cassie to spot the killer, who may be grooming *her* to be the next victim . . .

Please turn the page for an exciting sneak peek of Eileen Watkins's next Cat Groomer mystery

THE BENGAL IDENTITY

now on sale wherever print and e-books are sold!

Chapter 1

Todd Gillis bounced the keys to my Honda CR-V in his dark-stained palm, as if to remind me that he temporarily held my wheels hostage. "So, Carrie . . ."

"It's Cassie, actually," I corrected him.

"Oh, right. McGarrity?"

"McGlone." Todd seemed too young to have such a bad memory. But I guessed anyone's brain might be affected by this cocktail of exhaust fumes and motor oil cooking together in the July heat of the garage's repair bay. His short, dirty-blond hair rose in a kind of crest above his forehead—with the help of gel, or maybe axle grease? He radiated lechery and B.O.

I'd just come by to leave my four-year-old car for its sixty-thousand-mile checkup, and hoped to be on my way soon, but Todd seemed to have other ideas. With several other vehicles also parked in the bay, he'd managed to position himself between me and the glimpse of daylight beyond. There seemed to be no easy escape, unless I wanted to vault over a car hood.

Todd narrowed his eyes now to give me the once-over. "You said this is your first time here? 'Cause you look familiar."

"Maybe you've seen me around town. I have the cat grooming and boarding shop, on Wayfair Street." In the next instant, I regretted giving Todd even that much information.

He snapped his fingers. "The bikini car wash last month, out at the Roost. Were you one of those girls?"

"Definitely not!" I bristled. How often had he tried that line, I wondered, and did it ever actually work?

"Aww, don't say that. You're as pretty as any of them." He probably could tell, from the way my eyes frantically searched for an escape route, that he wasn't getting anywhere, and switched his approach. "So you're into cats, huh? Say, didya hear about the killer cat that's loose up on Rattlesnake Ridge?"

All I wanted at this point was to get back to my shop, where I'd left my assistant Sarah in charge. So it could only have been temporary insanity that made me take the bait and echo, "Killer cat?"

"Yeah! They say it's big as a mountain lion. Got hold of some old lady's dog, one of those Shih Tzus." He mispronounced the breed, maybe on purpose, to make it sound vulgar. "Ate it up, right in front of her!"

I didn't find this outlandish tale the least bit funny, and the wide grin that spread across Todd's grimy face confirmed my desire to spend as little time around him as possible.

"That's awful, if it's true," I said. "But someone probably made up that story. We hardly ever get mountain lions in New Jersey, or any other cats that big. Anyway, how soon do you think my car will be—"

"Ha, shows what you know! My dad told me that back in the seventies, there was a theme park not far from here that had all kinds of wild animals. Jungle World, it was called, and you could ride through. Sometime the big cats escaped and attacked people and pets. That's one of the reasons it got shut down. They got luxury houses up there now."

This was my first visit to the Gillis Garage, but Todd seemed to think that because we were around the same age—mid to late twenties—fate had brought us together. If this was his idea of seductive chitchat, it sure wasn't mine. Plus, he was a pretty big guy, and he had edged close enough by now to worry me.

Once again looking for an "out," I noticed a rather sinister figure stroll into the repair bay. A lean, middle-aged man with long, graying hair and lots of tattoos stopped in one shadowy corner. He folded his arms across his chest and glared in our direction.

Ironically, it made me almost grateful that I was no longer alone with Ted.

I tried again to cut our conversation short by

debunking his local legend. "Well, even if some big cat got loose back in the seventies, it wouldn't still be alive today."

"Maybe not the same cat, but it could have bred with something else, couldn't it? Don't they sometimes cross different cats to get new species?"

"Some breeders do, but certainly not with anything that big," I told him. "Well, as you said before, speaking of cats . . . I've got a bunch back at my shop that need to be groomed and fed, so I'd better get going."

"Sure, sure." He gave me a little more breathing room, but still partly blocked my exit. "Y'know, I don't usually like cats, but I wouldn't mind having one like that. Imagine owning a wildcat—one that could take down a dog!"

His enthusiasm for animal-on-animal combat began to turn my stomach, but I tried to find a non-confrontational way to discourage him. "Hybrids are very expensive, and I hear they can be hard to handle."

Todd leaned back against the door jamb and leered openly at me. "That's okay. After all, I can be pretty hard to handle, too."

Oh, to leap into my trusty CR-V and speed away! Unfortunately, Todd already had pulled it into the repair bay.

Behind us, the guy with the tattoos cleared his throat. "Hey, Gillis, if you're not too busy putting the moves on your customers, we gotta talk."

His boyish face twisting in annoyance, Todd told me, "I'll let you know when your car's done."

I saw my chance and sidled toward the exit. "You've got my number, right?"

"You bet I do, Cassie!" He winked.

Ugh.

I hurried out the door and across the garage's parking lot. Meanwhile, I could hear the discussion heating up between Todd and his customer.

"Man, how many times I got to bring this van back here before you fix it right?"

"Hey, whadya want from me? That thing's an antique. They don't even make parts for those anymore."

Sounded like Todd had never heard that the customer is always right. I had to give him credit, though, for talking back to a tough dude with flames and skulls crawling up and down his arms.

I covered the four blocks back to my shop at a brisk clip. I'd thought I lucked out, finding a place to get my car serviced that was within walking distance. Now I wondered if the convenience was worth dodging clumsy advances from Todd Gillis.

With a sense of relief I neared my own shop, on the first floor of a two-story building that originally served as a single-family home. It was over a hundred years old, and at some point the first floor had been converted for retail use. The last owner had operated a rather fly-by-night beauty shop and left a mess behind. I'd made a lot of renovations and given the exterior a coat of cream paint with blue-gray trim.

Now I paused on the sidewalk to admire, once again, my front display window. Large, quirky purple letters spelled out "Cassie's Comfy Cats" and a smaller font added "Feline Grooming and Boarding." I'd originally stenciled the lettering myself, when I'd opened six months ago. But my first window had to be replaced when a stray bullet went through it, during an incident at my shop that spring.

I'd expected running a business in this small, semi-rural suburb to be pretty uneventful. But in the short time since I'd opened, Cassie's Comfy Cats already had seen more than its share of excitement.

Glancing through the window now, I saw Sarah Wilcox behind the sales counter dealing with a customer. My petite, African-American sixty-something assistant looked relieved when I stepped through the door.

"Cassie, glad you're back," she said. "I wasn't sure how to handle this."

The young man on the near side of the counter turned to face me, also. A grayish plaid shirt and faded jeans hung loosely on his thin frame, and his pale, narrow face showed a trace of acne. He needed a shave and a haircut, too. I put his age about the same as mine.

On the sales counter between him and Sarah rested a rectangular, soft-sided black cat carrier. Even the mesh inserts were so dark that I couldn't really make out what was inside.

"You're the owner?" the man said, eagerly. "You board cats, right? Can I leave mine here, just for a few days?"

The request wasn't strange, but his manner was. His eyes bugged a little and his voice had a nervous edge. Still, a customer was a customer.

"No reason why not," I said. "We have room at the moment."

A couple of months ago, we would always have had room. But that spring we'd gotten some unusual publicity, and now our boarding facilities were sometimes filled to capacity. A large room toward the back of the shop featured more than a dozen "condos," each the size of a broom closet and with three different levels, for litter pans, food and water dishes and lounging.

"May I see your cat?" I asked. "Can you take him out?"

"Her." He unzipped the mesh door of the carrier.

Its occupant stepped out with a confident, fluid stride. She was a big, athletic-looking shorthair with a dark brown coat. Her long legs and slightly large ears hinted at some exotic genes.

A murmur from Sarah told me she also was impressed.

"Quite an animal," I said, while the cat allowed me to stroke her back. "What's her name?"

He hesitated. "Ayesha. Y'know, like the queen in *She?*"

I don't think he expected me to understand this reference, but I actually had seen the 1960s fantasy-adventure movie. One of my college boyfriends had a thing for Ursula Andress. My bad luck—a mere brunette, I also couldn't compete in terms of my chest or my cheekbones with Andress the Goddess.

"That's certainly regal," I said. "What breed is she?"

"No idea. I got her from a shelter as a kitten."

Ayesha, who had been scanning the counter

with her brilliant golden eyes, suddenly pounced on a pile of our brochures, scattering them to the floor. Sarah caught her before she could jump down after them. The blond man also helped get her under control.

"Has she had all her shots? Do you have any recent vet records?" I asked him. "She certainly looks healthy, but I have to be careful about bringing in any cats that might be carrying contagious diseases."

"Sorry. I don't."

Which raised another question. "Is she spayed?"

When he shook his head, I prepared to turn him down. I'd never yet had to refuse a customer, but my boarding area is pretty close quarters. A cat with FIV or another contagious disease, or a female in heat, could cause serious problems. "I'm very sorry, but we have rules. . . ."

The guy looked on the edge of tears. "Please, I'm desperate! My . . . my house burned down last night. I can't go back there, and I have to find someplace else to live that will let me keep Ayesha. I just need a couple of days!"

I worried that it might take him more than a couple of days to find new quarters. Still, I sympathized. I have three cats of my own, and couldn't imagine what I'd do if all of us were suddenly homeless. "You don't have any friends or relatives—?"

"Not around here. I came from out of state and I can't go back. Please, this is an emergency! I'll come get her as soon as I can."

I thought of the extra-large condo that my handyman, Nick Janos, had recently built on a wall opposite the others. I'd asked for it just in case we ever had to quarantine a boarder.

"All right," I told the blond guy. "Maybe I can keep her kind of isolated."

"That's great!"

He paid a week's board in advance, cash, and wrote down his name—Rudy Pierson—and a cell phone number. With his help, Sarah urged the lively Ayesha back into her carrier. Though a standard size, it almost seemed too small for her.

"Does she need any kind of special diet or handling?" I asked.

Rudy requested an all-natural food that I figured I'd have to get from the big pet-supply store on the highway. "She's well-trained, but she needs a lot of exercise." He glanced through the wood-and-mesh screen that separated our playroom from the front sales counter. "I can see you've got a big space with cat trees and wall shelves. She'll like that."

I nodded. "We let the boarders out there every day, in shifts."

"Terrific! Oh, and she'll walk on a leash. Y'know, with a harness."

"Really?" Sarah peered into the carrier.

"Anyway, thanks so much," Rudy said, on his way out. "You guys are lifesavers!" From the doorway, he cast a sad, backward glance at the black carrier, as if he feared he might never see his pet again.

"What a shame," said Sarah, after he'd left. "I wonder where the house fire was? I didn't hear anything about it on the local news."

"He said he's from out of state, so maybe you wouldn't have. Wonder how he found out about my place?"

"You're on the Web. If he's got a smartphone, he might have found you that way."

"Yeah, maybe." I shrugged off the small mystery. "Well, let's get Miss Ayesha settled. I'm going to put her in that big condo away from the others. Let's just hope she doesn't go into heat while she's here, or even our neutered male boarders might freak out."

Sarah put a pan with fresh litter at the bottom of the "quarantine" condo, while I filled one dish with water and another with high-quality dry food. Her Highness would just have to make do until I could track down some of the fare Rudy had recommended.

If it's a "natural" brand, Dawn even might carry it at Nature's Way. That would be convenient. I dropped into my friend's health-food store frequently, just to visit.

I toted the black carrier back to the condo area, where a few of the other boarders looked up or meowed in interest. Meanwhile, the lean cat's weight surprised me. When I unzipped the bag and lifted her out, I noticed again how muscular she was. Before putting her in her new quarters, though, I hesitated. Although Ayesha had short, sleek fur, in some areas it looked matted.

I usually groom boarders at a discount, anyway. Given Rudy's circumstances, I'd throw in the service for free.

"I want to deal with her coat first," I told Sarah. "It's kind of sticky or something."

My assistant followed me into the grooming studio. "Maybe from the house fire?"

"Could be. From the smoke, or maybe some other kind of fumes in the air." I set the carrier on my stainless-steel grooming table, let the new boarder out, and gave her fur a sniff. "Definitely has an odd, perfume-y smell."

Though lively, restless, and strong, Ayesha didn't fight the grooming process. Sarah was able to hold her by the scruff while I started working with a slicker brush. The cat's coat had a slightly stiff texture and it took a bit of effort to pass the brush through.

"What breed do you think she is?" Sarah asked. "She's an unusual color—such an even, dark brown."

"There is a Havana Brown breed," I told her. "I've seen them in pictures, but never in person. And Burmese are brown. But those are valuable purebreds. Rudy said he got her as a kitten from a shelter."

I switched to a comb, which seemed to glide through the hair more easily, but then noticed something weird.

Most cats have at least two kinds of fur—the silky or smooth guard hairs on top and a fluffier undercoat. The colors of the two can sometimes be different. Ayesha didn't have much of an undercoat, but her guard hairs changed color close to her skin. It wasn't the kind of "tipping" that occurs in some cat's fur, though. I'd never seen anything like this before.

I ruffled her hair back in several places, and always found the same thing. In some areas, the dark brown color went a little deeper. In others, like her belly, the light, golden shade showed up more. But it didn't follow any typical, natural pattern.

When I paused, perplexed, Sarah asked me what was wrong.

"Forget grooming," I said. "This cat needs a bath."

"O-o-okay." She sounded confused. "Think she got into something oily in the fire?"

"Let's just say, whatever she's got on her coat might not be good for her, and I don't want her licking it off."

We put Ayesha in the big bathing sink, filled it partway with warm water, and squirted shampoo over her. Again, she was a surprisingly good sport, as if she'd been bathed before. Wearing thin latex gloves, I massaged the soap deep into her coat and scrubbed gently with my hands. Sarah held the sprayer close to her skin, to rinse her without upsetting her too much.

Dark brown begin to swirl into the shallow bath water.

"What on earth—?" Sarah gasped.

"There's a reason we couldn't tell what breed she was," I guessed out loud. "And maybe a reason why Rudy claimed he didn't know. She's been dyed."

In spite of our efforts, only a little of the stuff washed out. Finally we gave up and towel-dried the cat. But not before we could just make out a faint pattern of leopard spots over her whole body.

"That's so bizarre!" my assistant said, with a

shake of her head. "Why would anyone dye such a beautiful coat?"

"Maybe to hide the fact that she's worth thousands?" I flashed back on Rudy's anxious and secretive behavior. "I'm betting Ayesha is a purebred show cat. And possibly stolen."

Connect with Us

Visit us online at
KensingtonBooks.com
to read more from your favorite authors, see books
by series, view reading group guides, and more.

 Join us on social media

for sneak peeks, chances to win books and prize packs,
and to share your thoughts with other readers.

facebook.com/kensingtonpublishing
twitter.com/kensingtonbooks

Tell us what you think!

To share your thoughts, submit a review,
or sign up for our eNewsletters, please visit:
KensingtonBooks.com/TellUs.